What people are saying about

Ezekie[illegible]

John Bennion's novel *Ezekie*[illegible] [illegible]erses us in the Utah Territory of the late 188[illegible] [illegible]time of hardscrabble farming, plural marriage, and outsider suspicion. A dead body in a ditch after midnight raises questions of murder. But deeper still, this is a novel about individual and communal values: What debt do we owe others, and what joy can we claim for ourselves?
Jack Harrell, author of *Caldera Ridge*

Aridity, Wallace Stegner wrote long ago, is the "ultimate unity" and "the one inflexible condition" of the American West, and survival there demands cooperation and community, which aridity will test to the breaking point. Nowhere has this been more true than in the West Desert of Utah where John Bennion was born and bred. Bennion's ruralist literary roots may reach toward Hardy and Lawrence, but go deepest into that desert dust he has never wished to shake off. Descended from 19th century British converts to Mormonism who sought to make the West Desert fulfill Isaiah's prophecy and "blossom as the rose," Bennion has soaked his imagination in the felt life of his patriarchal and polygamous forebears, and in this novel he summons out of the dust the voice of Rachel O'Brien Rockwood Wainwright Harker, a young polygamous wife, secret rebel, and apprentice sleuth, who discovers that "Only lust for water was strong enough to make a good person kill." Listen for the story she has to tell.
Bruce W. Jorgensen, writer, poet, and literary critic

Ezekiel's Third Wife

Ezekiel's Third Wife

John Bennion

Winchester, UK
Washington, USA

First published by Roundfire Books, 2019
Roundfire Books is an imprint of John Hunt Publishing Ltd., No. 3 East St., Alresford, Hampshire SO24 9EE, UK
office1@jhpbooks.net
www.johnhuntpublishing.com
www.roundfire-books.com

For distributor details and how to order please visit the 'Ordering' section on our website.

ISBN: 978 1 78904 095 1
978 1 78904 096 8 (ebook)
Library of Congress Control Number: 2018940334

A CIP catalogue record for this book is available from the British Library.

Design: Stuart Davies

Printed and bound by CPI Group (UK) Ltd, Croydon, CR0 4YY, UK
US: Printed and bound by Edwards Brothers Malloy 15200 NBN Way #B, Blue Ridge Summit, PA 17214, USA

Acknowledgments

I thank the many readers of the drafts of this novel, especially the group—Donna, Bruce, Valerie, Dennis, Levi, Althea, Gene, and Charlotte. I also thank Karla for her continuous encouragement and love.

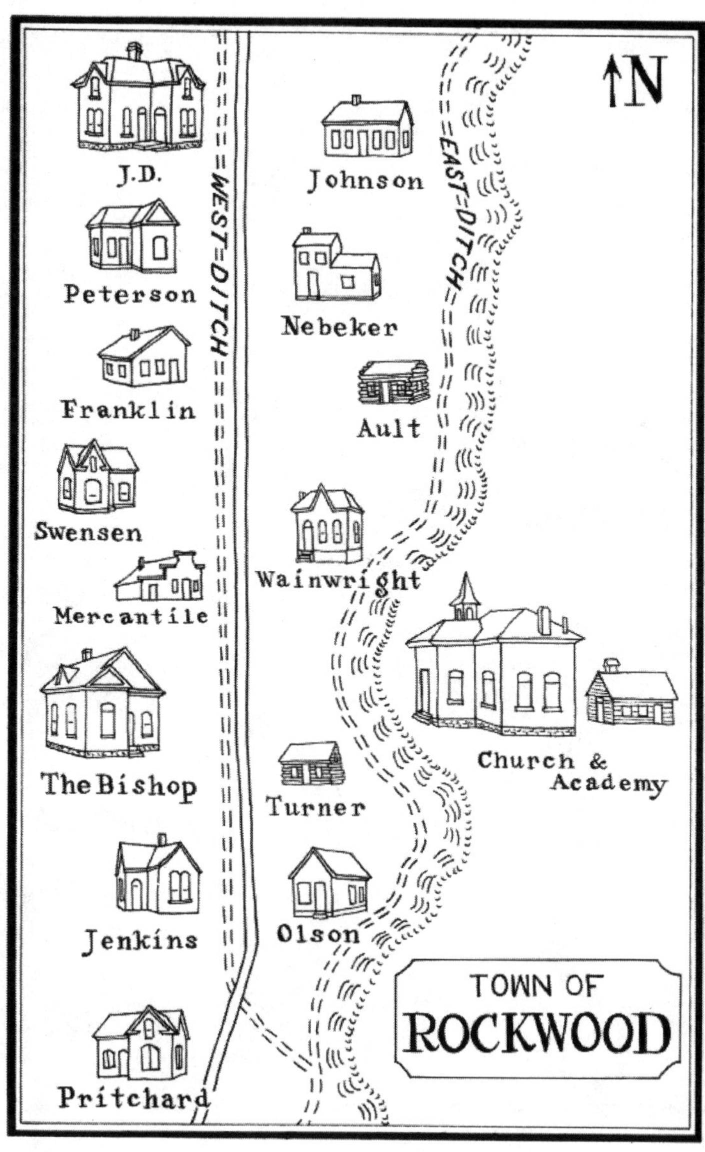
N
J.D.
Peterson
Franklin
Swensen
Mercantile
The Bishop
Jenkins
Pritchard
WEST-DITCH
Johnson
Nebeker
Ault
Wainwright
Turner
Olson
EAST-DITCH
Church &
Academy
TOWN OF
ROCKWOOD

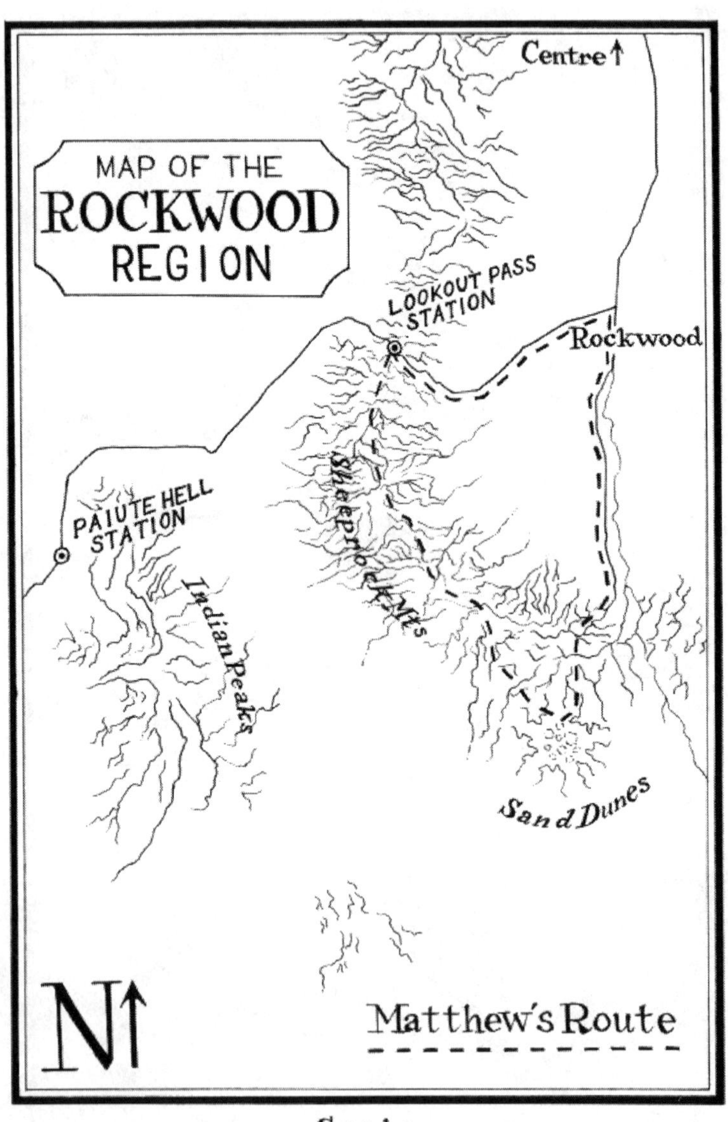
Centre
MAP OF THE
ROCKWOOD
REGION
LOOKOUT PASS
STATION
Rockwood
PAIUTE HELL
STATION
Sheeprock Mts
Indian Peaks
Sand Dunes
N
Matthew's Route
Scale
0
5 MILES

Chapter One

From the high barn window, I saw a jubilant flag of dust rise behind the freight wagon as it crossed the flat toward town. Matthew Harker, my secret husband of two weeks, would soon arrive for his freight delivery. That night, when I went out at midnight to irrigate, he would come to me and lie with me on the hay.

I finished forking the dried lucerne down into the manger and fairly ran down the ladder. I milked faster than a skunk sucks eggs. My feet did a dance under Beulah's belly and she shifted, nervous and wary. Finally, I stripped the last milk out of the cow's flaccid udder and carried the foaming bucket down toward the house.

The barn was built into the hillside above the houses of Rockwood town, so I looked across the rooftops northward at the freight wagon and its plume of dust; both would arrive within the next quarter hour. The air shimmered; it was only nine in the morning and already the whole desert was as hot and dry as a Monarch oven.

I stepped across the stonework water gate in the irrigation ditch, balancing with the bucket. As I tried to run through my fields toward the house, a bit of froth sloshed over the rim onto the dust. I stopped short, eyes fixed on the shape of the spill—an irregular oval, like a map of an imagined country, as ill-shaped as my own soul. Here I was running to catch a glimpse of a man none of my neighbors knew was my husband. *How did I come to this?* It felt like vertigo of the spirit as I thought back to my childhood in the Nevada minefields, when Utah Territory was as far from my mind as heaven. When I was ten, if some visionary crone had pronounced my future, I would have said she was drunk or deranged or both: "In another year, when you are eleven, you will travel east and become a Mormon." *Bollocks!*

I would have said (because I learned to swear when I learned to talk). "At eighteen years of age you will enter plural marriage with one man and his two previous wives, and one year after that, you will secretly take a second husband, a Gentile." *Perishing, bloody bollocks!*

But I had done all these things, acting contrary to legality and righteousness, with clear mind and purpose, so I might as well choke back any regretful thoughts. I started toward the house again: no moping over spilt milk for me, no matter what a gypsy woman might read in the pattern on the ground. What was done was done.

Walking fast, I swung the milk bucket round and round my body, shifting it hand to hand to keep from sloshing again. I flung open the back gate, crossed the yard and porch in a few strides, and entered the kitchen. Heart thudding so loud I thought my sister-wife Abigail could hear, I lifted the bucket onto the kitchen table, spread a cloth across the lip, and strained the milk into the ceramic pots. A little more splashed out, and Abigail glared at me. *Slow breath, slow, another.* Wouldn't do to have her see my hands shaking.

"Finished. Abby, if you want, I will tend the store for an hour or two so Zeke Junior can help you back here." It sounded like a rehearsed speech.

"Rachel, you're always one to rush over there when the freight comes." Abigail's face with her heavy jowls reminded me of an English bulldog. "What for, Rachel, my girl?"

What could I say to calm her misfortunate curiosity?

"I love putting the new stock away, handling it. Makes me feel wealthy."

Abigail snorted, her good cheer returning.

I forced my voice level. "You're the most guilty-making woman in all of Utah Territory. You should be glad I'm eager to work."

She shook her head and her jowls waggled a little. A different time I might have laughed. "Second most guilty making." She angled her head toward the other room where Sophia, the second wife, sat at her loom.

As if she could read our minds, hear our whispered words, Sophia called out, "I couldn't pray this morning. Some devilish spirit stopped my mouth." We heard the loom shift as she pushed down the treadle. "Evil is heavy on the air."

I had no doubt she could read my secret in the warp and woof of the rough cloth she wove. I stood in the doorway and considered her plump back, her blond hair twisted in a tight bun, her aura of savage righteousness.

Abigail smirked at our half-crazy, prophetic sister-wife.

"A sin in this town I can smell," pronounced Sophia. "God's wrath will be swift and sure."

Abigail leaned against the table, laughing so that her shoulders shook, and whispered, "'Tis 1891 and Sophia thinks we live in Old Testament times. What would we do without her words to keep us on the proper path toward heaven?" She wiped her eyes.

I was used to Sophia's eternal preaching, but lately she had seemed like one of God's own angels straight from the Book of Revelation. All week long, she had quoted scripture into my face. "Who can find a virtuous woman? For her price is far above rubies." *My virtue is my flesh,* I thought, but never dared to say, *which pleases my true husband, just as his pleases me.* "Strait is the gate and narrow the way." *My way is my husband Matthew, not my husband Ezekiel, who is as strict as a high-backed chair.* "Choose ye this day whom ye will serve, but as for me and my house, we will serve the Lord." *Yes, but I can serve the Lord by taking a second husband when my first is fled to England, useless to me.*

Just that morning Sophia had glared, as if she could read my thoughts and private acts in my face. "Rachel, *your* damnation slumbereth not." I had frowned back, wondering what Sophia knew. She dreamed dreams and had visions, like the prophetic women among the first Mormon pioneers. At night she sometimes wandered our rooms in her white nightdress, muttering, eyes staring but not seeing, as if she had already passed through the veil into Paradise.

Despite our sisterhood, the way she saw the universe was not the way I saw it. Her God was sterner than the one I prayed to, her pathway fraught with so many tangled commandments that I wondered she was sane at all. God's creation was paradoxical, I believed; life, difficult beyond words but also beautiful, a daily blessing. I could forgive Sophia her judgmental nature because her heart held only compassion toward children and the weak. She never blasted them with the word of God. She told them God loved them. I just believed I deserved the same charity.

Sitting on the bench near the door, I took off my manure-laden boots and put on my store shoes.

"Water first." Abigail handed me the two water buckets. My stepfather J.D., who lived just down the lane, had a well right outside his back door, which made it simple for his family to fetch water for drinking and washing. Ezekiel's wives, of which I was the least, had to fetch it at least ten times a day from the ditch that ran between the top of our fields and the barn. I grabbed the buckets and ran back up the pathway. Beulah angled her head toward me as if to say, "So soon? Please, give me another wedge of that lucerne hay." Turning right at the dry ditch, I soon crossed onto the Turners' property where the irrigation water was currently set. At their weir I put one foot on the bank and one on the edge of the stonework. I dipped the two buckets in the water, taking care not to swirl the mud. My right foot slid, and my shoe filled with water. Dust would coat my foot and turn into mud. No matter...if I didn't miss seeing Matthew.

I turned and staggered fast as I could with the buckets back through my fields and through the back door of the house. As I swung them up to the stand, the front of my dress snagged under one bucket. I couldn't pull free, because its lower edge had come down on my watch inside my pocket. I lifted the bucket, pulled myself free, and rushed to put lids on the buckets. I was sweating mightily from my run, so I grabbed the dipper and drank a cool cupful.

I turned to leave, but Abigail stood from the table and caught my arm, frowning now, serious in her role as first wife, Matriarch, which in the absence of our Patriarch Ezekiel, she took to like a cow to meadow grass. "Rachel, there's something you're not saying. You make me mistrust you when your face fills with pleasure at the prospect of lifting sacks of flour. If you flirt with the coach driver, it is a deadly sin."

Real fear settled in my belly. Matthew and I couldn't afford discovery, not now, not yet. We had to keep our marriage secret until we could earn enough cash money to leave Rockwood town on the train, hauling my goods and cattle. Maybe two more months would do it. I couldn't bear to leave with only the clothes on our backs, not after becoming accustomed to relative prosperity. We wanted to head for Wyoming, where water sometimes fell from the sky, where rivers ran full, and where cattle had enough feed to make their calves fat. All our property—cattle, horses, money—would make the difference between a good life and starvation on our new spread.

I also wanted to dissolve my bond with Ezekiel. Matthew thought this reason for waiting was insane. "You are not legally married!" Still, backward as it seemed, I didn't want to leave until I had an ecclesiastical divorce. Then I could leave without shame. Other women, weary of the Principle of Celestial Marriage, had gotten divorces.

I shrugged and turned from Abigail's prying eyes. Walking quick as I could, I pushed through the back door, cut through our small yard, out the front gate, and into the lane that ran down the middle of our village. I looked northward but could only see the dust of the freight wagon, not the wagon itself. Rockwood town had one store, one church building, and a single, one-room academy. Except for the church, which was set on the flat above town, all the buildings and houses lined the lane, eight to the east side, eight to the west.

I rushed across to the store we kept while Ezekiel was away in England searching for his family in the Lancashire Parish records. The prophet in Salt Lake City had sent him to collect names for proxy baptism of our ancestors. The idea was that all God's children, even those who died without being baptized into the faith, deserved a chance at this ordinance. I couldn't see the virtue in something so otherworldly when we three wives worked sixteen-hour days and barely scraped by. Tired of such a marginal return on my labor and sick of having only an absent husband, I had taken another man to my heart, defying the Mormon law that said only male priesthood holders could take a second Celestial mate. Many men had more. J.D. himself had five wives. Brigham Young had more than fifty, though I doubt that even he had the vitality to bed all of them. Was God jealous? Did he disapprove my disobedient act? Sometimes I thought he did, sometimes not.

I entered the board building, which was painted white with a false front. Black letters, square and proper, announced "Ezekiel Wainwright, Mercantile." I sniffed the odor of cinnamon, coffee, and molasses. Like breathing the air of distant lands.

Zeke Jr., almost as tall as me and even more of a thin stick, wanted to stay and help with the unloading, and I had no good excuse to get shut of him. Couldn't say, "Your mother wants you," when Abigail already suspected my wayward act.

Then as if I did not already have enough trouble, J.D. Rockwood, my stepfather, walked in and leaned against the store counter. "Rachel, I will be melancholy if the freight does not have the licorice I ordered." I loved his voice, with its hint of Liverpool accent. He smiled at me, which was all it took to make me feel like I was the most important person in the world to him.

He had taken my mother in, along with me and my two siblings, when we first arrived in Rockwood after we left Nevada. He had always been more generous with me than my blood father, a dirt-poor miner, had ever been. He was my contradictory J.D., hard as granite with everybody but his own wives and children, never gruff with us. As an agent to Wells Fargo, he was a terror to any criminal in Utah, but he would rather spend his days dandling a grandbaby on his knee. An excellent marksman, accurate at 500 yards with his old Sharps rifle, he had a weakness for candy. He was a bear of a man but light on his feet, wore a thick beard, carefully trimmed on the sides. Some said he could track a fly up a kitchen wall, but I had my doubts. He was first of the two men in this world whose respect I needed.

Deceiving him felt hazardous, because he had a hound dog's nose for sniffing out crime. I had to make every motion deliberate. I was no criminal, but he would think me one if he knew what I had done.

Slowly I took my watch out of the pocket of my dress. I saw that the silver cover was dented. When I opened it I found that the face was cracked, and it might as well have been a crack in my heart. It had been a gift from J.D. on my sixteenth birthday, a fine silver watch, with a chain that I pinned to my dress. I covered it with my hands as if to protect it from the glare of the sun. "The freight is on time today."

J.D. took out his own watch. "Yes, for almost the first time in my memory. Damnable erratic Gentile. He's generally an hour late." He reached to touch my watch. "I hope your timepiece 'taint ruined."

I shook my head and turned my back. "Just the glass." I plucked the three pieces from the face and lifted the watch to my ear. It still ticked. I tossed the fragments into the rubbish and laid the watch open on my palm. Turning, I found J.D. looking over my shoulder.

"I set the milk bucket down on it."

"I'll order a new glass," he said, smiling kindly. He held his hand out for the watch, but I shook my head.

"I'll do it. I am a grown woman after all and I can take care of my own needs."

He nodded, but then his smile faded. "I hope so, my Rachel. I worry about you three women alone with Ezekiel gone. I wish he had not been so eager to go. You let me know if you don't have enough to eat." He took my wrist in his hand. "So thin. Too thin."

"It's thin because I'm half antelope, not because I lack provender."

He chuckled, his hand heavy on my shoulder. I noted that his face had aged since my marriage to Ezekiel. His beard and hair had grayed. His aging seemed to have happened suddenly, while I looked the other way, even though I recognized that his fading toward white had been a slow process spread across the whole eight years I had known him. For the first time, he looked like an old man, one who would decline to his grave. I wanted to wrap my arms around him, hang on to his shirt and prevent him getting even one day older.

But before I could act on such foolish thoughts, the freight wagon stopped in front of the store. I stood in the doorway, my blood racing, while Matthew clambered to the back and handed down supplies—sugar, coffee, flour, and manufactured cloth—to J.D. and Zeke Jr. He gave me a careful nod and busied himself with his work. I watched his substantial shoulders move beneath his shirt. Good thick neck, but not too thick. Wide smile, white teeth. My comely man, pleasing to my eye. My husband and lover. As comely inside as out, kind, smart, funny, his eyes full of love for me, not just my body, but my whole self. He had known me since childhood, longer than any other human except for my mother, who was now in heaven. He was flesh of my flesh, not someone to share with a sister-wife.

Sister Jenkins walked down the street. She stood in front of the store and proclaimed, "We should not buy our goods from

Gentiles. The prophet says we should buy from our own people."

Matthew shook his head at Sister Jenkins, and she walked on. He glanced at me again, smiled a scant curve. I thought I might pass out from the blood rushing to my face, either that or climb the wagon and throw my arms around him. Wouldn't that be something in this tight Mormon village, a proper third wife embracing a Gentile man in broad daylight?

Then J.D. was at my shoulder, brushing past me. I shook myself, moved forward to lift a sack of flour, glanced up at Matthew, whose lips pressed together, brows bunched, and his whole body became taut. His face and body spoke the hatred he held for my stepfather.

J.D. called out to him. "Is the package I ordered up there somewhere?"

Matthew threw it at his feet, and J.D. nodded at him, seemingly unaware of any animosity.

Matthew thought my stepfather was the devil incarnate. Possibly few men loved their fathers-in-law, but his hatred was as far above the normal as the mountains were above the flat. Among the soldiers and freight men, J.D. had a reputation for having no mercy on those Gentile horse thieves or murderers he tracked as an agent for Wells Fargo. A couple months before, my stepfather had caught a man who had raped a Mormon girl. Found him and shot him in the gut, and the man had not bled to death, but his wound became infected, and he took two weeks to die. Matthew claimed it was the tenth man J.D. had killed. He said no man deserved to suffer so long, no matter his original crime. I tried to convince Matthew that taking a woman against her will was no light crime. I admitted freely that J.D. had a violent streak, but he was as kind to me as a bitch with her pups. He was the same to most women. Matthew was blind to his gentle side, couldn't be convinced of it, no matter how long I persuaded.

Just as quick, my husband was gone, driving on to Lookout

Station, four miles away, where he would spend the night with Ambrose and Libby Rockwood, who managed the station there. They were brother and sister-in-law to J.D., and Matthew had to be proper as a Sunday School maid with them. That night after everyone was in bed, he would run back to me. He couldn't afford to tire the freight mules and he couldn't borrow a horse from the stationmaster without good reason. But running eight miles was no hardship for Matthew. His mother was half Goshute and Matthew often took off his boots and ran, just for pleasure. Tonight he would run for my pleasure as well as his own.

"Your face is flushed, Rachel," said J.D. "Pray God you're not coming down with some sickness. You need more food. Or it may be that you're not getting enough sleep."

I shook my head, turning to help Zeke Jr. shelve the new goods.

What could I say to this man who loved God's commandments more than he loved his own life?

Chapter Two

After Matthew drove off, Zeke Jr. and I put away all the goods. Then I spent a lazy afternoon repairing my corral. The air was so hot that my skin felt it would catch flame; the lane between the houses of Rockwood town shone white-hot. Not just Sophia was touchy; people in town annoyed easily, even tended toward anger, as if the wrong word or act could cause one brother to strike down another.

The sun seemed bound and determined to transform our patch of Utah Territory into hell. Since early June, not a single drop of rain had fallen—nearly three months of drought.

It was almost enough to make me believe in Sophia's vision of a malevolent God. Just a year before, during the summer Ezekiel left for England, the weather had been too cold and wet for wheat, lucerne, and vegetables to grow; this summer was too hot and dry. God seemed to send moderate weather to the Gentiles, Infidels, and Heretics, not to his own true Saints living in Zion.

This year, through March and April, generally wet and yellow-green months, the ground had remained dust-dry, hard as adobe. The new leaves of the Lombardy poplars and Russian olives, which lined the fencerows and ditch banks, crackled when grasped. There was no grass to turn yellow, so the high prairie on which Rockwood sat became white or gray. *The colors of death.* I prayed every night for rain. Instead, the streams, already scant, flowed lower and lower in the ditches. Farmers struggled to keep even a portion of their fields and gardens alive. I felt like shaking my fist at the sky and returning to my Gentile life in Nevada, and I might have, except that Nevada was even drier, and my life there had been even more impoverished. It may be that hell is a relative condition, not such a bad place for those of us who have experienced it during our lives.

Through May and June, Abigail and I carried water, which

we poured across the dry seedbeds of carrots, beets, swedes, and maize. A crust formed which few sprouts could penetrate. Potatoes and corn showed a tender green and then withered. The lucerne, which we needed for hay to feed our cattle through the winter, decided to wait a year; a few dark green leaves tested the scorching sunlight, but the roots hoarded most of their strength. My cows up on the mountain range had little milk, growing as gaunt as their calves. We three women, wives of Ezekiel, became worried that our stunted wheat would not produce a harvest that would take us through the coming winter.

As June moved toward July, the weather had grown even hotter and drier, the white alkali desert shimmering in the distance, even the willows wilting, as if the whole town would explode into flame. Violent words and acts burst out on the streets and in church. People glared at each other as they watched the shrinking stream. I could see what was happening to us; lack of water was breaking apart our Zion community. Against my own better judgment, I found myself just as angry over water as everyone else. The lower half of my fields dried to mere dust.

The water master, Brother Swensen, who was also first counselor to the bishop of our congregation, warned that some farmers had been taking their water turn an hour or more early. "I'd rather the Saints die and be committed to their graves than to watch them steal from each other," he told everyone as he patrolled the ditches. He and the bishop worked out a twelve-hour rotation to replace the traditional twenty-four-hour one. They decided this new plan would help the water go further. They called everyone in town to an evening meeting in the church house to announce the change.

"I'll never get water to the bottom of my fields," said one man.

"When I have only half my water, who will take the other half?" Brother Olson hadn't listened carefully.

The bishop stood and motioned for everyone to sit down.

"Brethren."

Brother Turner rose anyway. "You are my bishop, the leader of my soul. Are you also going to take charge of my fields and water rights, too? Will you next take my wife from me?" Brother Turner's mouth twitched with anger, and he held his fists together before him, almost in the attitude of prayer. "You don't have any right to change what we all voted on." Brother Turner was a renegade in town, only coming to church meetings when he felt like it, which was as rare as rain falling. I could see his point—sometimes the commandments pronounced by the bishop chafed my own soul raw—but this was such a desperate situation that I thought we needed to pull together in the harness, somehow make it through this drought.

"We're going to try this new schedule," said the bishop. "We think that half the water twice as often will go further. We've considered the matter carefully in prayer."

"Who did you pray to?" asked someone in the back.

Brother Swensen stood. "We believe this will help. So as water master and as bishopric we have decided what is best for all of us."

The bishop sat down. "The matter is settled."

"You watch," said another brother. "This will bring even more *borrowing*."

As we left the meeting, downstream neighbors glared at upstream neighbors. The next night I caught Brother Turner removing a rock from under the gate to his ditches. He had placed it there earlier so that water would slip toward his garden. He and I nearly crossed shovels over this thievery. If we had come to violence, I knew he wouldn't have hesitated to hit a woman with his fist or use his shovel as a weapon. On my testimony, the bishop locked him in an empty room in the small schoolhouse for three days. Brother Swensen, the water master, had someone else arrested for breaking the dam of his neighbor. One brother knocked the son of another brother down in the ditch and held the boy's head underwater. The first claimed that the boy had stuck a board in the wrong water gate, causing the water to spill over into his father's fields. Neither the bishop nor the water master could find any suspicious wet ground in the supposed thief's orchard, garden, or field, so the bishop asked the accused dunker to give the father of the boy a lamb in restitution. The dunker apologized for being less than a man and dropping the reins of his own soul, but he refused to give any lamb. "How is the starvation of my children restitution for a lost temper?" The father swore that he knew the proper restitution for a blow to a child's jaw. It seemed that our whole village had gone mad, water mad. And I was right in the middle of it, my Irish blood rising so that I shouted at Brother Turner when I passed him one day in the lane. "Damn water thief!"

Now that it was August, the sun became even hotter, and the whole town was tense, ready to explode into flame. Every day I thought that violence would break out again.

By evening the air had hardly cooled. The sun heated my neck and cheek as I walked up to take the water from my next neighbor up the ditch, Brother Turner, who always argued about the time. I thought about flooding my fields, every drop of water precious, and about Matthew and I meeting in our barn after midnight, every touch precious. So my head was full of both worry and anticipation as I walked up toward my ditch at ten minutes to six that evening.

At the top of my fields, not far from the barn, I made the ditch ready to receive water. First, I removed the wooden dam from its slot in my side ditch and placed it in the gate across the main channel. I covered the dam with a sheet of canvas so that not even a trickle of water could escape during my water turn. Then I walked up around the bend of the hill east of Ezekiel's property, past the small, square academy building, under the church house, and onto Brother Turner's farm, which lay midway up the East Ditch. At six o'clock, the time assigned by Brother Swensen, I could take the water.

But Brother Turner stood above his own gate, scowling at the sun. I took out my pocket watch and showed him the time.

"Anybody can move the hands of a clock." He folded his arms across his chest. "By the sun, it's hardly five o'clock." He bent forward. "And your timepiece is broke."

"Just the glass is broken. You do this every water turn. It's full on six and by the time we get Brother Swensen up here it will be seven and you will have stolen an hour of water from me again."

I nearly hit him in the face with my shovel. I needed a good crop, especially this year. When I left town with Matthew, I wanted a little hay to ship north on the train for my own cattle and more to leave Abigail for Ezekiel's share of the cattle. If my plan with Matthew was to succeed, I couldn't spare this water.

Instead of becoming violent, I stepped down into the ditch, removed his dam of boards, so that the water could flow toward my fields.

He spoke without moving. "Damn your insolent hide. If J.D. wouldn't do worse to me, I'd put you in your place."

I smiled and bent to finish my work. It griped him that I stood up to him.

As I walked back down the ditch, I decided to check the dam again later. Most water stealing was stupid because it couldn't be hidden—a great patch of mud in a field was unmistakable evidence. But Brother Turner could claim, as he had after stealing water previously, that his garden was still wet from his own water turn. I pictured him sneaking out after dark, pulling back the canvas dam, lifting his water gate, placing a rock under it and going back to bed. Tomorrow he would say to me, "I can't help it if you can't set the gate right. I always check for pebbles and I always make sure the canvas is held down with several shovelfuls of mud."

In the desert, even in good times water was as valuable as

gold. This year its price was beyond estimation. Brother Turner had small children to feed; but still, I would not put up with his thievery. His wife—he had only the one—and children might have to take care of the irrigating while he was locked up again. No one but Sophia seemed to worry about them; all summer she had kept them in eggs and milk.

I walked back down the ditch, checked my dam (not even the smallest leak). Then I passed down through my field and reentered the house, which was crowded with Abigail and Sophia and their children, nine of us at the kitchen table. The table had three loaves of bread, a couple jars of jam, and a pitcher of milk. Sarah looked up at me and grinned. "Aunty Rache, please sit by me. I saved you a place." Abigail smiled at her daughter.

"No, sit by me," said Marianne, Sophia's child.

"If you slide apart," said Abigail, "she can sit by both of you."

Sophia prayed, "And we are grateful for this milk and bread"—*and this spot of jam for the bread*—"especially when so many in town have less." When I was a child in Nevada we never had jam, except for a jar one Christmas, which we spooned straight into our mouths until it was gone. Eyes open, I saw all the heads bowed, the two other wives, Zeke Jr., Marianne, Sarah, Stephen, the rest. "And bless our father and husband Ezekiel far from us in England. Bless him to finish his work and return quickly to us." Abigail nodded at Sophia's prayer.

Zeke Jr. grabbed his bread first, broke it into the bottom of his bowl, scooped out some jam, and poured milk across it. With his mouth full he said, "I want to be a freight driver when I grow up. I'll crack my whip across the backs of those mules."

I glanced at Abigail, who watched me. She said, "You don't want that. You want to be an important farmer like J.D., Rachel's father."

"I do too want it." He pretended to crack a whip.

I grinned at him. "You'll be so good at it that you'll be able to flick a fly off the ear of the lead mule."

"Don't encourage the boy," said Abigail.

"Keep his feet in the paths of righteousness," said Sophia.

I ate my food slowly, my head still full of Matthew, who would come to our barn right after I moved the water from one side of my fields to the other.

I took my plate to the dishpan. "I'm going to check on the water."

Abigail nodded. Brother Turner wouldn't steal water until full dark, but I wanted to be by myself to think about Matthew. Dusk was thickening and I could see the glow where the moon would rise. I stepped off the back porch and walked up through my fields. Ezekiel's fields. In a few months I would have my own.

I glanced down the lane at the shadowed houses, all filled with righteous townspeople. Oh, how they'd raise their hands to shocked mouths if they knew. "Rachel O'Brien Rockwood Wainwright Harker," I whispered. Could a woman garner names and husbands like birthrights?

My Irish-born father would call me *sleiket*, a creature too sly for her own good. What I had done was contrary to the laws of the Church, but not contrary to the laws of nature or of God, despite what men on earth said about the order of heaven. For millennia women had taken new men to themselves when their husbands left them.

At least that's what I kept telling myself.

Often the voice of my stepfather, J.D. Rockwood, thundered in my head, reading the scripture in church meetings when I was seventeen: "if a man receiveth a wife in the new and everlasting covenant, and if she be with another man, and I have not appointed unto her by the holy anointing, she hath committed adultery and shall be destroyed." A woman in Hamblin, sixty miles to the north of Rockwood, had disappeared after being discovered with a man not her husband. Had literal-minded Mormons slit her throat and buried her in the sagebrush? I didn't know. But I knew I didn't want to put it to a test. I certainly didn't want to force Matthew or J.D. into the position of protecting me against the brethren.

I stopped at the weir and watched the water flowing into my field. Water would make the lucerne grow. Lucerne, with its thick, rich leaves, made excellent hay for cattle in the winter. I walked up the ditch a short way to our orchard.

The night after our wedding two weeks earlier, Matthew and I had first lain together. I had been astonished that he could love me, a woman who was thin as a stripling boy and olive-skinned like my Manx mother. He had kissed me long and slow, and his lips were sweet as nibbling strawberries. My man. My own man, who loved me and none other on all the face of the earth. Then he had pressed harder, his tongue rough and smooth against my own. His kisses were nothing like Ezekiel's austere pecks, dry as a father's.

I had stripped Matthew's clothing but his hands shook too much to help me with my buttons. We lay skin to skin, and my mouth moved against his open mouth, tongue dallied his curious tongue. A tingling warmth spread through my body as my belly pressed firm against his. I held his hips between my thighs and celebrated the prospect of holding him forever. His hands pressed the small of my back, his mouth ready to swallow me, and I knew he wanted me, Rachel, as a lover, not just as a body to engender a child on. Nearly swooning from the blood beating in my head, I wanted to please him more than I wanted breath. I needed the pleasure of taking him inside, holding him inside me, him pushing deeper and deeper, the sacrament of sweet flesh, precious as God's smile from heaven, both of us shuddering as body and spirit knit, glorious as angels singing hallelujah.

Swaying as I stood in my dark field, I savored that remembered loving, when I would have new love that very night. I touched fingertips to my lips, to each breast. A touch lower. Mormons didn't cross themselves, but I didn't know how else to reverence my body, which would that night please Matthew, my husband, my lover. I wondered if I was with child, something Ezekiel had been unable to achieve after a month of clumsy labor. If I was pregnant, it made our leaving in six or eight weeks doubly necessary. It would not do to have my belly swell a year after earnest Ezekiel had left for Liverpool. I could not say, "Well, his seed must have lain dormant this past year." Not even superstitious Sister Jenkins would believe that lie.

Chapter Three

Wrenching myself awake, I shoved the quilt off and swung out of bed—still half in my dream, half in my black and suffocating bedroom. A flaxen-haired angel had stood at the foot of my bed, proclaiming destruction: "Viper! Thy damnation slumbereth not!"

"Sweet mother of Jesus!" Soon as I said that Catholic curse, which no good Mormon would utter, I clapped my hand over my mouth.

Had I been asleep or awake? Had I been visited by an angel or just by Sophia walking asleep again? I didn't know. The vision had quoted Sophia's favorite scripture but had stood sideways to me, speaking as if to someone not in the room, while Sophia never flinched from the face of sin. One of God's own angelic warriors was less fearsome than Sophia in her ire.

Whether the apparition had been dream or spirit or flesh, the sound of her voice made fear-sweat drip down my neck.

I strode to the window and saw from the angle of the moon that I had overslept. I grabbed my pocket watch from the bed stand and struck a match. Twelve twenty-five. Matthew would have already run the four miles from Lookout Station, already spread the saddle blankets in the loft of the barn. Poor Matthew, forced to wait almost a half hour for his pleasure with me. I smiled. Having a whetted appetite never hurt anyone.

Tying my hair back, I slid into my frock without bothering to put on a petticoat. I had no need for one under a dress I would soon remove.

I folded back the quilt, folded it twice again, and hugged it close. Aunt Mary, J.D.'s first wife, had pieced it from scraps of my own mother's dresses—Mary's gift on my marriage to my first husband, Ezekiel Wainwright, but tonight I would spread it in the barn loft for Matthew. My mother, a wanderer and a rebel, would smile down from heaven seeing her former skirts put to such use.

I crossed my room and opened the door quick. I knew from past experience that if I opened it slow, it shrieked like a harpy in labor. Listening at the top of the stairs, I heard only the wind in the chimney and summertime crickets out the window. If we opened the windows at dark, the house generally cooled off enough by ten or eleven for all of us to get good rest. My sister-wives and their half-dozen children slept the sleep of the blessed.

I didn't dare carry a candle or lantern, even though the stairs were black, steep, and narrow. Barefoot, I crept down, and each step sounded loud enough to wake the whole house, or at least Sophia. Any moment she might rise again before me like a white spirit. I had an excuse for leaving: the water needed to be moved from the south field to the north, but I could relax better with Matthew if nobody was awake and curious enough to wander outside and find my shovel lying unused.

I rushed down the short hallway toward the kitchen and back door, which I swung open. After stepping off the screened porch, I hurried past the springhouse, where we kept our milk cool. The jugs of souring milk, the dishes of butter, and the wheels of cheese were not as abundant as in J.D.'s house, but still these provisions were a comfort to my soul. I moved the quilt to my right arm while I lifted the shovel from where it leaned next to the back gate. Because of the waxing moon, once I was outside, I needed no lantern.

Glancing at the sky, I saw that, six and a half hours after I had set the water, Cassiopeia had not yet sunk to the Sheeprock Mountains, which curved around the town ten miles to the south and which looked like a giant knife-blade: point at the east toward Rockwood Creek Pass, hilt at Lookout Pass in the west, where the station manager thought Matthew was asleep in his bed.

From the back gate I saw that not all of the houses were dark;

just across the lane a light showed in the Swensens' window—probably his third wife awake with her colicky child. Again, I felt exposed crossing my field in the moonlight, carrying a quilt, which I could never claim was a tool needed for irrigation. Matthew and I and the youngest Sister Swensen were the only wakeful souls that night, and I hoped she wouldn't be curious about me slipping into the barn at midnight. For any of these saints, *my* new marriage was adultery, a sin second in seriousness only to murder. I shook my head, but the uncomfortable thoughts persisted. What if I had mistaken the heat of lust for the confirming spirit of God? What if He was angry at my license? I shook not just my head but my whole body.

I glanced up at the barn, wondering if Matthew was watching for me from the loft window, just as I had watched for the freight wagon coming earlier. I twirled my dress for him. Coyotes yipped up on the flat, and one howled, sounding like a human infant wailing. I had never feared the night, but my heart chilled, making me peer at the corners of my dark field. I shook myself, hoping none of my neighbors had seen Matthew sneak into town. Then the danger would be real.

The night air was so dry as I strode up through my field that I could hardly smell the plants. It was probable no one in town would get even a second crop before September frost. I snagged the hem of my frock on a stunted thistle.

Yearning for Matthew but fearful as a doe, I lifted my skirts and ran toward the barn, safely distant from the house. I would check the water, move it to the other side of the field, and then run to my lover. He would have the rough saddle blankets warm already, but he would smile as I unfolded my soft house quilt. He would lift off my clothing and we would give each other pleasure. Despite the warm night, I shivered, ready for the wonder of his hands moving slow across my skin.

I looked for his face in the hay door high in the barn, but I couldn't distinguish him. We would have three hours before the water trickled to the other side of my field and I directed its flow onto the orchard, and finally, early the next morning, onto the garden. When I changed the water to the orchard, he would have to leave town and run back to his bed at Lookout Station so he could drive the freight wagon.

Near the top, I stepped out into the short lucerne. My fists clenched with anger. The ground was merely damp; dampness wouldn't grow lucerne; only a real soaking would do. Water should have been standing in the field. I had another field and the orchard to water and the first patch wasn't a fourth done yet.

I hurried across the top of the field. First, I would warn Matthew what had happened, and then I would walk up the ditch. I would rouse Brother Swensen, the water master, perhaps the bishop or J.D., and confront the thief. I walked quickly toward my stonework weir, a dark wedge of water just below the straight young willows of the creek. I had to constantly work to keep willow shoots from getting a purchase on my ditch banks. Ahead I saw something white, a piece of canvas perhaps, draped over my water gate as a dam. Whoever was stealing water wanted all of it, not just a trickle. I strode forward, shovel lifted to brain someone for robbing me of my water.

Closer to the weir, I stopped short. It was no canvas but the dress of a woman, stuck down in my gate. Her pale hair and her white clothing caught the moonlight. Dread clutched at my throat, because she looked like the apparition in my room. I hurried forward anyway. Her body blocked the water from coming onto my fields; her arms dangled across the sides of the wooden frame. A wind roared in my ears as I flung down my shovel and quilt and splashed across the muddy upper corner of my field. The woman's feet stretched along the bottom of the ditch and her white nightdress billowed. Her head slumped forward. Her hair, blond like Sophia's, fanned in the water.

I knelt in the mud on the bank and lifted the woman's head—Sophia, sunk shoulder-deep in dark water, her white skirts swirling. A meaty gash opened in her cold face, forehead to cheek. No blood dripped from the wound. Her face looked cold, white as stone. Her face was wrong, unnatural, like the moon rising red. Just that day she had been alive, preaching at me. Even now, she could open her gray lips to chastise me again.

The canvas dam across the main ditch was still in place, so the water had backed up to form a pool, with some water going around the dams and flowing on down the ditch. I grasped Sophia's lifeless hand and pulled, but her clothing was so heavy I couldn't budge her. I wedged my fingers under her chin—no heartbeat. I touched her arms, face, and lips—all cold as ditchwater. The cut had bled out; what remained was thick and syrupy. The blood, mud, and water smelled so dank that I nearly choked.

To my shame I thought, *Now I can never leave Ezekiel's family. Abigail will not survive on her own*. We had been getting along so well, and now my sister-wife was dead. My mind howled. Sophia's face was as white as that on a porcelain doll. I gripped her shoulders and lifted her partway out of the water. Shaking her shoulders, I hissed in her face, "Live. You cannot be dead. Cannot."

Chapter Four

The previous March, a month after I married Ezekiel, our benign, young patriarch had fled Utah Territory for England. Conveniently, the trip, to do genealogical research, also put him out of the reach of U.S. deputy marshals hunting polygamists.

He had wanted to get me with child before he left. Despite Abigail's frowns, he came to me every night during his last two weeks at home, working over me, not considering either my pleasure or comfort. He reminded me of a red Hereford bull in his lack of tact, romance, or care. His face, sweating above mine, looked as if he was in pain.

Then he had climbed on the train, looking pale and haggard from his labor over me. But my monthlies came on schedule, well before he had traveled across the ocean to reach England. Whether it was my lack of fertility, as Sophia suggested, or some other cause, his seed had been cast in vain. Nothing happened inside my womb. Which was all right by me. I didn't think my favor with God depended only on how many children a man could get on me.

I continued as before, tending the cattle J.D. had given me as a wedding gift, watering Ezekiel's fields, visiting with J.D. on Sunday afternoons, talking about everything from the nature of the universe to the books we read, or our various hunting trips together. He was the only man who spoke to me as an equal, and even he didn't do that all the time. It soon seemed as if I had never had a husband, except for the fact that I lived in a house with two sister-wives, who had not been happy to be ignored by their husband while he sniffed after a younger woman. Every night my arms curled around my pillow, a flour sack filled with corn shucks; it should have been a husband. Growing up watching animals mate and engender more animals, I had learned a healthy respect for my own urges. My nights with

Ezekiel had not been the height of pleasure, but they had also been too short.

I thought, riding after the cattle, or up all night irrigating, or turning and turning alone in my bed in the still-hot adobe house, that I had turned twenty with Ezekiel gone and I would be twenty-two before he came home. I, who was to be a Savior on Mount Zion through my industry and my womb, was childless and would be manless for at least another couple of years.

Early spring, before we knew how hot and dry the summer would be, Ezekiel sent a letter that shook us three women from crown to sole. Despite the fact that the previous fall the prophet Wilford Woodruff had proclaimed the end of polygamy, bowing to the pressure of the Federal government lest the Church be destroyed, Ezekiel had written that he would bring a young woman back from England to become his fourth wife. This against both the law of the land and now the law of the Church. His fourth fiancée was a Wainwright, a distant third cousin, daughter of the caretaker in the rectory where Ezekiel had been copying names. He wrote of this new woman's childlike faith. Childlike face, thought I, reading the letter. Blooming breasts. I imagined a girl as pale and soft as a moon.

Abigail and Sophia held a conference at the kitchen table. I stood with my back to the swinging door between kitchen and dining room, a smile curling my lip.

"And where does he have in mind to put her?" said Abigail, the practical one. I knew Abigail had saved money toward a new bed with a cotton and spring mattress. "First wife, first night home," she had repeated often, a year and a half before his return.

"She's hardly older than Zeke Jr.," said Sophia. "What is he thinking?"

I said, "He's thinking of the Lord's commandment to raise up a glorious posterity." I giggled and they frowned at my lack of reverence. "We need another house. Three more houses."

"How can we build another house?" asked Abigail. "We work all the time and can barely survive. How can we take on more work?"

Standing there, I saw my own marriage differently. Whatever we were of a family—three women and six children—involved less than nothing of Ezekiel. Instead of a man seated like a king in the middle, this family was three women at a table deciding how we would organize ourselves so that the desert would not starve us. Three women managing loom and cow and ewe and child and narrow ditch and straight rows of corn, smooth sheets of lucerne. This was what home manufacture, and self-sufficiency, and becoming a Savior on Mount Zion meant; this was the sum of all the words of the prophet—three women planning around a table.

That afternoon, sitting on a bank with my horse, Babe, grazing close and my twenty red beef cows trying to fill their stomachs with wiregrass, I reconsidered my life. I'd had a bellyful of Ezekiel, or rather I hadn't even had that. What made it that a man could legitimately love two or four or fifty women, but a woman could love only one man? My own mother had married J.D. when she still had a husband living in Nevada, and no one had been too concerned about the finer points of the law. The way men read God's word made the difference. They said God commanded them to take many wives. Said it was my duty to marry Ezekiel. But I'd had enough of duty. I knew it would be thought grievous sin, but I was ready to move beyond the beastly Principle; I wanted to live alone with my man in my own house, even if it was a miner's shack.

I pictured Ezekiel bringing that child-woman to our home. Her face might grow glum as she discovered she would not have solitary possession of Ezekiel or his house. Even if he had carefully explained that there were three other women, she still would not believe that she would have him only one week a month, living tight in a small room in a crowded house with ears and eyes and mouths all around her in the dark. Romance would have kept that vision from the girl. I would do almost anything to avoid participating in her disappointment when she arrived in town.

Since the age of eleven, I had known that obedience to the Principle of Plural Marriage would earn me a queenly crown and throne in heaven. Where would I find the faith to shuck off plural marriage as my mother had shucked off her unprofitable life? Wilford Woodruff had declared plural marriage was no longer required of the Saints. Brother Franklin had abandoned his second wife, leaving her to fend for herself. She had returned to her parents in Hamblin. It was rumored that Brother Nebeker had stopped sleeping with his second and third wives, only giving them sustenance. Through the winter he had built a second house, where they lived with their children. J.D. and the bishop held steady, changing nothing about their many-branched families.

Ezekiel would soon take a new wife. What could I do? It seemed clear to me that there might be many ways for me to choose a righteous path.

Mere days after these events Matthew came for me, just as he had sworn he would when we were both eleven and my mother fled Nevada. It felt like an answer to prayer. Before long we were married.

Chapter Five

Standing over Sophia's body in the ditch, I pondered how to lift her. I bent low and tried, but my hands slipped, unable to get purchase on arm or wrist. Her limbs seemed already stiff, which denied hope she was alive, but I needed to make sure. If I warmed her, she might open her eyes. It was possible. It was just as possible that the sun would rise at midnight. I tried again, but her clammy flesh was too slick.

"Matthew!" I screamed, and just as quick wished I hadn't. J.D., my stepfather, would examine the ground around the body and read Matthew's tracks running toward me as clearly as if the story had been printed in the Hamblin *Herald*. Could I tell J.D. that one of the Three Nephites, ancient undying disciples of Christ, had helped me pull Sophia out of the ditch? "Rachel, my girl, what have you to do with this man?" he would ask, if my tracks and Matthew's mingled, mine laid over some of his, his over mine.

Then I realized Matthew's danger, much more than the uncovering of our secret. J.D. would blame a stranger hiding in the barn before he would suspect any townsman of this murder. He didn't know Matthew as I did, didn't know his gentleness.

I took several deep breaths. Then I set my heels and hooked my fingers in the sleeve of Sophia's nightdress. I put one foot in the ditch, but it sunk deep in the mud. I pulled hard and Sophia's sleeve ripped from shoulder to elbow. I fell backward, landing on my rear. I rolled to my feet and pulled again on her bare arm, but my hands just slid off. I wrenched my foot out of the mud and got down in the ditch behind Sophia. I pushed, my shoulder against her back. My teeth grated on each other as I turned her in the water, which rushed past me, soaking me to my waist. Then with a final lunge, I rolled her onto the bank. The water poured through the gate, draining into my field. I turned Sophia face upward and then sat in the mud on the bank, her head in my lap.

No hint of pulse. Her face in the moonlight was a repulsive gray. I slid lower on the ditch bank and pulled her closer, my arms shaking from fear, effort, and cold. I kept thinking that if I could only warm her, she might open her eyes. I rocked back and forth, no longer sobbing, but feeling tears run down my face.

How long had she been in the ditch? At least an hour, I guessed. Even if I had waked on time to change the water, I could not have seen her attacker and stopped him. Had she really stood at my bedside, robed in the white gown she wore now and warned me with scripture? The dream must have come after her death. My mind swirled like muddy water. I held my cheek against her cold cheek, my arms around her, willing her to warm again.

Who had struck her down? With the drought, it was possible that even in this village of righteous brethren someone could have been angry enough to swing a weapon at her. I was neither a brother nor decidedly righteous, and I had wanted to knock Brother Turner down. I looked over my shoulder at the dark houses below me. Had Sophia caught Brother Turner putting a board in our water gate so that the stream would back up toward his property? If so, he might have struck her.

I stared at the barn, where Matthew might still wait for me. Sound carried far in night air. Why hadn't he come running? Watching the great doorway of the barn, I clutched Sophia tighter, as if I could hold her spirit from leaving her body. Soon the field would be full of the brethren, pronouncing who they thought had killed Sophia, strutting up and down along the creek and trampling over any tracks. But J.D. would be the first notified. He would come quickly, even in the dark, to scan the ground by lantern light. He would find the tracks of Sophia's murderer, just as he found whatever he sought. As an agent for Wells Fargo, he had recovered a lost thoroughbred horse, lost gold from the stage which had been held up, recovered countless other thieves and lost animals all across Utah Territory.

If no tracks led from the body to the barn, J.D. would have no reason to search there and discover signs of Matthew. But I had been a half hour late. Had Matthew walked from the barn to the ditch to watch for me? I peered at the dark ground but could see only the receding sheet of water. And what would I do if there were tracks? Tracks could be brushed out of dust or sand, but not mud. My stepfather knew I wasn't stupid; I couldn't mar tracks as if by accident.

But if Matthew was still hiding in the barn, I had to warn him away. Turning Sophia from my lap, I laid her on the bank and walked around the wide sheet of mud into the orchard. I passed through the darkness to the edge closest to the barn. "Matt," I called. "Matthew Harker." I wouldn't call loud; I didn't know who else might be out checking their water. "Matt. Go away. Don't come out. Go away." I waited and listened. Nothing moved except for my horse Babe shifting her feet and the milk cow Beulah rising at the sound of my voice. I heard no answer, no other sound of any movement.

It was useless to enter the wide, dark doorway or to climb the ladder to the loft. Either he had never come, which was a hopeful thought, or he had come and left again. I bowed my head. "Please God, arrange it that Matthew stayed at Lookout Station."

Slowly I forced my mind toward the unthinkable. If Sophia's be-damned dreams had led her to Matthew and she had confronted him, flinging the bitter word of God in his face, would he have responded with anger? No, he wouldn't have cared. But if she had called me adulteress, whore, a slut of Babylon, could her pious serpent tongue have incited him to murderous rage?

Impossible! But either he or one of the good Saints of Rockwood had killed her. Both alternatives were unbearable. But there she lay, no life in her, the bloody wound across her face.

I started back toward Sophia's body, stopped, moved toward the house, stopped again, turned toward the barn. J.D. would know by the water flowing into the field and by the drying of my tracks just how long I had stood here dithering and he would want to know why. Should I run for J.D. or Abigail, for the hunter or the healer? Sophia was dead but going for the healer would give Matthew more time to run—if he had been here at all.

I dashed down through the fields but then remembered my quilt, still lying in the field. I ran back up toward Sophia's body, lifted the half-sodden fabric, and hurried toward the house again. I climbed to the upper floor, then didn't know what to do. The quilt would drip all over the wooden floor and mark it. I ran back down the narrow stairs and flung the quilt across a bench in the cold cellar.

I was so panicked that I could hardly breathe as I lifted my hand to beat on Abigail's bedroom door, to jerk it open. Abigail struggled up out of the sheets, showing only her wide, white face. "Who is it?" she cried, her voice wavering with terror. "Mother?"

I ran to her bed and put my hands on her wide shoulders. "Rachel. I'm Rachel."

Her face was only a pale shadow. "Quiet, girl, you'll wake the children. You'll be the death of me, rushing in like a spirit from the beyond." Her hand touched my face, my arm. "You're wet, wet and muddy. You've soiled my bedclothes."

"Sophia," I hissed.

"Don't wake her," said Abigail, her voice gruff. "She couldn't sleep last night." Finally it sank into Abigail's thick head that something was wrong. "What is it, Rachel? What has you rushing around waking them that needs their sleep?"

"Sophia." I tried to breathe. "Let me speak. Up at the ditch. Cut on the forehead with a sword edge." I seemed to move in a fog. Why did I say what it was that killed Sophia? All I knew was that the cut was deep and extended from the top of her forehead to below her cheekbone. "She's dead. I know she's dead."

Abigail swung her feet to the floor. She clutched my arm and thrust her face close to mine. "No! Not Sophia. Did you—"

"What are you saying?" It seemed to me that she was still babbling, still mostly asleep. Then I realized she thought I had struck Sophia down. I put my hand across my open mouth. "Abigail, I didn't kill her. How can you think it?"

But I did know. Many times before the three of us became sisters in mind as well as by God's law, I had wished Sophia dead. I had screamed it into her face.

Abigail sat back on the bed, still trying to gather herself. Then she stood and pulled her dress on without taking time to remove her nightgown. "Go for J.D. No. Show me first. Maybe you were mistaken. Perhaps she still lives."

I lit an outdoor lantern, my hands shaking. Mostly I didn't want to see Sophia's ghostly face by moonlight. Abigail rushed out the door behind me, waddling in her haste. I lifted my wet skirt in one hand and the lantern in the other. "This way."

At the bank of the half-drained weir, I held the lantern above the body. Abigail bent over Sophia and turned her ear to Sophia's mouth. She pushed Sophia's pale hair out of her dead face. I lifted the lantern higher and glanced at the bank opposite. I could see no tracks between the barn and us. No evidence that Matthew had come down toward the weir, but water had flooded over the bank and could have washed the tracks away.

I looked across at the tangle of willows on the bank of the creek above the water gate. Leaning against them as if flung there was a shovel, the old broke-handled shovel I had carried to the barn in July for Matthew to use when he helped me irrigate. I started across. Abigail clutched at my arm. "Don't muddle the tracks. J.D. will want to look at them."

"She could have been killed with that." I pointed at the shovel.

"Yes, she could. But first things first. Leave it to J.D." She bent over Sophia.

I was anxious about leaving anything to J.D. when Matthew was involved. J.D. was kind to the righteous but had little charity for those he deemed wicked.

Abigail looked up at me. "Rachel, get a holt of yourself. I need your help." She tried to lift Sophia. "Let's get her to the house." I set the lantern on the bank, settling it so it couldn't tip and start a fire in the dry weeds along the ditch. Abigail and I locked hands behind Sophia's shoulders and lifted her. Then we locked our other hands behind her knees. We lifted and her head flopped back. Together we carried her through the field. Halfway down, Abigail tripped and we both let go, dropping Sophia's body on the ground. Her body lay twisted in an unnatural manner, and her hair spread out around her head. I lifted her to a sitting position and knelt next to her. I put her arm around my neck and held her clammy hand with my left hand. I put my other arm around her body and Abigail did the same from the other side.

"Now," I said, and we lifted Sophia and stumbled the rest of the way to the back gate.

Zeke Jr. stood in the open doorway, holding a lantern. "I woke and you were gone, so I came outside and called for you. Why didn't you answer?" He walked out onto the porch.

"Open the gate," called Abigail. "Please be quick. She's very heavy."

"What are you carrying?" He stepped off the porch, crossed the yard in a few steps and shoved open the back gate. When he saw the body, he became immobile, eyes wide. But he had wits enough to turn and run across the yard ahead of us. He opened the door, and we carried Sophia's body past him through the kitchen.

"Put her in my room," said Abigail. "We'll never get her up those narrow stairs." Zeke Jr. opened the door to his mother's room and stood aside. "Strip the bedding off, Zeke, will you?" His mother's voice was soft for him. He pulled off the bedclothes and dumped them on the floor in the corner of the room. Then he set the lantern on his mother's dresser and disappeared. I wanted to go after him, make sure he was all right after what he had seen, but my arms were still full.

I maneuvered Sophia's body toward the bed.

"Not yet," said Abigail. "She'll soil the mattress."

"Hell! Let it be soiled."

"No!" We lowered the body to the floor.

Abigail rushed into the kitchen and spread newspapers and a layer of rags across the bed.

"Now," she said. We lifted Sophia and laid her out. Abigail held the lantern close, and I saw that the cut was not a clean one, not made by a sharp weapon like a sword. The flesh was smashed, bruised all along the blow, and slightly curved. I touched my fingers to the wound and pressed lightly. Her flesh felt like the surface of a pudding; the bones of her face were certainly broken.

"Rachel, do you think someone thought she was stealing water?"

"Doesn't make sense. It was *our* water turn. But it does look like the mark a shovel blade would leave."

Abigail looked at me. "Maybe she caught someone stealing water *from* us."

Nodding, I pictured Brother Turner swinging a shovel at Sophia. His small face was dirty and his mouth grimaced. His eyes gleamed white. I realized that my dislike didn't make him a killer. Many in town faced starvation with the coming winter. A few had borrowed and more would borrow water, and many would defend their act, maybe with violence. Or maybe the killing had not been over water at all. Brother Turner's face was replaced by Matthew's. I winced as if struck. His mouth grimaced with viciousness, his eyes were small and devilish.

All the children in the house crowded into the room. "I woke them," said Zeke Jr. "Everybody's here now."

"Oh, Ezekiel," Abigail said, "this is too much for these babes.

You should have let them sleep."

His face fell and I thought he would cry, but he pulled himself together. He thought of himself as man of the house, I knew. He turned and took Marianne's hand and tried to get her to leave. Abigail joined him, trying to shoo the young ones out of the room, but they crowded past to look. Surprised by the body, they fell silent but soon started whimpering.

"What cut her that way?" Zeke Jr. asked.

"Something dull," his mother said. "Not a sword or a knife."

"She was hit with a shovel," said Sarah, Abigail's ten-year-old. She had tears on her face but was now calm, a calmness I found frightening. "I've seen that same curved shape in the mud."

"I don't know, Sarie." Abigail turned to me, her mouth a frown, questioning.

The younger children wailed behind us. Sophia's oldest child, Marianne, who was five, pushed past the others and took her mother's fingers. Just as quick she dropped the water-soaked hand. "Who is it?" the girl said. "She shouldn't be in Aunt Abigail's bed. Wake her up and tell her to go home to her own bed." I picked Marianne up and moved her away from the corpse. Tears ran down my own face. I felt terror, as if Satan or one of his servants had taken over the town.

I heard the back door open, and someone crossed the room. The first Sister Swensen came into the bedroom and put her arms around Abigail. "I saw you rush up into your field. Then I heard the children crying."

"Sophia," said Abigail. "Face bashed in."

"Not Sophia," Sister Swensen whispered.

"Dead," said Abigail.

Sister Swensen clucked and waddled to the bedside. Her head darted forward as she looked at Sophia. A squat woman, white-haired and wearing her white nightdress, she looked like a huge hen. "Horrid, horrid. Who could have done this?"

I knew that if I was an honest woman, I would have already gone after J.D. My arms wide, I herded the children away from the body. Abigail shut the door on Sophia and Sister Swensen and then sat at the kitchen table. She lifted Marianne onto her lap. "Children," she commanded, "gather round. Aunt Sophia—" She looked at Marianne. "Your mother has returned to Father in Heaven. Right now her Grandfather and Grandmother Jorgensen are welcoming her into Paradise. Jesus and the prophets have hugged her and led her to a place where she can rest and learn and watch you be happy. Her only sorrow now is your sorrow." Tears streamed down the faces of Zeke Jr. and Susan—Abigail's older two children. The smaller children started wailing again, Richard and Little Mary joining Marianne and Stephen.

Sister Swensen came out of the bedroom at the noise. "Poor chicks. The poor chicks." Then she clucked, "Chuk, chuk, chuk." Despite the tears in my eyes, I laughed, a bark like a dog. The two women and the children stared at me. I wrapped my arms around Marianne, and the women held the other children, who wept in our arms. I clung to their warm bodies, trying to erase from my head the feeling of my hands and arms on their mother's cold, dead flesh.

Chapter Six

I separated myself from Sophia's girl. "I need to go after J.D."

But first I ran up the stairs and shrugged out of my sodden, mud-laden frock and slipped into a dry dress, a tan cotton one. I started for the door, then went back to grab my watch and put it into my pocket. I felt the dial—one ten. Without doubt, J.D. would ask me about times. Passing Sophia's room, I shoved open the door. Her quilt had been folded down, but as far as I could see, the bed hadn't been slept in. Finally I rushed back down the stairs.

Striding up the lane toward J.D.'s house, I felt a lump in my gut from my fear that Sophia had somehow discovered Matthew in the barn, and he had struck her down. It seemed more likely that Sophia in her white dress had come suddenly out of the night and surprised someone stealing our water.

I beat on J.D.'s back door. Finally he swung it open, wearing only his white garments, the holy underclothing given to all Mormons when they first enter the temple. His hair and beard were disheveled.

"Sophia's been killed."

"You say she's dead?"

"Yes."

His face twisted with shock and anger. "My Lord in heaven. Where is she?"

"We took her to the house, laid her on Abigail's bed."

"Where did you find her?"

"In our ditch. Sitting in the ditch."

"The ditch? You mean down in the water?"

I nodded.

He disappeared inside but returned in an instant with his trousers on. Mary, his first wife, appeared in the door behind him. She was fully dressed.

I turned and the three of us walked back down the street. Inside our house, I showed them the body. J.D.'s broad shoulders seemed to fill the bedroom. He touched Sophia's face along the line of her cut. "Her cheekbone is broken." He moved his fingers up to her forehead. "I'd wager her skull's cracked." Then he lifted behind her head. "Neck's broken. A terrific blow." He moved her jaw from side to side. "Rigor mortis has not set in. She was killed only an hour or two ago."

He motioned with his fingers above the cut. "'Tis the same curve as a shovel." He examined Sophia's hands and arms. "Tsk. She didn't even have time to lift her arms to ward off the blow."

He turned to me, his face terrible. "Ah, Rachel, how can this have happened in Rockwood?" His hands fisted against his thighs. "Among these good people. Among the people of God."

I thought that violence had happened among every people since Cain slew Abel in Adam's family. But I wondered if it felt the same every time, as if the very fabric of the universe had rent and stars fell from the sky.

J.D. walked out of the room. "Let's go up and have a look at the ditch." I followed him as he grabbed a lantern from the kitchen, lit it, and walked heavily up through the field.

If Matthew had done this, I would protect him. The guilt from that knowledge of myself sat on my soul like a leaden lump.

Far across the lucerne, I saw that the lantern Abigail and I had carried up was still burning—a small circle of light. It looked so forlorn, as if it was Sophia's soul half raised toward heaven, half caught where she had been murdered.

"I forgot my lantern." We walked quickly across the top of the field to the weir. I avoided looking at the barn, wishing I had actually gone up into the loft to check for Matthew, and at the same time grateful that I had not. My tracks would be curious to J.D.

"Oh, my Rachel, how can we survive this tragedy?" He laid his hand on my shoulder and I watched his face, which moved from anger to sorrow. Speaking, he hardly moved his mouth. "A woman dead and one of the Saints the killer." I bent to retrieve my lantern. Where was Matthew now? Not knowing would drive me mad. I wanted to be a visionary woman, a seer, knowing where my husband was. I pulled myself back to the present need.

"She was sitting there." I pointed downward. "Right in the side gate."

"The tracks are all muddled. Here are deep tracks in the mud."

"I had to pull her out. That's where I stood; then I knelt there to roll her out onto the bank." I shivered again thinking of her clammy skin. "I went for Abigail and the two of us carried her down."

"You should have come for me first."

I opened my mouth, shut it again. Holding my voice quiet, I said, "I couldn't leave her there in the ditch."

He shook his head. "She fell there?"

"She was sitting backward. Her arms were out to the sides resting on the bank, and she sat right in the gate."

"My Rachel, I am asking you as clear as I can: Do you think that she might have fallen there?"

"Or floated that way, with the water pushing her."

"You said her arms were up on the sides." He shook his head once, sharp. "Of course, she could not have floated there." When I was a child, he never criticized my judgment. Same as with a horse, never responding with anger, never hasty. But once I became a grown woman in his eyes, once I wanted to help him with his detective work, he often became short with me.

He picked up the other lantern and lifted it high. He touched the crown of his head with the fingertips of his left hand, rubbing the bald spot there in a circular motion.

I imagined someone killing in anger. A man without a face. After such a killing, the person would clutch his shovel and run.

But stopping to place the body in a sitting position in the water gate. A warning? Was it a message: never steal water again?

A couple of men in town were capable of such anger, and then coolness afterward—Brother Turner, Brother Pritchard, Brother Jenkins. Of course J.D., who had killed before as an agent to Wells Fargo. I looked at his broad back, the white of his temple garments. But he had killed enemies of God, not a woman with two children to love. Whoever had done this had been either so angry he lost possession of his own soul or crazy out of his head.

He said, "You came up at what o'clock?"

I opened my pocket watch, which was still ticking despite the dampness on the silver case. "A half an hour ago. Just after twelve thirty." Almost the truth.

"You came up to set the water last evening?"

"Yes. I walked up and switched it over at six o'clock."

"So she was killed during your water turn."

"Yes."

He glanced at my face and I felt it heating up, sure as sin he could see my secret written there, like pen on parchment.

J.D.'s fingers traced his habitual circle on the crown of his head. "I'm frightened that she discovered someone stealing water and said harsh words that provoked him. She never was one to mince her words, not her."

I didn't know if Matthew had killed Sophia. I doubted it; but if he had, and no one knew he was here, no one could accuse him.

I let out my held breath.

More likely it was someone pushed too far by the drought. Brother Jenkins had gotten angry enough to strike Brother Pritchard's child. Could Sophia have caught him taking water, slipping it under the dam at the main weir upstream? Or Brother Turner, who also had a temper and who lived directly above us on the ditch?

I looked over the houses in town. Light shone in the Swensens' house, and in the Turners'. As I watched, a light came up in the bishop's house. Was the killer hiding in one of the dark houses I looked over, hands over his face, mortified at what he had done? Or was he one of those whose lanterns were lit?

I wiped both hands down across my face; it was horrible to think of someone in town killing Sophia, more horrible to imagine Matthew's face twisted with murderous anger. In daylight we could simply walk the ditch and discover who had mud in his fields—not necessarily the newest mud. A man who had killed in anger would surely gather his wits and shut off the water he'd been stealing.

Turning back, I glanced at the barn. *Father in Heaven,* I prayed again, *bless that Matthew's tracks are nowhere near*. I looked across the weir and pointed to the shovel in the willows. "J.D."

He glanced up. "Yes. I saw it, my impatient Rachel. All in good time." He stopped short of the sheet of mud around the wooden gates and ditches. I stood shoulder to shoulder with him as we examined the ground. The bottom of the lantern made a round shadow that made it difficult to distinguish what was track and what was uneven mud. His hand was up, rubbing his crown again as he thought. The water flowed through the east gate and out of the ditch into my lucerne field. Despite the horror that possessed me, it still felt good to have water spreading across my field. I shook my head, wondering at my instinct toward making things grow that was deep as life itself, deep as death.

Curious about who had laid down tracks along the ditch bank, I stepped toward the edge of the mud where the water had pooled. About ten feet up the ditch from my water gate, the path along the bank was dry. When I tipped my lantern slightly, casting its light sideways, the tracks showed clearly, shadows in the prints and light on the edges. I bent nearly double and stepped slowly, following the tracks as they continued up the bank. Many people had walked up the ditch and back down, but I could distinguish several recent ones, crossing over all the other tracks in the powdered dust.

Stepping carefully in the weeds just off the pathway, I followed the tracks past a huge sage bush, big as a small tree. Here the topmost track was the rounded toe of a work boot, slightly wider than the heel. I knew Matthew wore square-toed boots, and for a second my soul lifted. The left heel was also worn badly, and I knew Matthew wouldn't let his boots go like that. I noticed that the right heel had been repaired. I peered up the ditch as it curved around the hill on which the chapel was built. Around that curve was the Turners' property. Holding the lantern high, I started following the ditch upward.

"Rachel, are you marring those tracks?" I stopped, irked that he thought I was so stupid. When I first came to Rockwood, he said over and over how bright he thought me. *Look at that girl do her arithmetic,* he said a dozen times. *You wrote that? You are a natural genius.* I lapped it up like honeyed milk.

"I'm walking to the side of the path. There's a set of tracks here, and I want to see how far up they go." I would bet one of my new calves that they ended at Brother Turner's doorstep. He had stolen before. Desperate as he was, he might have done it again.

J.D. joined me and bent over the pathway, also tipping his lantern so the light cast downward. "The last ones were men's work boots, looks like. 'Tis clear they were made recent." He bent lower and squinted. "But this dust is so dry, I can't tell how many hours ago, whether it was tonight or last evening." I followed J.D. as he moved down just to the side of the ditch, taking care to stay back from the pathway. I tried to see what he could see, something about the way dirt fell from the sides of the prints into the depression made by the foot. "Someone walked down the path and went back up sometime last night." J.D.'s feet sank into the muddy field. I stepped exactly where he stepped. "Too recent to be somebody taking the water a week ago." He rubbed his head.

"You'll make yourself even balder." I immediately bit my lip.

He stared at me without smiling, but then he lowered his hand, hooking it in his beard. "The water was taken from the west ditch and put in this one two days ago. Somebody came down here recently. Could be last night, could be yesterday."

"Couldn't be yesterday." I pointed to where one of the booted tracks crossed mine, going up to take the water from Brother Turner.

"Right you are, Rachel. But they still might have nothing to do with the killing. Might be someone going for a stroll or Brother Swensen checking the water." He rubbed his eyes. "I can't see like I used to."

"You should get eyeglasses."

"No, not Brother Swensen. The print's much too large." He tried to step back but bumped into me. "Give me some room, Rachel. I must have room to turn around." He stepped carefully back toward the weir. "Who would have thought that I'd have to memorize the tracks of men in Rockwood?" He pointed down to where I had run through the muddy water toward Sophia. "Your tracks when you found her?"

"I think so." I bent. "Yes."

"Barefoot," he said. "I question the wisdom of a man going off to England when his own wives can't afford shoes."

"I choose to go barefoot." I could open my mouth and add, *Go barefoot to my husband.* The words were on my lips, ready to spill out. Those words would save much distraction with untangling the mystery that night. But they would not come. J.D. would think our lovemaking lascivious sin. He would never, even if he lived to be a hundred, understand. Nothing had changed about my need for secrecy.

"And then the fool wants to marry again when he can hardly support one wife, let alone four. After the prophet has said we should take no new wives. Tsk." He shook his head sharply, and then leaned forward again. "Your tracks and Abigail's." He pointed to his left, to the bank below the main gate. "Abigail *chooses* to afford shoes."

He looked across the dark field toward the house. He walked forward and picked up my shovel that I had dropped in the field when I first saw Sophia's body. "Yours?"

"Yes." If he walked a step farther he'd see my double tracks when I retrieved my quilt.

"And Sophia's tracks?"

He finally turned and walked toward me. We both bent and swept our lanterns back and forth across the ground. No tracks, except for mine and Abigail's, appeared where the pool of water had stood. I stepped slightly to my left, examining the uneven, shadowy ground for any track before I put each foot down. I saw my barefoot tracks and Abigail's shod tracks but no others.

"Have we confused your tracks with Sophia's?"

"I doubt it," I said. "My feet are longer." I prayed that Matthew had also wakened late in his bed at Lookout Station and had never arrived here. But he would need to pay attention. If he came upon us suddenly, I'd have a difficult time explaining the sudden greeting of a handsome and strapping man.

"Here," J.D. said, tipping the lantern slightly and kneeling. "What are these?" He pointed to bare tracks going around the edge of the mud—mine as I walked through the part of the orchard nearest to the barn to warn Matthew.

I said nothing.

"Not Sophia's."

"I walked up toward the barn after I found the body." I said nothing else.

He stared at me. The shadows made by the lantern made his face even more stern. "What made you walk closer to the barn after you found the body? Did you hear something?"

"No." I felt the blood rushing to my face. Luckily it was too dark for him to see me blush.

He stared at me. "Did you walk up to check on the animals?"

I didn't know what to say, so I said nothing.

He shrugged his shoulders. Then he slung the lantern low and circled in a clockwise direction around the weir and the patch of mud adjacent to it. "There are no other tracks in the field. Except for horse tracks." He pointed in the ditch bottom below the gate in the main ditch. Grass was cropped to either side. "Days old. Pritchard's damn horse, I'll wager. Nothing to do with this." Brother Pritchard's horse was forever climbing out of his ramshackle corral and grazing the ditches. "I think he lets him out on purpose to graze." Sour-faced and thrifty, Brother Pritchard was forever repairing his horse's damage to the ditch rather than simply fixing his corral.

I examined the ditch and bank. Some hoofprints at the edge of the mud were shallow, made before the bank overflowed; some sank deep into the bank. "These tracks were made after she died. After the water overflowed." I looked at him and he nodded. I wished Pritchard's wayward horse could talk, could say what it had seen as it wandered the bank, before and after Sophia died.

J.D. continued his circuit of the water gates. He jumped the ditch and came back toward the weir on the other side. He paused at the path to the barn, which cut straight across the top of the water gate. A week ago, I had laid tracks there when I went from changing the water straight to Matthew. It wouldn't matter if J.D. found those old tracks because I went to and from the barn at least twice a day to milk the cow or do other chores.

But then my soul seemed to wilt in my body as J.D. pointed to another set of tracks, leading directly from the barn—the square toe and flat heel of boots like the kind Matthew wore. I knew, because they were different from any I'd seen—different from those sold by any Mormon storekeeper in Hamblin. J.D. went down on hands and knees in the dirt, examining and memorizing, putting the glimpses of the boot together like a puzzle. "Fresher than those round-toe boots."

I cast my eyes down. Next to my toe was a barefoot print,

shorter than my own foot. "J.D., I found Sophia's print." I pointed to her tracks coming from the barn. J.D. scurried toward the weir, one arm holding the lantern high. "Both sets of tracks go from the barn to the weir." J.D. dropped to one knee and bent forward, examining the ground. "He was running. She was walking." He looked toward the barn. "He was chasing her and she didn't hear or see him coming."

"She was hit in the face."

"She may have heard him and turned." He pointed to the sheet of mud surrounding the water gates. Then he rubbed his eyes again. "I wish we could see the tracks where he caught up to her."

"You must be mistaken." Despair flooded me like a sickness in my blood. Feeling that I might fall, I put my hand out and pushed against the air.

"What? The tracks are clear. She walked to the weir. He ran to the weir. There's what he killed her with." J.D. pointed to the old cast-off shovel. "Her body was there in the weir. What other explanation is there?"

I imagined J.D. roping Matthew, dragging him behind his horse until he was dead. My hands fisted tight at my sides.

"Here are her tracks going up to the barn door." J.D. pointed to the curve of a sole, the imprint of her toes. "Just like yours over there in the orchard. Going toward the barn. Very fresh. I imagine we'll also discover that he was a stranger in town. I've never seen boots on any of the brethren that would make these tracks. My Rachel, I have a powerful feeling this is our man."

He had never before talked about feeling when looking at tracks. He knew or he didn't know. His eyes weren't as strong as they once were; he had started forgetting things.

I looked down at the tracks. I wasn't as good as J.D., but I could see the flat barefoot tracks walking up and then back down, and I could see the toe-only tracks, Matthew running. I pictured Sophia walking up across the fields, asleep or stuporous, unseeing. She must have wandered to the barn, back down to the weir. It seemed clear that Matthew had run after her and killed her as she heard and turned. I followed their prints down to the weir and slumped to sit on the water gate.

As a boy, Matthew had been closer than a brother to me. He had nothing of the cruel or malicious in him. His face was open and clear, and he was slow to anger. He seemed just the same now, eight years later, still gentle and careful. But what had five years as a soldier done to him?

"Yes." J.D. got down on one knee. "'Twas someone who came out of the barn who killed our Sophia." I wanted to drag him to look at the other tracks, but J. D didn't let anyone force him.

As if I were a raven or a magpie circling the weir, I imagined myself looking down from the air at the muddy banks and the swirl of tracks leading to and away from the body. Unless an angel had swooped from heaven and struck Sophia down for her vision of God as stern and hateful, Matthew had probably killed her.

It still made no sense. For what seemed like the hundredth time, I sifted what I knew of Matthew.

Chapter Seven

Until I was eleven, my mother, my two siblings, and I lived with my first father—a dirt-poor, west-desert, Gentile miner—at Osceola, Nevada, on the border between Utah Territory and Nevada. Matthew's father and Goshute mother had worked a mine nearby. Both men complained constantly that the other mine infringed on his claim. Each miner's name for the other was "That damn trespasser." Somehow Matthew and I had ignored our parents' dispute and had run wild together through the piñons and cedars after finishing our chores.

Both of us stayed outside as much as we could, so winters were purest hell, stuck in a bitter cold shack that the wind blew through like it blew through brush. My main memory was sitting with my brother, sister, and mother as close to the cook stove as we could. Once we took the racks out of the oven and laid a rug inside. We took turns crawling in that warm cave. I burned myself—rear, shoulders, and forearms—but it was worth it to be surrounded by pure, lovely heat.

I learned to read and write from my mother, sitting as close to that stove as I could get. Later there was a board schoolhouse, but that building was even colder than our shack. There were two small stores, a hotel, a restaurant, a livery, and a smithy, all slapped together. Most everyone in town thought only about digging gold, silver, lead, or tungsten out of the ground.

Spring was like a revelation, summer purest joy. Soon as it was warm enough to stay outside, Matthew and I spent every hour running and playing under the cedars and piñons. We made miniature ranch spreads in the duff under the cedars, fences of twigs, pebbles for cattle and horses. We built tiny houses and barns from slabs of bark. I even built an outhouse once. We had corrals a yard across for taming horses and doctoring and marking calves. It was nostalgic even then because my father's first desire on coming to America from Ireland was to get his own ranch. He settled in Oklahoma Territory, but when the farm failed, took off for the mines of Nevada.

"I wish we'd never left Oklahoma," my mother said a hundred times if she said it once. Matthew's dad had done the same, given up on a hardscrabble place for the dream of gold. Both men always dreamed of going back to ranching but never could get enough money together.

Once we were chasing each other, and I tripped, falling forearms first down a slide of shale. I sat at the bottom holding my red and dripping palms up, blood running from my shredded forearms. Blood splattered the rocks. Matthew ran to me, took off his shirt and tore it into strips to wrap my arms. He led me back to my mother who smiled at him for his doctoring work. "You'll be a doctor when you grow up."

"Cattle rancher."

We lived together every summer until we were both eleven. One night my father's drinking friends dumped him on our doorstep, and for the first time my mother left him there. It was spring, and I had slept outside in colder weather, so I wasn't worried about him. She stormed back and forth in front of the cook stove. "Mother lode!" she shouted. "There is no mother lode. I have to drag him home twice a week. Dammit, it's been *every* night all this week." She was still pacing when we went to sleep. The next morning she laid a few clothes, what flour we had, and a pot onto the bed. She wrapped our earthly goods in the bed quilt, then tied it with a couple of my father's belts. When my father woke, she said, "We're leaving you, Timothy." I didn't even think of questioning her, the way she looked at my dad. He must have felt it too, because although he swore and raged as my mother stolidly finished making a small pack for each of us children, he didn't lay a hand on any of us to prevent our going.

I barely had time to run and say goodbye to Matthew. I

grabbed him and pulled him behind his shack, took his hand and sliced both our palms with my pocketknife, mingling our blood in a promise to seek each other out in eight years—to rejoin what adult foolishness had torn us asunder. The last I saw of him was his mournful face and his hand, still bloody, raised to wave goodbye.

My mother swung her makeshift pack across her shoulder, and we set out—walking mile after mile around Wheeler Peak and across horribly barren desert. We made it all the way to Bloomington, near Fort Deseret. Then we headed north, riding on a freight wagon whenever a driver took pity on us. Three weeks after leaving Osceola we came to Rockwood town, which seemed more like heaven than any place I had ever lived.

I didn't forget Matthew, but I had assumed he forgot me, assumed that he had become a drunken miner, just like every man I knew in Nevada.

But he never forgot, and eight years later he came for me.

On a May day hot and dry as July, a little more than a year after Ezekiel left for England, I rode Babe to the Rush Lake Station to look at a new purebred Hereford bull the stationmaster, Jared Cook, was using. I stood before the animal, which was as deep and heavy as a rhinoceros.

I told him, "I would like to run my cattle with yours next spring." We came to an agreement and I turned to leave when the Wells Fargo freight wagon arrived. On top appeared a ghost, half familiar. "Do I know you?" I said. He wore the same smile as Matthew, my childhood friend. I shook my head and turned away, turned back. "Are you Matthew Harker?"

He pulled back his horses. "Yes. Rachel O'Brien?"

"Rachel Wainwright," I said. "Eight years. I thought you'd be governor of Nevada by now."

"Eight years. I thought you'd remember that long." Then someone shouted from inside the station, and he allowed his mules to step forward. "You should never have left Nevada," he said over his shoulder.

Breathless as a girl, I watched him pull his mules to a stop in front of the station. He handed the reins to his partner, and while the stationmaster brought out the mail, he walked toward me. As a boy he had been quick as a weasel, darting under the cedars, flashing a white smile backward over his shoulder. Now slower, thicker-bodied, he was familiar but magnified, startling as a revelation. I couldn't take my eyes away. In my memory he was still a boy, not this tall, broad-shouldered man—this wide-smiling man. His sandy hair had darkened to walnut.

"I have come to honor the oath we swore eight years ago."

"How...did you find me?"

"Luck. Purest good luck." He smiled and I had to look away. "And persistence."

"I don't believe it." My face flushed hot.

"Believe it. Ambrose Rockwood, the innkeeper at Lookout Pass Station, told me you were here. I've come to take you away from these Mormonites."

"I'm married."

"Legally?"

"Before God."

"This false marriage changes nothing as far as I am concerned."

I took a step away from him.

"People in Osceola area think that your mother took you to the East, or even back to the Isle of Man. But I didn't give up. All the time I was in the army, I thought about you waiting for me. I knew that even if your mother took you across the ocean that you, Rachel O'Brien, would never change. You'd still wait for me." He smiled, apparently sarcastic, but I saw the tears standing in his eyes. "I thought your love was as steady and dependable as an ocean liner."

"Children's affection. Not love. I didn't imagine you changing, either. In my mind you're still ten."

He looked at me, sharp, then.

"When I was discharged from the army, I despaired of ever finding you. I thought that if I took a job with the freight lines and the stage, with Wells Fargo, that I might hear word of you. I've asked in every city between here and the Mississippi." He took another step toward me. I took another step back. "Then Ambrose told me you live right here in Rockwood." He took another step forward.

"Matthew. Stop."

"When he said you'd bound yourself to a Mormonite, I thought at first that it must not be you, because my Rachel would never give up on me, never forget me." He turned his back, and I had to hold my hand from touching him on the shoulder. "I went into a slough of despondency thick as quicksand. Even though your marriage, being the third to one man, is not legal in this territory or any other, I also knew Brigham Young taught his people to hate all Gentiles. Once in the habit, those who follow him can't give up their hatred."

Matthew was partly right. Bishops still warned their people not to buy in Gentile stores. It was fine to sell to Gentiles, to get rich from the Gentile miners and settlers coming through the state, but not to buy from them.

"I can't abide a people so bigoted."

I smiled. "So you're bigoted against the Mormons?"

He shrugged.

"Your father died a few years ago. He never remarried, and he always talked with longing about his children and bitterness about his wife, who had abandoned him."

"He probably remembered us when he was falling down drunk, because he didn't have anybody to beat on."

Matthew shook his head. "He was a broken man. He loved you."

I remembered my father with a face powdered with rock dust, his eyes bright and fanatical. Or drunk.

He stepped toward me. "You didn't wait."

I felt my face flush again.

"Are you blushing for shame that you didn't wait for me? For not thinking twice about breaking your oath? You mistrusted me, mistrusted your own word, sealed with our blood. You should have waited the full eight years before giving up and marrying someone else."

I climbed on Babe and turned her toward Rockwood. "Goodbye, Matthew Harker."

"No woman will replace you," he called after me. "You haven't seen the last of me, Rachel O'Brien."

I didn't turn back. Matthew's face had been clear and strong. He had grown to be a goodly and a winsome man. As I rode away I thought about Ezekiel, pious, spindly, and pink. I felt cheated by fate or God or my own desires; I didn't know what to blame.

That night I walked up to the barn and lay across the back of my horse, Babe. I thought about the man Matthew had turned into. How had he found me despite my mother's act of losing herself among the Mormons? I shook my head; the boy was still in my thoughts. I remembered running away from my cabin where my father, mother, and we three children lived. I nearly swooned as the past rushed back on me, Babe's mane clutched in my hand but my head in Nevada. Even after eight years of forgetfulness, my interest in Matthew had remained hidden inside me like fly eggs in meat.

The next week when my water turn came, Matthew's voice came to me out of the dark orchard. He stepped out on the other side of the ditch.

"Go away. I'm a married woman." I figured he had copied down the water turns from the list posted on the front window of the Merc.

"Your marriage is not a legal marriage."

I couldn't see his eyes, but I spoke toward his shadowy self.

"In the eyes of my God, it is legal. My connection to a righteous man will carry me to heaven—make me a Queen, a goddess in heaven. Would you, Matthew, drag me down to hell?"

"Yes," he said.

"I am married heart and soul."

"But let's not talk about that. Walk with me."

I didn't know what to say, but for sure and certain I couldn't say no.

"Two new miners have taken over our parents' claims. The new miners fight over territory just like our fathers did. Rachel, nothing is new underneath the sun."

In the dark our shoulders brushed, and my shoulder tingled. An anxious, pleasant want stirred in my gut. My body certainly recognized that there was a fine-looking man close, even if I couldn't see him in the dark. I thought about Ezekiel thousands of miles away across the ocean.

"I have a small herd of horses."

"I have cows, twenty of them, a gift from my stepfather, J.D. Rockwood."

He was silent for some time.

"You lived with that devil?"

"You know I did. He's not a devil."

"Bewitched you."

"Tell me about your horses."

"Two are Morgan crosses, great for plowing. I've been thinking about Wyoming. I've heard there is still land available for homesteading."

"Sure, you should go there, Matthew. I picture you plowing behind those horses, breaking your ground. I was frightened you'd tunnel yourself into your father's hole."

"Not this son. Just when he wanted me to give him serious help, I became itchy and the wanderlust took control, so I joined the army. Air and wide sky for me." He leaped the ditch. "Married to a Mormonite." I thought he would touch my arm, and I moved back. "But that's your style, running away from me through the cedars. I've slept in every stage station between here and San Francisco, and between here and Omaha. I still dream about you, about every other night. Maybe every third night." I heard a forced laugh. "But you've certainly stopped dreaming about me."

"You don't know the first thing about me, Matthew Harker."

"I sure like Ambrose. But I don't understand how one brother could be kind as an angel and the other cruel as Satan. Ambrose's the one who told me where you live."

"Dammit, Matthew, give it up. I am not leaving my husband and my town, no matter how much you hate J.D. Rockwood."

"I also have a great affection for Libby. You know she thinks her dogs are her children. She sits them at the table when we eat there."

"I know, Matthew. They are my aunt and uncle. I know all about them."

"I've told them I admire you, and they think the better of me for it."

I shook my head, not knowing what to say. Finally I blurted, "I have a horse. Babe."

He followed me up to the barn and Babe was at the fence. Matthew moved slowly into the pen, held his hand flat for Babe to smell. Soon he was moving his palm across her shoulders, belly, and flank as if she had known him already.

He said, "She's a good horse."

"Good judge of humans."

As suddenly as he came, he leaped the fence and was gone. He hadn't even touched my arm.

I felt my soul caught on the end of a tether, like the bouncing, clawing bobcat that J.D. had once roped and dragged home.

Nobody had wooed me like Matthew had just done. Not the stammering town boys, and certainly not pious, methodical Ezekiel. Eight years Matthew had nourished his love for me, fed it, and made it grow. Clearly this was a rare devotion, not something to set aside easily.

The next day I noticed a quickening inside, like a space made for a child I hadn't yet conceived. I was not only curious about the contours of Matthew's face but about the changes in his mind and soul. He was sure of himself, his mind still weasel-quick, but stable. I smiled as I walked between house and field. Imagining myself as Matthew might see me, I knew myself as a mahogany-haired, sharp-faced, slender woman—pleasing to his eye.

That night he walked through my dreams, his round boy-face grinning through a patriarchal beard that stretched down to his belly. In the dream, Matthew's beard, unlike Ezekiel's, was blond, silky smooth. I ran after him through the cedars, as I had as a girl, but now we wore no clothing and I was full grown. In the dream, I climbed after him up through the branches of a cedar, finding him bedded down on top of the tree—lithe, free, unpredictable Matthew. Waking, I turned and turned on my bed.

I regretted my marriage to Ezekiel. My husband was rightly named; he was an Old Testament man, a brittle stick.

The next time I changed my water, Matthew sat on the bank as I pulled the board dam out of the water gate to let the water flow down toward my second field. He shadowed me as I followed the water rushing out onto my stubby lucerne. "What if Sophia had come to change the water?" I asked him, smiling. "Would you have come after *her* with your devil's words and black heart?"

"No. Only after you, my blood sister. There is only one moon in this man's sky."

"You have less ambition than any man I know."

"Ambition? I doubt that's what drives Mormon men."

I smiled at the idea that Ezekiel was possessed by lust. He had had to close his eyes to mount me, and as soon as he was on top, he had gone to work rocking his body like sawing a log. An act of passion it was not, not that and not love. Duty.

Matthew stood ready to run back to Lookout. It pleased me that he ran four miles each way just to talk to me. I smiled after his broad back as he leaped the ditch, trotted up the dusty hillside so he could circle the town and return to his bed. He was a gentle, smart man, good with horses. He walked along the ditch with me for a month but never touched me. He certainly knew when to rein in his animal self; he probably also knew when to release his passion. I could wait another year or I could have him now. He would be perfectly willing, under the fruit trees or in the barn.

Then I felt foolish for dreaming adulterous dreams about a Gentile, a minnow in the kingdom of God.

"I've loved you all these years," Matthew said to me.

Love? I *had* loved Ezekiel, as much as I was able. Held respect and affection for Abigail and Sophia; especially I loved J.D., my stepfather. But how did love solve my dilemma?

The next week, walking along the ditch with me, Matthew said that Mormonites were stuck in the Old Testament, that Christ had done away with slavish obedience to duty. "Your every act proves me right. Come with me to Wyoming." Then he had leaped the ditch and leaned forward to kiss me; I hadn't moved away. His lips pressed mine once quickly, soft. The touch burned in my memory.

Riding Babe on the flat above town, with my cattle around me, I had allowed adulterous and apostate thoughts to settle into the swept room of my mind. I felt myself to be a stranger in a familiar land. Then we received word that Ezekiel had taken another wife, and I made up my mind.

So on a Monday in mid-July I told the two wives I needed to find a market for my calves. I traveled westward, passing Lookout Station, where J.D.'s brother Ambrose lived. I told him the same half-truth concerning why I ranged so far from home. I stopped at Paiute Hell Station, eleven miles away. There I contracted with Captain Jardine for my fall calves and I asked him to marry me to Matthew. The captain's ironic smile (he knew I was a Mormon woman marrying a Gentile man) made me wish I had traveled farther from Rockwood town, but he swore he would tell no one.

Despite the danger, I convinced Matthew to continue through the fall driving for Wells Fargo, saving his wages. I would also hold as I had been, living with Sophia and Abigail. In September I would ask for a divorce from Ezekiel. In October, when the calves were grown, I'd claim half of the profit—my rightful due after doubling the herd J.D. had given me. With money in our pockets, Matthew and I would meet a night train and ship my half of the herd and Matthew's horses north on the train into Wyoming.

"No Mormonites for five hundred miles," Matthew had said of Wyoming, thinking that in embracing him, I was eagerly abandoning my people and my God.

I wasn't leaving God; I was simply leaping out into the unknown with a hopeful heart. I was like my mother, who had found the faith to leave her impoverished, drunken husband. Or like Eve, who at the dawn of the world had abandoned blissful ignorance and embraced knowledge. Strong women of a practical trust in God. I had broken the Church's law by marrying Matthew, but I knew the Father would judge me fairly.

That night I sat inside Ezekiel's house with my family of woman and children, who, in the absence of husband, had gradually become flesh of my flesh. The night before, Sophia's baby girl had been restless and Sophia had sung to her for an hour, rocking and holding the child tight, her face kind. She saved her wrathful face for adults, those who had volition to abuse; it was never for the pure and innocent.

Watching her, I had known that one day soon, I would have

to turn my back to her and Abigail and the children, these people I had come to love. I couldn't keep an extra husband secret for long in a tight Mormon village. In a couple of months I would walk away from house and town, the town that had welcomed my mother when eight years earlier she had fled from my violent, impoverished, Gentile father. How could I leave these sister-wives?

Well, I could do it because our joint marriage was sprung, twisted out of true. Before Wilford Woodruff had issued the Manifesto, it had seemed noble to go against the law of the land in obedience to God; but since the prophet had given in, the Principle seemed a useless aberration. And I could leave my sister-wives because I had Matthew to replace Ezekiel. Matthew, a splendid man, whose arms and clever parts wanted me more than Ezekiel ever had. I could flee my compound marriage and never look back. *His sacred, sweet arms wait for me*. The words hissed in my head like the snake in Eden, but a snake I had transformed into something pure. *Secret but not sinful!*

I felt it in every part of me that my love for Matthew was not evil. In this Mormon town men had multiple wives, but wives had only a part of one man. I grinned in the dark at the irony. *I have a man to myself, when many women have only part of one.* With a heart and blood that had always rushed rapidly as a shrew's, I constantly hungered for second helpings of food and now for a second helping of man. And this new husband fit me, flesh-to-flesh and soul-to-soul.

Through the two weeks since our marriage, I finally decided that constant fear was not worth any amount of money that calves and work could bring. I also wanted Matthew with me every night—my hands and cheek on his smooth chest, my mouth on his broad mouth, his slow, gravelly voice in my ear. I began to doubt my decision to delay leaving for Wyoming. All week I had feared discovery, especially by J.D. Any lie I had ever told him withered on my tongue. That very night I had decided to tell Matthew that we should leave, but I had come to that decision everlastingly too late.

Now I had waited so long that Sophia was murdered and Matthew fled.

Chapter Eight

Still standing next to the weir, I heard a shout from the foot of my field, near the house. Turning, I saw a light bobbing up toward us.

"J.D." From the Scottish brogue I knew the man was the bishop, who had immigrated from near Edinburgh twenty years earlier. Tromping heedlessly through the middle of my lucerne, he ran straight through the standing water, making deep footprints in my field.

"Brother J.D., is Sophia truly dead?" He rushed up to J.D., who held his palm flat against the bishop's chest.

"Tracks. You're befouling the tracks." I saw tears glisten on the bishop's face.

"Oh." The bishop stepped back. "I canna think without fuddlement. I canna stop thinking about her wee bairns. Do ye know who did it?"

"Someone with a square-toed boot."

"No!" I shouted, still sitting on the edge of the water gate.

The men turned and stared at me.

"Rachel, you read the tracks as well as I did. I do not understand why you think it was not this man who was in your barn."

"Are you certain of this, J.D.?" The bishop's beard wagged up and down as he talked.

"Yes. I am certain this man ran after Sophia."

"There is another set of tracks." I pointed again toward the ditch pathway.

J.D. turned away. "I was frightened it was one of the Saints."

"Sophia's dead," I told the bishop. "That's all we know for sure."

"Ach, to be sure Abigail needs me." The bishop ran back down through the field.

J.D. lifted the lantern to examine my face.

He leaned closer to me. "What has possessed you that you must read these tracks in a contrary manner?"

I couldn't open my mouth to say the first word.

He glared at me then turned, walked to the willows, and lifted the shovel, examining it in the light from the lantern. "Mud. Only mud. It may have been washed carefully and then stuck in the bank."

"That's our shovel. If he really killed her with it, why would he wash it? Why wouldn't he just cast it aside? Even bloody it doesn't show who killed her."

"Maybe he was washing it while he decided what to do. Then he just cast it from him." With his face down like a hunting dog, J.D. examined the ground next to the willows. "Here! He ran away this direction." He walked through the mud, heedless of his boots.

The weir seemed to whirl around me, and I leaned against the shovel, so I wouldn't pitch myself into the water. Matthew, a killer? He had walked with me under the fruit trees in the orchard for seven weeks and had never touched me until I invited him to take my hand, to hold and kiss me. He was not cruel or stupid. He would not be easily angered, even by Sophia's bitter tongue. More than that, if he had been provoked to kill in anger, he had no reason to lift Sophia into the water and prop her in the gate. As J.D. had made clear, she could not have simply fallen that way.

Our first idea was right. This killing was about water. But J.D. on a track was like a horse with a bit in its teeth.

"Here!" He circled through the brush, exclaiming with a "hup" or a "hey" when he saw a new track, as if he were at the cattle auction. He ran up the hillside, the eastern edge of the valley in which Rockwood town lay. "The tracks go straight up here."

Then he stopped. "I can follow these later. I want to check

Ezekiel's barn. Perhaps this man left something behind that will help us figure who he is."

I felt my heart laboring, as if twisted into a knot. I wanted to call out to Matthew, make certain he was actually gone from town, not just hiding on the hillside.

Tipping his lantern, J.D. followed the boot tracks backward toward the barn. "Probably was just as you said. He sought a place to sleep." He moved slowly, pointing to the square-toed tracks and back at Sophia's barefoot tracks. Her tracks stopped short of the barn. "She walked up the path through the fields. Maybe she heard something like you did. Then she continued closer to the barn, turned, walked back to the weir and was killed here." J.D. followed Matthew's tracks backward to the barn door. "He's not running here. Could have walked quietly so she wouldn't turn and see him."

"Could be disconnected to her killing. Like those other tracks."

J.D. shook his head. "He ran directly after her."

He walked into the barn where he might find the bed Matthew had probably prepared for us. I lifted my skirt and ran into the barn after J.D. "Father." He turned. "What about those other tracks?" I pointed out the door at the western bank. "You need to follow them down. It wouldn't take long to sort out the last two or three sets of tracks. See who's been here recently."

"Could be anybody's." He lifted his lantern. "These were directly following Sophia. Running after her. The shovel is right there. This is a sure thing, Rachel."

Earlier that night, when I had peered across at the barn from the orchard, calling to Matthew, he had probably already fled. Even if I had crossed the ditch and walked into the barn, without a lantern I would have missed seeing his tracks, which were already laid down, running after Sophia. Sophia could have seen him enter the barn. She shouted at him, her voice shrill as a knife. He ran after her and swung the shovel to silence her.

I wished my imagination would shut down, leave me to what I thought—that he was incapable of killing.

But it wouldn't. Then I realized that if J.D. had made a mistake about the tracks leaving, and Matthew still hid in the barn, he might strike out at whoever came upon him.

"J.D., he could still be there." The pitch of my voice rose as I spoke. "He might still be hiding there."

"He's long gone. But I will be careful." He stepped into the deeper darkness of the barn. Following him inside, I stopped. Had I heard someone moving above me in the loft? Perhaps it had only been the soft wings of the owl that lived there. J.D. held his lantern high, illuminating only my horse, Babe, and the three milk cows. I looked up at the wooden ceiling, the floor of the loft. J.D. climbed the ladder.

"J.D."

"The killer slept here." Something fell from the ladder. I ran forward and found a pile of our saddle blankets, the bedding Matthew and I had used for our marriage bed. I also found an army blanket. J.D. came down the stairs. "His bed was laid out, probably not slept in. Army deserter or thief from the army." He lifted the edge of the blanket and showed me the white U.S. Army letters. "He borrowed your saddle blankets for a more regular bed, heard Sophia outside the barn, ran out and killed her. Could have been you when you came up to change the water. Could be that Sophia saved your life by coming up first."

He squatted and felt the fabric of the blanket. "New." He walked to the barn door and handed me the blanket. "Now let us discover where he came from." He strode back to the barn door and circled back and forth around it. He turned straight north, toward the Aults' place, below ours. He jumped the ditch and strode down the path past the Nebekers' and Johnsons' places. Soon he came to the north edge of town. I followed more slowly, carrying Matthew's army blanket, which smelled like him. At first J.D. had moved reluctantly to discover the tracks, thinking they belonged to one of his neighbors; now he moved with vigor. "Right now he's probably running hard as he can away from here. I'll bet we find a horse has been stolen."

To Salt Lake City, I thought. *Anywhere J.D. can't track you.*

I lifted my pocket watch and looked at the hands in the light of the lantern. Barely one forty. If Matthew had started running at about midnight he could be six or eight miles away by now.

J.D. walked down the ditch toward the lower edge of town. Suddenly he stopped and rubbed his fingers in the circle on his head, what I had always thought a curious motion. "You change the water, not Sophia."

"You know I do."

"Why do you think she was out here in the middle of the night?"

"I've been wondering that myself." I tried to keep my voice level.

"Did you hear dogs in town raise a ruckus? Seems they would sound a warning if a stranger was in the barn, even here across the fields."

"I didn't hear any dogs." Matthew had fed meat to our dogs and made friends with them, so they wouldn't bark.

"And I thought you were a light sleeper. Anyway, she must have heard something. Sharp ears cost Sophia her life."

I felt the universe turn around me again. "Looks like Ma... "—I swallowed—"...the man with the square-toed boots did it."

"Yes."

J.D. walked through the sagebrush below the last house of town. "Here's where he came in." He looked back at me. "What?" he said. "You're still shaking."

I considered telling him everything, but he would think me an adulteress, worse even than an apostate or a Gentile. "I thought he might still be hiding somewhere here. It scared me."

"Hours after he killed her? Not likely. If you're frightened now, why did you walk toward the barn earlier? There was no way you could have known he'd been there. I had to look at the tracks to find that out. But it still was foolish for you to go wandering after a murder."

He turned away from me, pointing toward a patch of alkali dirt, white in the lantern. "The ground is too hard here to see tracks except in full daylight." He cast around, walking back and forth across the edge of the alkali. "I hate this awful business, but at least I won't have to accuse one of these impoverished brethren of killing Sophia. Hup. Here they are." Holding his lantern, he followed Matthew's backward tracks toward the Lookout Road, where I knew Matthew had come into town. Would he guess whose the tracks were once he knew they came from Lookout?

"You go back to the house. I know Abigail's going to need help. And send somebody after Brother Ault and Brother Johnson. One other—Brother Nebeker. Get them to saddle up and be ready to go after whoever slept in the barn. Tell Mary to have King saddled." He stopped. "Her two small ones, oh, dear Lord in heaven, those poor children."

"No. I'm going to track with you."

"You will just delay me." He glared at me.

In a minute more we came to the bridge across the western ditch, which followed the old creek bed. From there the lane turned into the road to Lookout Station. "Just as I thought," J.D. said. "Here are his tracks coming from Lookout Station. These tracks were certainly made by no townsman." He trotted along the road while I waited at the bridge. "Still here. Still here." His voice was gleeful as he pointed at the dust of the road. Westward was Lookout Pass and west of that eight more miles on the freight route was Paiute Hell Station, where Matthew and I had been married.

It still didn't make sense that he had struck Sophia down. Even if she had discovered him, he had not wanted our marriage secret. "Polygamy is sin," he had argued. "I have taken you out of sin." Also he had wanted to be with me nightly, not only when the schedules of freight wagon and irrigation matched. If Sophia found him by accident, he would have felt free to announce our marriage. He would thank Sophia for releasing him from his promise. He would not think to kill her.

I thought about riding after Matthew right then, leaving my cattle, all my belongings. I thought about being married to a murderer.

J.D. called out. "The tracks back this way are barefoot. He ran from the west wearing no shoes and stopped here to put on his boots. Crazy." Matthew, half Goshute, always ran barefoot, like his mother's people. But when he came to town, he always wore boots so I wouldn't think him uncivilized.

J.D. walked back. "It's definite, Rachel. The tracks come in from outside town. He walked here along the Lookout Road." He turned toward me. "So this stranger comes along the Lookout Road and goes into the barn to sleep. He gathers your horse blankets to make a better bed. Two questions: Why wouldn't he just knock on the door and ask for a place to sleep, and what possessed Sophia to walk toward the barn where he was sleeping?" His hand was up, rubbing his crown. Stimulating his thinking. "Did he ask her for a place to sleep and she walked up to show him? For some reason, he turned on her?"

Now was another chance to tell J.D. everything. I took a breath. "Came in so late that he didn't want to wake us? Went into the first barn he saw?" I couldn't make myself say that I had taken a second husband. "Sophia's always walking about at night."

That had been my main worry on the nights I lay with Matthew. In the middle of our lovemaking I had listened for the creak of the barn door below us. Very distracting.

J.D. turned on his heel and we walked silently back up the lane. We passed J.D.'s own house, lit with a lantern in the kitchen. He continued on past the Aults' house, the only one in town still dark. Then we came to my house, which was lit with half a dozen lanterns. Through the window I could see that several other people had joined the bishop in our kitchen. J.D. paid no attention to them as we strode up through my field and back to the weir. He jumped across the ditch and looked up toward the barn.

"He must have heard Sophia or Sophia heard him. So he left the barn," said J.D. "Running after her." He pointed again at the prints, which in the light from the lantern showed only a pit of black, just the toe, digging deep, no heel. I noted where the square-toed prints crossed over Sophia's bare ones. "And he clubbed her with the first thing to his hand. But why? 'Tis bewildering. If he wanted to have carnal knowledge of her, why hit her with a club?"

"Wait. You don't know his tracks weren't made later. I still say that you don't know that he ran after her when she was alive."

J.D. jumped across the ditch again, following Matthew's tracks as he left the weir, left Sophia's body. He studied the ground carefully inside the top of the orchard. Head low, as if he were a hound following a scent, he walked up the hill after the square-toed prints, the lantern swinging in his off hand. I marveled that he could see the tracks at all. "I'll get a better idea where he's headed from here."

I hesitated, looking toward the round-toed tracks. People in Rockwood were generally too busy or tired to go walking for pleasure. It was likely the tracks were laid down by a water thief.

But J.D., that stubborn, stubborn man, was going after Matthew.

I held Matthew's blanket against my chest. J.D. would never turn back from a trail once he set himself to it. Once, he had killed a thief who had stolen Brother Pritchard's stallion. J.D. tracked the criminal toward Centre, which lay in the open desert between Rockwood and Hamblin. He had shot the man without harming either saddle or horse. When the body had been brought back on a wagon, the head was only a mass of flesh, bones, and buzzing flies. If J.D. caught up to Matthew, Matthew would be dead. I had known J.D. for eight years and knew how deadly he could be. But I worried that saying Matthew was my husband would only give J.D. another reason—adultery—to kill him.

"J.D.!" I was desperate to have him turn back.

"Yes?" He stood halfway up the hillside. He bent forward, his hands on his knees, as if he was out of breath or weary. I came up on him. His breath rasped in and out. I had never seen him so out of breath. I touched his hand and it felt cold as clay. He waited, his hands still down on his knees, for his breath to come back.

"Papa. Are you all right?" He wasn't. I could see he wasn't. "You can't rush off like this."

Then he lifted himself upright and strode up the hill again, as if shortness of breath had not afflicted him.

"I will follow until this damnable Gentile establishes a clear direction, and then I will run back for my horse and shirt and the other men. The square-toed prints are very clear in the soft soil."

I walked quickly up the hill and stood next to him. My heart was in my throat because I hadn't contradicted him since I was a hotheaded teenager.

"You go help Abigail. She needs you."

I shook my head. He wanted me to take the woman's part, rather than helping him track down the killer. "No. I'm coming with you."

I owed him much, even obedience generally. If it came to a choice between him and Matthew, I didn't know what I would do.

Chapter Nine

My mother felt the same about J.D. as I did. Before she met him she was a wanderer; after finding J.D. she wandered no more. As a girl she had wandered from the Isle of Man to Ireland, wandered from there with her new husband to Liverpool, New York, and Oklahoma Territory, from there to Nevada. The spring I was eleven she decided to move on again, wandering away from my blood father.

Arriving in Rockwood town, my mother had been destitute, except for us three children. She asked where she could stay, and Mary led my mother, my sister, my older brother, and me to the Rockwood backhouse, a cabin behind J.D.'s three-story mansion. He was the richest man in town, which my mother must have divined out of a careful look at his property as we walked down the middle of town.

We helped with feeding the animals, cleaning the house, and cooking; we ate at J.D.'s table, full-bellied for the first time in any of our memories. Then at Mary's instigation, J.D. married my mother, despite the fact that she had another husband. It was as if my father was dead to us. We still lived in the small house, and he rarely came to my mother at night. We had solid walls around us, cupboards full of food and a closet with extra clothing. We lived in a green valley, never as green as Ireland, but green from irrigated fields, orchards, even a flower garden or two. Tall Lombardy poplars had been planted as a windbreak and for beauty. J.D. had even imported a new tree, something I had never seen before—Russian olive, which gave up a beautiful flowery perfume. The odor drifted across town through July and August. We walked along ditches full of water. The earth wasn't pitted with mines, was not marred with stone and dirt rubble.

Through the fall, pumpkins and Hubbard squash fattened in the garden. We bottled corn and beans. The first frost was almost a relief because we could leave off picking and slicing.

Against the thick wall of our house, more than a cabin, was a stack of solid cedar wood taller than my head, enough for a full winter. We would never have to go out on a blizzard night to scrabble for twigs or cast-off boards on a mountain scoured of firewood by a thousand miners. Our father had never seen his way clear to take a day away from digging in the dirt and borrow a wagon to bring a big load of wood to our shack, so we were always cold. Not so in Rockwood, the town settled by J.D. and named after him. People thought about the future. I had to go outside in the winter, with my chores to do, a cow to milk, pigs to slop, fences to build, but I had a thick wool coat and good boots and a hat knit by Mary. That first winter it felt as if we had died and gone to heaven.

So it wasn't a great leap for me to move from my gratitude for a full belly and a warm kitchen to thinking about matters of God and religion. We all listened as Mary taught us newcomers the gospel. J.D., who was as broad-bodied and steady as a wall, and Mary, tiny and fair as an angel, disproved my father's claim that all British were evil and tyrannical. I had looked up into Mary's kind face and imagined that the God she preached must be just as generous.

My mother's face did not enliven at the good news: angels revisiting the earth, the Priesthood of Abraham restored, a modern-day prophet. Still her mouth whispered "yes" whenever Mary asked a question. "Yes, I believe God the Father and the Son appeared to Joseph Smith. Yes, I will consign all my earthly belongings to God and be baptized." I remembered that my mother closed her eyes as she listened, appearing as a woman asleep.

Unlike my mother and my brother, wanderers and doubters both of them, I believed every word taught by the woman who became my Aunt Mary. She sat in her rocking chair with us children sitting at her feet, my mother in a stiff-backed chair just opposite. I can still hear her voice—clear, melodious, calm—weaving a picture of the universe that seemed both strange and familiar. Before this earth was formed, the children of God had lived as a great family in heaven—Father, Mother, and children. The ordinances of baptism, receiving the Gift of the Holy Ghost, the temple endowment, and Celestial Marriage were narrow gateways leading back to Their presence. I imagined God the Father, God the Mother, Christ, and Adam positioning the stars, stirring the material of the universe, with the Holy Ghost flowing like water between Their fingers, all of Them together shaping the earth and heavens, just as Matthew's Goshute mother weaved baskets of reeds.

The Saints, like their parents the Gods, felt the urge to create—to multiply and replenish. They raised large families, and they organized the desert so that it would blossom. They dug ditches, planted trees and fields. As a girl of twelve, I loved walking the lanes or ditch banks, knowing that the industry, ambition, and harmony of the Saints established a solid hedge between me and the wilderness. The pattern of their movements as they walked through their fields or to church, as they herded cows and sheep, wove a tapestry that swaddled and comforted me.

On the day of my baptism I watched Brother Peterson picking apples while his daughters cut them into slices and spread them on the shingled roof of their house, covering them with cheesecloth. The first Sister Swensen used an axe to open a huge Hubbard squash that she had retrieved from the granary, while Brother Swensen tempted Brother Pritchard's wayward horse with a bucket of windfalls. I stepped around Brother Olson's ancient sheepdog sleeping in the dust of the lane. Brother Johnson used his team of horses and a system of ropes to roll a wagonload of grass hay onto his stack. The whole town hummed with work. Although my stepfather was the richest in town and the Turners—small, bitter-mouthed people whose ancestors came from northern England—were the poorest, no one was destitute. No one suffered hunger of the order of the miners living on the border of Nevada. Of course, disagreements and differences existed in the town, but everyone joined at the white, wooden church on Sunday, singing together the hymns of Zion, eating together the sacramental bread and drinking the wine. It was a few years later that I learned they were not perfect, that they had disagreements over water, food, and land, just like everyone else.

Although I am sure my mother had no such transcendent feelings as my own, she had a rare order of faith, a way of seeing that had enabled her to pluck her children out of ground in which we would have surely perished. She had imagined herself leaving a man who wallowed in drink and who was more visionary than any Mormon I knew. Her practical faith had led her to plant a thick-bodied man of God firmly between her children and starvation, picturing herself as the fifth wife to wealthy J.D., straight and stern as a brick wall, a man who never deviated from any path he set his foot to.

Courteous to my mother, J.D. doted on me, her older daughter. After Aunt Mary taught me to read, J.D. ordered books for me. After I dressed one day like a boy and came out to work the cattle, he bought me Babe, a tall, black mustang/thoroughbred mare, a horse that could go all day and still be strong at evening. My brother watched all this and left town during the night before his sixteenth birthday. I pictured him mining in California, wandering northward to Alaska and mining there.

My sister and I embraced our Mormon lives like a gift, becoming new beings and leaving girlhood behind. My memory of Matthew faded with other childhood fantasies, especially after town boys came courting. My younger sister had, at the age of sixteen, married a member of the high council in Hamblin, and I felt some urging from J.D. and Mary to follow her example. When I grew to a marriageable age, Ezekiel Wainwright had come courting. I had known Ezekiel since moving to Rockwood town. He had married Abigail before I had ever entered J.D.'s household. When I was fourteen he had married Sophia, and then when I was nineteen he courted me—two women as unlike each other as a clucking hen and a sparrow hawk.

While I deliberated, J.D. took me to Centre, a town fifteen miles from our own. We were to get supplies and to return a stolen horse. His main reason was to convince me to marry Ezekiel, to embrace the Principle of Celestial Marriage. Embracing an abstraction was easy, but to embrace Ezekiel, who was thirty years older than I and who already had two wives—that was a different question. So we had a grumpy trip, J.D. preaching to me, and me spitting back at him. While we were there two federal deputies, who had been assigned to go from town to town and arrest polygamous men, had been killed. Obviously a Mormon had done the killing. J.D. had allowed me to help him as he looked into the crime. Unwillingly allowed me. He tried to rely on tracking when I wanted to talk to people, figure out who had the mind to do such a deed. We had come to harsh anger between us over how to best proceed. But finally we figured out who had done it. After our success, I thought that J.D. would then allow me to work with him, to be a partner as he helped track down bandits and stolen horses. But two things became clear—that he didn't want to work with anybody, and that he especially didn't want to work with a woman.

So I left home for a while. I moved to Hamblin, fifty miles from Rockwood, to look for a husband, a man of my own. Because my own sister's house had no room, I lived with J.D.'s sister. Hamblin, the biggest town I had lived in since I was a small child in Dublin, is a mining town south of the Great Salt Lake; immigrants from all over live there, and not just Mormons. J.D.'s sister was married to a man who thought the Principle was an abomination. I went to dances, and some of the young men held me in their arms, but none of them pleased me enough to want to spend eternity with them. Maybe I didn't give them a chance. I was courted by several older men and that was even less attractive. The thought of allowing any of them carnal knowledge of my body made me want to shriek. If I was going into the Principle, I was going to do it so I could live near J.D., and have a reasonable chance at prosperity.

For a time I considered giving up and returning to the Gentile life of my childhood, where the government didn't come after men who slept in the beds of several women. But I reminded myself that those Nevada miners often despised the women they used to satisfy their urges. They did nothing to support those they considered whores. Even if the system of plural marriage was imperfect, it did provide for women, like my mother after she left my father.

I lived there through a summer, missing J.D. and my home so much that I returned to Rockwood that fall. With a brightness of mind and dread in my gut, I made up my mind to marry Ezekiel, a good man, if simple and too quiet, too ruddy. One February day I just said yes to him. Yes to staying in Rockwood town near J.D., yes to having one third of a man, not a whole man to worry about and only a third of his attention to suffer. They said the Principle was God's commandment, the only pathway to the Celestial Kingdom. I didn't believe that it was the only way. In fact it was a penance for many women, like scourging their flesh, to share their man with other women. I believed that such women would come to hate God, angry that He required them to live in misery for their husband's glory. Despite these evils, I went into my compound marriage to Ezekiel and his two other wives with my eyes open, a practical decision, one God didn't require of me, but one that pleased J.D., the bishop, and Mary, J.D.'s first wife and my second mother. It was a sign to them that I would bend my shoulder to the yoke of righteousness instead of running away like a wild colt.

In Ezekiel's household I had food in my belly, even if it wasn't as good as what I had eaten with J.D., and a hope for heaven, even if it was distant. Any man I would have married in my previous life would have been a drunken, heathen gold-grubber. During this time, before he returned and proved me wrong, I figured that even my childhood friend Matthew probably swung a pick every day and passed out on the floor of a bar every night.

I had faith that Ezekiel would eventually grow into a stalwart Saint like J.D., becoming nearly a god on earth. But after his whining about the deps, the federal deputies who put polygamists in jail, after his escape to England, his taking another wife against God's will, and this wife a mere child, I disbelieved Ezekiel could ever become a man anywhere near J.D.'s stature. So then I found another, trying to have him and keep my friendship with J.D. intact, for sure a perishing hazardous plan.

Chapter Ten

Tracking my husband Matthew, J.D. held the light low and strode along the hillside. He bent forward, examining the tracks, and I heard his beard scratch against his garments. "Here! Rachel, see…he took his boots off again. Why would he do that?" If he figured out why, it wouldn't take long to follow that logical trail to Matthew. Although there were other Goshutes in our valley and in other valleys westward, few of them owned square-toed boots.

I followed my stepfather's footsteps, thinking about his stubborn determination. It had lifted him from poverty. Born the child of a farm laborer in England, destined to spend his life making someone else rich, he joined the Mormon church and immigrated to America, where he grew to a man who owned vast stretches of desert land, thousands of sheep, hundreds of cattle and horses. He rose high in the councils of the Church, and men and women listened carefully when he spoke. He would depart this life in glory, bearing with him decades of experience, having garnered a posterity of five wives, fifteen children, and twenty grandchildren. He had thwarted his natural destiny by multiplying every talent God entrusted to him.

Still, I had wished a thousand times that he was less dogged. He was obsessed with uncovering evil and sin.

I had been fifteen when J.D. shot a horse thief. It had made me furious at him. I called him a beastly murderer, without a heart. My words started tears to his eyes; he had disappeared for the rest of the day, riding the hills on his horse. Mary had come to me and told me that when the Prophet Joseph and his brother Hyrum were killed by a mob in Carthage Jail, J.D. had been seventeen, a bare-faced youth, newly baptized into the Church, new to America. After the tragedy, he had walked out from Nauvoo with a thousand others to meet the cortege carrying the coffins back home. The wagon had been covered with brush to keep the sun off the coffins. J.D. and his older brother had wanted to grab their rifles right then and go with a troop of other boys and men to hunt down the murderers. Mary said that Willard Richards and others spoke to the people of Nauvoo, urging them to let the law take care of the killers. These words of peace sunk deep into J.D.'s heart.

Later, when the bodies were laid out in the Mansion House, J.D. had been one of those to walk through and gaze down at the pale face of the prophet and the ruined face of his brother, nose smashed to pulp. Despite his youth, Mary said, he realized that revenge wouldn't stop the pain he felt. Mary told me that when he'd had to kill, eight times now, he'd had days of remorse after each one.

Remembering her words was small comfort. I knew that despite this reluctance to kill, J.D. wouldn't hesitate if he thought the man he hunted was guilty of murder himself.

I imagined Matthew lying dead, shot by J.D., and I staggered as I followed my stepfather along the hillside. I shook my head, which felt full of buzzing bees, repetitive pictures and ideas swarming. J.D. paused, tipping the lantern back and forth. Below us in our yard, I saw a couple of lanterns, a group of dark-shouldered men and women in white dresses.

"You'll kick into a cactus barefoot in the dark." He turned west along the rim above the valley. "His first impulse was to return the way he came." J.D. pointed down toward the bridge where he had discovered Matthew's tracks coming from Lookout. "But he turned and turned on this spot; then he turned north again. So before he could think straight, he wanted to go back west toward Lookout Pass or Paiute Hell Station." J.D. followed northward along the hill. He pointed. "Here the Gentile started running—probably heading toward Hamblin, where he can escape on the train. We can stop him with the telegraph."

Matthew. His name is Matthew.

I glanced again at the houses spread below us. Matthew had looked down on the same houses, but then they were all dark, the people inside sleeping peacefully—all except for Sophia's killer. What earlier sound had drawn her from her bed when sensible people stayed abed?

Now nearly everyone in town was fully awake. Lanterns were lit in every home, points of yellow light to either side of the lane. The delicate scent of my lucerne, nearly ready to cut, wafted up the hill.

Suddenly J.D. stopped.

"What?"

"Just give me a minute. I was all right, seeing Sophia dead, but now..." By the light of the lantern I saw his eyes glisten with tears. "Those two children, those small children."

He wiped his face on his white sleeve and strode after the tracks. I followed, working hard to keep up. It was not the first time I'd seen this flinty man cry.

Mary had told me about the death of their second child, Isaac, three years old, in 1848 on the trek west from Nauvoo. The wagon train camped on the Platte River, which had seemed shallow enough for a child to walk across—not more than half a foot deep but acres wide. They had all been busy finding a spot for the livestock to graze, getting dinner started, laying out the bedding. Mary realized she hadn't seen Isaac for maybe thirty seconds. She called for J.D. in a frightened voice and he had run from the oxen he was tending to. J.D. came over the bank and saw Isaac downstream. Mary said that the child appeared to walk on clouds reflected on the sheet of slow water. As J.D. ran down the bank, Isaac slipped into a hole and was carried downstream in an invisible, deep current. As Isaac's head went under, J.D. ran farther down and splashed out into the river. He thrashed forward through the mud and water, and he nearly didn't get out himself. A teenaged boy swam out, tied to a rope, and found the hole Isaac had fallen into, searching there and farther down the stream until dark. They never found Isaac's body.

Mary said that she and J.D. both knew that a child so innocent had been taken straight to heaven. Standing on the shore with a blanket around his shoulders, J.D. swore an oath that he would live his life so perfectly that he would have that child again. Perhaps in the Millennium, the time between Christ's return and the Judgment, Mary said, he and she would know the boy and could watch him grow into a man. That story and countless others helped me love J.D., made me see him not as the demon hunter and tracker Matthew saw him as but as the man who had saved my mother and me.

J.D. stopped again. "The tracks are gone." He turned around, lantern held high, and cast back and forth. I saw only an anthill, prickly pear cactus, stumpy sage, and shadscale—and our own tracks, of course. Walking back fifteen paces or so, J.D. pointed to the ground. "There he is, the barefoot devil. I lost him because he turned around. He's going back to the side of his own trail. Look. Here he's confused. He turns to look down the hill toward Rockwood, turns north again toward Rush Lake Station and Hamblin. Here he whirls around and around on the hill." J.D. turned with the lantern, just as Matthew had.

I felt dizzy. Was this my stepfather or my lover spinning on the hill? One thing was sure, Matthew had been so petrified that J.D. Rockwood would soon be after him that he couldn't think straight.

"This Gentile darted one way, then another, like a rat caught on an open barn floor. The pattern of his darting will reveal his mind. What do we know? He came from the west. Straight west is the notch of Lookout Pass, beyond that, west and south, is Paiute Hell Station. No one at Lookout but Ambrose and his unfortunate wife, Libby. So the killer had to come from farther west. He is either a pothole miner, a ranch hand, a traveler coming from California or Nevada, or a soldier from Paiute Hell Station." He looked at me. "I favor the last because of the new army blanket."

Somehow he had missed thinking of the freight driver, a miracle, because he had thought of just about everyone else in the whole territory. He held the lantern in his right hand; his left massaged his scalp in a circular motion. He seemed to address Matthew: "Did you know what you were going to do? Did you know you'd find a woman alone? Did you plan to kill her?"

J.D. stopped at the crest of the hill, his head down. "I'm so tired, Rachel. Maybe I'd better start looking and stop thinking."

"Wait until morning. We can sort out the tracks." I touched his arm.

J.D. moved suddenly, pacing back along Matthew's trail. "No," he shouted. "Look, Rachel, he turned down toward town again. Maybe we're following a crazy man. Maybe he just killed her for no reason. Maybe he's just wandering without sense." I watched a shudder pass through his body. "I can't abide the idea of someone killing dispassionately, without cause. A person like that has wilderness for a mind. I can't stand to think of Sophia, poor Sophia, so fair of face and hair." He looked up, distracted. "Fair of face if not of tongue. She is dead now. She always had a word of fierce piety in her mouth, as if she thought that God was the leader of some ancient army. At the same time she knew that true religion and the undefiled was aiding those less fortunate than her. Nothing will bring back that contradictory woman. But capturing and punishing her killer, containing the horror of her death by putting a name and a face to him, identifying the conditions of her death—these acts will help us bear our sorrow."

"Another killing will help you feel better?"

He could hardly hear me. I had never seen him so distracted.

"Nothing will help her children. The babe will be raised in a loving manner by Abigail. She's a gruff but deep-hearted woman. And by you, Rachel, who since childhood has been as wise as a serpent but harmless as a dove. I'm more worried about the first child, the girl Marianne, who has known her mother and will suffer her loss."

It seemed to me that J.D. had slipped the tether to his mind. I could hardly speak for the tears in my throat.

He kept talking. "Rachel, help me watch over that child, make sure that Abigail does not slight her in any way. Perhaps you, since you have no bairn for yourself, can take over the two children, raise them as your own." He moved his mouth in a prayer. "I swear to you, God, that I will protect Sophia's daughter Marianne, make sure she is raised well and married well. I pray that her mother is wandering a grassy meadow in Paradise and can hear my promise."

We backtracked above Ezekiel's place, the church building, and the Turners' fields. "Here he goes down toward Brother Olson's barnyard. I'll wager my right hand that a horse is missing. The stranger is a fool not to have taken your horse. Babe was penned right below where he was sleeping. If he'd taken her, we'd never catch him. Brother Olson's nag will give out on him before this night is over. This Gentile is a wavering fool, a panicked killer. He will be easy to apprehend."

Wavering maybe, a fool to marry me, but a killer? My mind still balked at that idea.

J.D. followed the tracks into Brother Olson's barnyard and climbed over into a split-pole corral. I hoisted my frock and followed. "I still wonder why none of us heard dogs barking when the man came into town. Only Sophia heard." J.D. hit his fist against his thigh. "If only I had waked and gone out to investigate. He that hath ears to hear, let him hear."

Any second I expected him to light on Matthew, the freight driver. "That is the man," he would say, and every hope I had would be dashed to the ground.

J.D. walked across to Brother Olson's small adobe house and banged on the door. The old Swede finally came out. He was stoop-shouldered and his head hung forward from his body.

"Tragedy in town," said J.D. "I'm surprised you didn't wake."

"Nothing wakes me. I sleep like the dead. You know this, Brother J.D."

"Not even when a man comes into your corral and steals your horse?"

"What?" Brother Olson stared at J.D. "You say my horse is missing? Damn."

"I'm not sure," said J.D. "Maybe you should come and check. Someone killed Sophia and maybe ran away on one of your horses."

"Killed?" said Brother Olson. "Oh, no, not Sophia. Such a pious woman." He looked up at J.D. "Not one of the Saints?"

"No," said J.D. "A Gentile stranger sleeping in Ezekiel's barn."

My fingernails dug into the palm of my hand.

"A Gentile. Then Satan sent him to silence Sophia. She was always speaking out against evil." Brother Olson pulled on his boots and, still in his long, white underwear, rushed out to the split-pole corral, his head bobbing forward with each running step. "Oh, my Sven is missing, my best horse of them all." I nearly laughed, because he only had two horses. He sat on the ground. J.D. walked to the gate, held his light, and found where the horse had been led out of the corral. Brother Olson stood and ran into his house, returning with his rifle in one hand and his trousers in the other. "I will get the bugger. I will come with you and get the bugger."

"You need to stay and help Abigail."

I knew that J.D. didn't want Brother Olson following with a gun because he was so reckless. Once while deer hunting, Brother Olson had trotted his horse through some brush when a deer broke cover in front of him. He tried to aim, his gun bouncing, and shot his own horse in the back of the head. No one knew what direction he might shoot if he was frightened or angry.

J.D. started to walk away, but then turned back. "No. As soon as it is light get a telegraph sent to Jardine. Do you have paper and pencil inside?"

"I do not," said Brother Olson in an offended voice.

"Well, you can remember this. Send to Captain Jardine about the murder. Tell him the killer came from Paiute direction." J.D. paused, thinking aloud. "Say it could be one of his soldiers—no, don't say that. I don't know who it was. Just say that the killer came from the west."

"Yes," said Brother Olson. "Please bring back my Sven. I have left to ride only my old plow horse, Lars."

"And send to the sheriff in Hamblin. Tell him what happened and tell him to watch the train station."

J.D. started after the horse tracks. I followed. He bent low with his lantern and walked through the brush, which snagged at my frock. "Go home, Rachel. Your place is helping Abigail with the children."

I shook my head.

Matthew had ridden at an angle up the hillside. We followed the tracks straight south. They dropped off the hill above town, crossed the creek and went up the road south toward Rockwood Creek Pass. "We've followed for three hundred yards and there are no more changes in direction. We have a clear track now."

Matthew had ridden south? He had no chance to escape J.D. running that way. No town big enough to hide him lay in that direction.

"We have him," said J.D.

He turned and walked back toward town, banging on the doors of the men he wanted to ride with him. He no longer paid any attention to me following, so I stopped in the lane in front of my own house and watched his back. He stopped only when he came to his own house. He stepped inside and he came out almost immediately, wearing his hat and buttoning his shirt. Then he disappeared into his barnyard, probably retrieving his horse.

I stared southward at the dark line of mountains where they dipped to Rockwood Creek Pass. Matthew had ridden in that direction, through unfamiliar territory in the dark. Unlike Babe, Brother Olson's old nag would not be sure-footed. That shambles of a horse would stumble at every gopher hole and half-buried boulder. Matthew would have to keep kicking him into a trot, or an occasional awkward, swaying lope. It was infuriating. Why hadn't Matthew stolen Babe, a horse that could stay ahead of J.D.'s tireless mount? Any man with half a brain would have done that.

I thought about the tangle of tracks on top of the hill. They had been a mystery to J.D. but made perfect sense to me. Matthew had started toward Lookout Pass, feared being too easily tracked there, started toward Salt Lake City, feared for our plan, and decided to lose J.D. in the sand dunes ten miles south of Rockwood town.

From the dunes Matthew had three options. South across the sand was one route to eastern Utah, traditional home of outlaws, country so tangled with canyons, sand, and thick brush that J.D. might never find him. Matthew was no outlaw but would he think of going there? Straight east were the Mormon communities of Nephi, Provo, Spanish and American Fork. For sure Matthew wouldn't go there. West was desert, and northwest was Lookout Pass, where Matthew had stopped with the freight wagon for the night.

Standing in the lane trying to figure why Matthew had gone south, I thought of another possibility and my breath caught in my throat. He might plan to ride southward and then cut back north. Try to get back to Lookout Station before dawn. If he could get back to his bed, he would be safe. If he could do this, no one would know that he had left in the night. If he couldn't? All our plans were lost. If he didn't show up to drive the freight wagon, J.D. would suspect him, put a name and face to the tracks simply because he was the only person in a hundred miles who had disappeared. We would lose our chance at our cattle, I would be marked as an adulteress. And Matthew would be hung as a horse thief and murderer.

Why had he stolen Brother Olson's horse, when he could run faster than that nag? Waiting in the lane for J.D. to gather his posse and ride after my husband, I came to an answer. He might plan to leave Brother Olson's horse in the sand. The poor beast would wander there and Matthew's pursuers would waste time tracking a riderless horse. Matthew would leave the sand dunes by foot, somehow disguising his prints, and return to Lookout before he was missed—a six-mile run, little more than an hour for Matthew under normal conditions. But the track behind the mountains was over rough ground—rocky, passing over the low foothills of the mountains, including shale and some dropoffs into the canyons. I had ridden there looking for cattle. That could take two more hours.

Sure as I knew my own name, I knew this was Matthew's plan. He planned to be sitting drinking coffee and eating Sunday breakfast with the station master, Ambrose Rockwood and his loco wife and their family of dogs while J.D. was still trying to figure out which way he had gone.

I went through the times again, just to make sure he could be safe. If he had left around midnight he had almost six hours before the first glimmer of dawn. He only had to go about eleven miles, something he could do blindfolded. His plan would work, if nothing went wrong.

Standing in the lane, I shook my head. Something always went wrong.

I remembered how Matthew's voice had wavered with passion and fear as he spoke about J.D., and my gut grew cold. Matthew would do anything before he would allow himself to be captured by a man he thought was Satan's minion, evil incarnate. If he went with J.D. peaceably, J.D. probably would not harm him. But why would he go peaceably with all that nonsense in his head?

"You could have made a dozen different choices, Matthew," I said aloud in the dark lane, "but I wish you Godspeed. Run with all the power of your ancestors. Run as if your life depended on it."

My mouth twisted. His life did depend on it. Possibly mine too.

Chapter Eleven

I knew how Matthew thought, not just because we grew up together in Nevada, but also because his method of wooing me was to tell me stories. One night, before we were married, we sat under the trees in the orchard, waiting for the water to finish spreading across one of my two fields of lucerne. Matthew sat in the crotch of an apple tree, so high in the branches that I couldn't see his face.

His disembodied voice sounded in the darkness. "I've heard tell that J.D. uses the power of his devil's priesthood to see tracks invisible to normal eyes."

I laughed out loud. "His devil's priesthood? I didn't know you believed in children's fairy tales."

I thought he'd laugh, but he didn't. "They say that even at night he can see footprints as if they have phosphorus painted on them."

"He's the best tracker I've ever known, that I can say. But there's nothing supernatural about it."

"It can't be godly to be able to tell from a track what his own brother Ambrose says he can tell."

"To me he's been the kindest man I've ever known. How can a man who is so kind have a compact with the devil?"

Matthew snorted. "I saw at Hamblin Station that man he gut shot. Took the man *two* weeks to die. He hates anybody who isn't a Mormonite."

"You're talking nonsense."

"Sign that *you're* not thinking straight when sense seems nonsense."

"I've got to change the water." Before Matthew could say anything, I stepped out into the moonlight and moved the dam so that the other half of my field could be irrigated. That setting would have lasted until morning, so I should have just gone back to bed. Instead I walked back under the trees. "He's a good man. You can't see that part of him, but I can."

"You've been bamboozled, tricked, fooled, connived against. You're the one who believes fairy tales. I mean, you believe all this claptrap about Joe Smith. That's proof you've been fooled."

"You don't respect me if you say this. I believe no claptrap. I believe like Joseph Smith that humans have unlimited potential. He believed we can grow forever."

"What about the temples? I talked to a man, another driver, used to be a Mormonite. He said that they perform rituals with dead bodies in the temples. And that every person who goes in the temples swears an oath that he will murder the prophet's enemies. That's what drives J.D. Rockwood, these oaths."

"Matthew, I tell you it's not true. This is my father you're talking about."

"Your father died in sorrow in Nevada."

"What evidence can I give you that would convince you you're wrong?"

"None. What evidence can I give you that you're wrong to be a Mormonite?"

"None." I knew that, given time, I could talk him out of his narrow ideas about my adopted people. But I wished he wasn't so stubborn.

"I've heard that J.D. and the other Danites, back in Missouri, slipped out at night to kill Gentiles. That's the reason they were kicked out of that state."

He was right about the Danites. I knew from talking to Mary, who would answer honestly any question I asked her, that in 1838 a brother named Sampson Avard organized the Daughters of Zion, the Danites, and had led them on midnight raids of revenge against the enemies of the Mormons. The Prophet Joseph soon excommunicated Avard, but for decades afterward the reputation of the Saints had been damaged by the stories of "Mormon Destroying Angels." But Matthew was wrong about

J.D. being a part of it.

"J.D. was in Liverpool when the Mormons were in Missouri."

"Mormonites were kicked out for murder and polygamy. The Mormon religion is old and savage. Blood atonement. They wanted to deny Christ and return the world to an Old Testament condition."

"Matthew, I won't listen to any more of this."

Those old times of violence against Gentiles were over. When Elder Orson Pratt said in a Salt Lake conference that revenge on Gentile Missourians passing through the state was wrong, J.D. had been relieved.

As if he could read my mind, Matthew asked, "What about the massacre down south? West of Cedar City at Mountain Meadows. John D. Lee led some Indians, or God-fearing whites who knew better, against a party of Missourians in Mountain Meadows."

"J.D. wasn't involved."

"How do you know?"

"I know. And those Missourians were not innocent. They claimed credit for murdering the Prophet Joseph. They said they would poison every spring in their path across southern Utah."

"Who told you that?"

"It was what the Saints who lived down there claimed, and they would have ample reason to lie. But my point is that J.D. thought the massacre foolish, wicked, and cowardly."

Matthew said, "You're smarter than this—to believe what you're told."

"So I should believe what *you* tell me?"

"Consult your native intelligence. These soldiers at Paiute Hell Station and the Wells Fargo men I work with tell me that Mormonites believe some sins can be requited only with blood—blood atonement. They said the Danites were still strong. They said that J.D. Rockwood was first in line at the killing at Mountain Meadows."

"None of this is true." I rose and walked down to the house without saying goodbye to him.

The next water turn, he was back again, talking to me out of the branches of the apple tree. "Hello, Rachel."

I expected him, so I wasn't startled. To be honest, I hoped he would be there. "You come to tempt me from an apple tree, you devil. You want to make me hate my own people."

"I will not bring that up again. I don't want you to leave me and go back to your house. I want to talk and talk and talk to you. I don't want to offend you."

I smiled and listened. He talked about how he felt when my mother took me away from him. He told about his time in the army, his year as a freight driver looking for me.

But I never was able to convince him his fear of my stepfather was misguided.

Another night when Matthew came to me, he started talking about J.D. again. I stood to walk away.

"Wait! This doesn't cast your beloved J.D. as a devil or even as a villain. Just as a good tracker and detective. I just want to know if it has any basis in reality."

"Talk on."

"The story is that one man was clever enough to almost get away from J.D. by running away to the sand dunes that lie over the mountains southward. I heard that the driver of a stage bearing gold from the O.K. Silver Mine saw a man on the ground with his horse standing over him. The driver stopped and walked over to help the downed man, who immediately shot him, took the gold, and ran away south."

"Wasn't J.D."

"I know," said Matthew. "Wells Fargo telegraphed J.D., who tracked the bandit killer to the sand dunes, where he lost the tracks. They said J.D. was ready to give up and head home, when on the hillside opposite he saw the glint of a rifle. He sneaked up on the man, captured him, and hauled him to Salt Lake, keeping part of the gold for himself."

"This is the only thing you've told me with any truth in it. J.D. did everything you said, except he didn't keep any of the gold for himself. He gave it back to Wells Fargo. I know the rest of the story is true because I was fourteen at the time and he told it to me firsthand."

"He must be some tracker."

I frowned. "Now you're trying to butter me up. This time the truth is even better than the story. Knowing the killer was close by, J.D. hid himself in the cedars and waited, wakeful through two nights, until his quarry relaxed. Then he saw the glint of sun on the rifle and took his man."

"If J.D. Rockwood was pursuing me, I sure wouldn't wait at the dunes like that other fool. It would be stupid to just wait for J.D. Rockwood to show up and capture me. I'd leave my horse at the dunes and run away in a direction that devilish tracker couldn't guess."

"He could still track you. He can track any creature across any surface."

Matthew shrugged. "So truce?"

"Truce." I didn't have the heart to try to convince him his plan wouldn't work. J.D. could track across the sand…unless the wind came up immediately.

But I knew that if he underestimated J.D.'s power to track, my stepfather had no concept of how much ground Matthew could cover on foot. I knew he could run all night and not get tired. I knew this from direct experience.

When we were both young in Nevada, his mother had told him a story about a Goshute man who ran horses to a standstill. We had tried it once when we were both nine. We found a small herd of mustangs and had picked one, the slowest one, a little brown mare, to follow. The herd went over a hill and we topped the hill not long after. We followed them across a wide flat. They kept running ahead. I had given up before an hour of running, but Matthew had kept on after I went home. Later he told me he had walked or trotted after the mustang all day, with the mare walking or running ahead. Whenever she was in earshot he talked to her. Finally toward evening he laid his hand on her wither, but he couldn't figure what to do after that.

Eight years later, walking with me along the irrigation ditch, he told me other stories. "My mother's people, the Goshutes, are great runners," he told me. "Long ago they ran down antelope."

"No. That's impossible."

"Not impossible. They set up a giant pathway two miles round by turning limestone rocks over so the white underside showed. Then they chased the antelope. Those animals follow each other's white tails when panicked, so they would run toward the white they saw on those rocks. The hunters stationed small groups of boys around the racecourse. The first group would run with the antelope for a while; then the second group would take up the chase, running a relay. Finally, when the antelope tired, the runners herded them into a brush corral and thinned the herd." He grinned at me and I could see his white teeth even in the dark. "More recent some of the young men ran with the stage westward from Paiute Hell Station. They easily kept pace with the horses, even turning cartwheels and showing off. Then the stage would stop while the passengers gave food or coins to the boys as payment for the show."

"Better pickings than running down antelope?"

"Stage horses run slower. No white man thinks of the Goshutes as human. They think of my mother's people as an order of monkeys."

"Except the Mormons. They have tried to befriend the natives."

"Like they did in the Black Hawk War?"

"They are the Lamanites, ancient people from the Book of

Mormon, descendants of the Children of Israel."

Matthew laughed out loud.

"Quiet. Someone will hear you and I'll be in big trouble."

"Proof. I have proof of what most white people think of Goshutes. There was a group of soldiers stationed at Paiute Hell Station. They were supposed to keep the peace. How were my people who were all spread out and who had no good weapons supposed to break the peace? And if they decided to steal a cow or something, how was one group of soldiers supposed to catch them in five hundred miles of desert? A stupid proposition, both offensive and useless. So these soldiers, frustrated because they had no action and angry because of the occasional theft of some outlying rancher's poor cow, found out there was a small group of Indians camped on a spring on the other side of the mountain. They rode their horses over there and, when they rode up, the men and women walked toward them with palms raised as a sign of friendliness and peace. Those soldiers opened fire and killed them all. Shot every one of them dead. Women, children, babies, all but for one girl, that the captain took back for 'questioning.' He questioned her for several days in the privacy of his own room, but when he got tired of her body he took her up a gully and shot her in the face. He didn't want any witnesses, because their official story was that the Goshutes had attacked the soldiers, opened fire on them without warning.

"Well, before that, when the soldiers were still gunning down the small group, one of the Goshute men who had been out hunting returned to see the last of his small group murdered. He came up just as they were finishing the slaughter. Well, he froze for a second, but then he took off running and they chased after. He could have run all day, but he ran toward a small group of cedars. They circled the grove, knowing they had him. While they waited for him to give up and come out, they fired into the grove. When they finally gave up and walked into the grove, guns ready, he had disappeared. My mother thinks he knew of a cavern covered with a rock. The cavern tunneled through the hillside and he got away.

"So he joined the Goshute boys who ran for the stage. Only when he begged he didn't want food. He wanted bullets and lead. 'So I can hunt to feed my family,' he told the passengers. The soldiers were finally transferred, maybe to get them away from the area of their massacre before someone suspected them. Well, this lone Goshute man, he followed them, just out of range of gunfire. That night, when they stopped for the night at Deep Creek, north of where you and I grew up, every one of them was killed."

"This story doesn't make sense, Matt. If there were no witnesses, how did anyone know that the women and men walked out peacefully?"

"My mother told me the story, and she never told a lie."

I wanted to ask him where the girl was when the soldiers were chasing the lone man who saw them killing. Had she just stood patiently until the killers finished chasing the witness to their crime and came back for her? I wanted to tell him that there were as many holes in his story as in my blood father's winter underwear, but Matthew was in no mood for me to contradict what his mother had told him of the horror. And anyway, the essence of it was probably true. The whites had been as cruel to his mother's people as Matthew thought J.D. was to all Gentiles.

I decided that fear and hatred constitute the true creed of the people of this earth.

Chapter Twelve

Back at Ezekiel's house, several men and women stood in our yard—Sister Pritchard, the bishop's wife, a few others. They turned their heads and stopped talking as I draped Matthew's blanket across the fence and opened the gate. Through the window I saw Abigail still inside with Mary and Sister Swensen. I stepped into the kitchen.

"Where you been?" asked Abigail.

"With J.D."

She nodded. The woman on each side of her held her hands.

I walked through the kitchen into the room where Sophia's body lay face up. She still wore her soaked white nightgown. I sat in the chair and stared at her, my hands clenched in front of me. Soon J.D. would ride after my husband, unless I figured a way to stop him. Time seemed to slow down, so that every breath took several minutes.

Someone shouted, and I walked onto the back porch. Brothers Ault, Nebeker, and Johnson had come with their horses. J.D. led his King, a tall black, tireless horse. He was as fast as Babe, faster, and either his lope or his trot would outstrip Brother Olson's worthless horse. King pawed the ground, clearly eager to start moving. Behind the saddle were large, square saddlebags, which held J.D.'s equipment for hunting down criminals—his lantern, spyglass, and ropes for tying up his quarry.

"J.D.," called someone from the kitchen door—Abigail. "I pray you catch her killer."

"We will do our best." He turned to the men with him. "One moment."

He strode inside, and I followed him into Sophia's room. He stood at the foot of her bed. "When I first saw her body laid out on this bed, heard her children wailing in the kitchen, I felt the same despair I felt in Nauvoo when we were forced out of the city and across the Mississippi in the winter. Hopeless. As if, here in the heart of Zion, God had turned his back on us, his Saints. Looking at her, I thought that our forty years building a place of holiness and safety in the desert was for nothing. I felt that Satan and his workers reigned everywhere on this earth."

I looked at his face and saw he was shaking with anger.

"This stranger, this Gentile soldier who came into our village and killed a gentle woman who heard a noise and walked up to investigate. This act will be avenged."

He was in a white fury and nothing I said would make any difference. I saw his burning hatred and couldn't open my mouth. If I told him this Gentile was my husband, J.D. would turn from me and follow Matthew anyway. My only hope was to go with him, talk to him when he was calmer.

When he left the room, I walked behind him to where the men sat their horses.

"What did you discover?" asked the bishop.

"Gentile in Ezekiel's barn. He killed our Sophia."

"Which way did he run?" The bishop stood behind us, in the doorway.

"South."

"We need to get going, J.D.," said Brother Nebeker. "He's getting farther away every minute."

Brother Ault nodded. "I don't like waiting for no man, not even you, J.D."

I pictured J.D. following Matthew, relentless in the dark. "No!" I clutched his arm as he took King's reins and mounted. I wanted to tell him all, feared telling him all. I couldn't think what to do except hang onto his sleeve. "You don't know he did it."

He let his hand dangle toward me, let me clutch not just his sleeve but also his hand, his huge warm hand. "A stranger in town? Clearly he did it. He ran after Sophia. The shovel was there. Show me the tracks of the person who did it if he didn't."

"The other tracks."

"No. Not related."

If I went along, I could keep him from doing violence to my husband. "Let me go with you." He took back his hand.

"Why?" he said. "You're not ready and you're needed here."

I could think of many reasons to go, but none I could say. "Give me two minutes. And I'll ride with you."

"J.D.," said Brother Ault. "We can afford no more delay."

"No. No. No. No." By the time J.D. finished he was shouting. "You have a dress on, no horse, and this is man's work. Man's work."

"Talk to him first." I pressed the knuckles of each hand up against my cheekbones. I couldn't say, *Talk to my husband first. Don't shoot my husband without talking to him first.*

The long scabbard that contained his rifle hung down next his leg. He kicked his horse and rode ten steps and reined him in. When he turned, his face was calmer. "Of course I will, my soft-hearted Rachel." His beard thrust out as he turned the horse again and rode up the lane, crossing toward the weir at the top of my fields.

I watched him go. The time was gone when I could believe that he would ever let me work with him. Now the mere suggestion that I wanted to ride with him made him furious. I walked back through the kitchen, which was empty, and into Sophia's bedroom, where the women had gone. I staggered, picturing a rifle aiming, nearly heard an audible shot.

I clutched at my watch and opened it. Just past two. With Matthew's head start, they might never catch him. I thought about riding after in the dark, but what would that do? Could I stand between Matthew and J.D.? Maybe if I had more courage.

"We can't wait," said Abigail.

I stared at her. "What?"

"She's already almost too stiff to dress." I stared at her, not comprehending what this strange woman with the bulldog face might be talking about. "Rachel. Oh, Rachel, this has been a serious shock to you, has it not?"

I looked at her, then at Sophia, at the black mark from forehead to cheek, the cut deep as a small ditch across her face. Sister Sorenson was unbuttoning Sophia's nightdress, which seemed a great affront, to undress a grown woman. Finally, I shook my head and came partially back to myself. J.D. was gone. He would catch Matthew, no matter that logic said Matthew might be safe at Lookout Station before long.

Moving half-consciously, I helped the other three women lift the body as they peeled off Sophia's nightdress. My mother's body had also been cold to the touch. The two sisters brought in basins of steaming water and began washing. Abigail worked on her face, washing the crusted blood away with hot water and soap. Then she stitched the edges of the ragged gash together. I panicked again. J.D. never deviated from a course he had set himself on. I slumped against the wall and then slid to the floor.

"We'll have to have the funeral tomorrow," said Mary, busy with her basin and rags. "The day after at the latest. In this weather she'll hardly last longer." She turned toward me. "It's been a difficult night and it's going to be an even more difficult day. We just have to bear it."

The words passed through my head, hardly registering. I sat with my knuckles still pressed up against my face. I wanted to go to Matthew. I wanted to ride Babe ahead of J.D. and follow the tracks to Matthew first. We would make our way to Salt Lake City and mix with some company taking the northern route to California. We could go to San Francisco or Alaska or South America or Europe.

How could I find my husband? How could I track him down in the dark faster than J.D. could? I had no faith in that possibility. He was in God's hands now.

Abigail took my hand and lifted me. "Her two babes. Go to them. They must be comforted."

I think she thought they might give me as much solace as I could give them. She had no idea that I was distraught about more than Sophia's death.

In their upstairs room, I rocked the children. I held the blonde child Marianne, who held Baby Stephen. The small girl was helped by helping her brother. I tried to keep my own hands from shaking, so she wouldn't feel my own fear. Sophia's dead face, the cold feel of her skin. She had slipped away from her body, the mother of these waifs, no light in her eyes, nothing to animate her tongue. The word sounded again in my mind with each beat of the rocker—*dead dead, dead dead, dead dead. Matthew might soon be dead.* I tried a song I knew Sophia had sung to the children. "Lead, Kindly Light, amid the encircling gloom. Lead thou me on, lead thou me on." I wondered if the song would cheer Marianne or just remind her of her loss.

"Heaven is too long to wait," said Marianne.

"I know," I said. "Far too long."

I rocked and hummed. Strands of her hair had pulled loose and tickled my face, but I couldn't move to push them back. Marianne tucked her face against my shoulder.

With one hand, I held her cheek against me, and with the other I groped for my watch, my hand still shaking so much that I had to try three times before I could open the face. Only two-twenty. I had thought that more time had passed.

Marianne sobbed once, and my shoulder was wet from her tears. The poor child. The unwilling memory of lifting Sophia's body forced itself back into my mind. I remembered again my arms around her cold flesh as I shoved against her, turning her out of the ditch, my cheek against her own cold cheek.

I remembered seeing my own mother's body—stiff and unfamiliar on the bed. My mother had given up her habit of drink when she became Mormon; the only thing she imbibed as a member of J.D.'s household was a sip of sacramental wine, and that in church on Sunday. But the years of hard life had weakened and aged her. After settling in Rockwood, she had gradually grown more and more tired, sleeping ten or twelve hours each night. Then one morning she didn't wake up. I had risen to build the fire and sat on the edge of my mother's bed. Her face had seemed calm and happy, but when I touched her cheek and found it cold, I became frightened.

Aunt Mary had been awake also, working in the kitchen in the large house, close to the backhouse where I and my mother and the other children lived. Mary came quickly and held me, helped me see how peaceful my mother looked. Mary explained to me, just as Abigail had explained to Sophia's two children, that our mother had simply gone home, returning to the arms of the Heavenly Mother and Father who created us all. She would be close when I wanted her.

I found Aunt Mary had spoken the truth. Whenever, during my teenage years, I'd had some trouble or another—difficulty with Babe's training, my lovesickness for Brother Swensen's son who returned from Brigham Young Academy and attended to me, Babe's physical sickness after she foundered on moldy barley, trouble with my brother who refused to obey Mary—I always felt my mother near, not speaking to me, just offering comfort.

As she lay in the coffin in the white board church, my mother's mouth had curved up slightly—the closest she had ever come to smiling. I believed that at last she had stopped wandering. My mother's smile had been so different from Sophia's horrid grimace, framed by her blood-soaked hair.

It seemed like forever, but I knew it was just a few minutes before Stephen allowed me to lay him on the bed and Marianne curled in my lap. I continued to rub the girl's neck. I heard Abigail and the other women moving below, washing the body, but the two children kept me from joining them. In the morning, someone would find my sodden quilt. How would I explain that? Any little thing could give Matthew and me away. It became clear that he and I had built our house on shifting sand.

I hoped that he would change his mind and run not toward Lookout, where he would be too easily found by J.D., but toward a town, Provo or Nephi, Salt Lake City if possible, populous enough that he could lose himself. He would contact me somehow, and I would join him. If he had killed Sophia, would I have the courage to turn him in or would I follow him? Would I help J.D. locate him in the city, make sure he hung for his crime, or would I help this criminal escape? "Heavenly Father, make him innocent and let him be safe from J.D." I frowned at my prayer; praying to change the past was useless, because it was already laid down.

I tried to imagine Matthew riding Brother Olson's poor horse bareback, with just a twine bridle. By now he should have gotten to the sand dunes, which in this moonlight would have looked as if a huge, luminous cloud had settled on the ground.

"Matthew," I said, sitting in the dark holding Sophia's little girl. "Your little ruse will not help." I felt disoriented, as if my soul swayed in and out of my body.

When J.D. arrived at the sand, he would just cast about and find Matthew's foot tracks. Hopefully Matthew would be an hour gone before J.D. arrived and found Brother Olson's horse standing right next to Matthew's foot tracks. Clutching the girl, I shook my head, disoriented. For a while it had seemed that I was the one running from J.D., I the one looking over my shoulder for any sign that the best tracker in Utah Territory followed close behind me.

Matthew had been going, riding and hopefully running, for more than two hours before J.D. started after him. He told me he could run from Lookout Station in about forty minutes—that was four miles. I could hardly believe he could run that fast, but he swore he could. Going round by way of the sand dunes was a little more than twice as far. Logic said there was no way J.D. could catch up to him before he was safe in his bed at Lookout Station. Still, my stomach didn't rest easy.

I felt like dumping the child on the bed, running screaming through the town, riding Babe toward J.D. to keep him from harming my husband. But without a different story to wave in front of J.D., like a red cape in front of a bull, he would not slow or stop his hunt. I could change nothing unless I could prove that another man had killed Sophia. Marianne whimpered and then sighed. If I could hold still for another few minutes she would be deep enough in sleep that I could leave. *Breathe and breathe, will myself calm, will us all calm: J.D., Matthew, the other men tracking Matthew. God bless us all with Thy peace, with careful thought.*

The physical evidence—Sophia's body in the weir, the shovel close at hand, and Matthew the closest one to where she lay—pointed square at Matthew. So who else could have had reason to kill her? As I stroked Marianne's head, my mind was clearer than it had been since I found the body. I knew that Sophia had not stolen water and been killed for it. If it was a killing over water, it must have been done because Sophia caught someone else stealing our water and he hit her in anger at her accusation. The Turners had the most reason to steal the water because they were the poorest in town. They were also the only ones who really could steal from us. Anyone else would signal their guilt with a muddy patch in their field or garden. First suspect was Matthew, second was Brother Turner. Who else? Brother Olson took the water before Brother Turner. The ditch was full and would be a temptation. But after a full day of the worst kind of heat baking the ground, his ground would be dry on the surface. Any new mud would proclaim him a guilty man. He would be a fool to do it. He was a fool, but it would be easy to discover whether he was that much of one, if only I could leave Sophia's two children sleeping.

The main problem, though, was that Sophia lay on our own property, not on that of either of those two brothers. Then I realized that if one of them swung the shovel in anger, he would not want her lying dead on his own property. He would certainly have carried her away from the scene of the killing. If he had done so, the prints would be deeper, because he would be carrying the weight of two. As soon as Marianne went to sleep, I would check for mud in the yards of those two; then I would examine the round-toed tracks carefully, determine how deep they were and where they came from. I couldn't ride with J.D. or stop him, but I couldn't do nothing. If he brought Matthew back alive, something I hardly dared hope for, I would have to have proof positive of who the real killer was.

Chapter Thirteen

I shifted with one sleeping child tight against my thigh and the other across my lap. I imagined six sets of tracks, maybe more—nearly as tangled as Satan's mind. The round-toed track that had gone up the ditch toward Turners' and Olsons'. My tracks, Sophia's, Abigail's, J.D.'s. Also Matthew's. Other tracks lay underneath those, people walking up and down the eastern ditch. I knew it was unlikely that a quiet Mormon farmer had killed Sophia, but the body had been set up in the water gate like a warning. Matthew would have had no reason to place the body so oddly. My brain twitched from one idea to another, like a trapped mouse.

I had to get up to look at the tracks. I shifted again and Marianne opened her eyes. I held still, singing softly, "Marianne, go to sleep, my Marianne, my lovely dear, go to sleep."

Soon she shut her eyes again.

If it was a water killing, it was not the first in Rockwood town. Thirty years earlier, a bishop had struck down his own first counselor, a Brother Samuels, in an argument over water. The bishop had left town, and I had heard recently that he had died in California, a wealthy almond farmer. As a teenager, I had listened to stories about the dead man, who, they said, still walked the ditches, appearing to people who tried to steal water.

Sophia had been struck down with the curved blade of a dull shovel. Possibly the shovel caught in the willows, perhaps another shovel, one now washed and hidden safely in the shed of one of the brethren. If I could find a wet shovel, I could have an idea of who to question, but how could I go through every man's shed in the dark? I looked out the window and at the broad side of J.D.'s house, across his fields. Mary was here, helping Abigail, and J.D. was riding after my husband, but one of the other wives, Matilda perhaps, had a light burning.

Rockwood was a town of good people, who, except for times of drought or severe cold, got along fairly well. Yet Sophia lay dead. If I entertained the idea that someone other than Matthew had killed her, then a killer at that moment stared at his lantern or at a dark wall, knowing he had struck a woman down. Only lust for water was strong enough to make a good person kill. Murder, which was the worst sin a person could commit, made the killer liable for Outer Darkness, total isolation from all of God's light. This shadow-faced killer would be in unspeakable torment.

But who could he be? My mind returned to Brother Turner, who could have been stealing water from us, had stolen it before. I disliked him more than I had ever disliked anyone, but that didn't make him a murderer. If Sophia had caught him putting a board in my gate so the water would back up toward his own gate, would he strike her down? It didn't make sense for him to strike the only one who had befriended his wife and children when he was locked up for stealing water before. I thought about my own anger at him the night before when he argued with me about the time. With only a little more provocation, I would have swung the shovel. I admitted that most women and many of the men in town would hesitate, and once hesitating, would not complete the act. I numbered those who seemed capable of this kind of anger: seven men and one woman. Inexact science, I knew, but it helped to have some idea of who could have done it if Matthew had not.

I pictured Sophia sitting in the gate, the swirl of tracks around her. I shook my head in the darkness. My mind was simply mulling again the same inconclusive ideas, circling and circling. I needed to follow the round-toed shoe upstream. I wasn't the tracker J.D. was, but if I studied the parchment of the ground carefully, I could read the unconscious message written there. Once more I tried to move, but Marianne sat up and clutched at me. The tracks would have to wait. My legs twitched with frustration.

Dear God, please protect my husband when I cannot. I prayed in my mind. Matthew's smile, his long patience with me as he waited for me to decide to marry him. He had not changed in the eight years we had been apart. I'd sooner suspect myself than Matthew, sooner believe that my own hands were bloodstained. At that moment, maybe in answer to my prayer, a sense of peace came over me. My legs stopped twitching, my heart seemed to slow. I felt calm. I knew powerfully that he had not killed—could not kill—an innocent woman. It would be as likely for the sun to shine at midnight or for a woman to give birth to an owl. It had not happened. I foresaw that I would leave my home with Matthew, would choose him over J.D., choose any place he decided to go over Rockwood, my home for eight years. The tension drained from my body. I was no longer divided over Matthew. He was innocent.

I shifted my watch out of my pocket, held it in my sweaty hand and laid my fingers across the dial. One hand short, one long. Two thirty-five. Time seemed to spin fast, because so much had happened since I had discovered Sophia's body, and slow, because a week of minutes and a month of hours had passed since my life had changed by finding her dead.

After the children were finally sound asleep, I walked downstairs into the room where Abigail, Mary, and Sister Swensen sat with Sophia's body. She was washed and dressed, her hair combed. Her cut was stitched together, and they had put something, cornstarch maybe, along the line, making it more horrid than before.

"Asleep?" asked Sister Swensen.

"Yes. It took Marianne a long time."

Mary laid her soft hand against my neck. "You could use some rest yourself."

Looking through the bedroom doorway, I saw that the kitchen

was lit from outside by several lanterns. Half the adults in town seemed to be standing in the front yard, talking over what had happened. Soon I would go out and see who was missing. The killer might hide in his dark house, anguishing over what he had done.

"Sarah," I said to Abigail's oldest daughter, who stood in the doorway, her face still horrified. "Can you go up and sit with Marianne and Stephen? I don't want them waking alone."

She looked at her mother, who nodded and asked, "So you will watch with us?"

I shook my head and left the room.

"Rachel?"

I ignored her. I had work to do.

Walking into the kitchen, I picked up my lantern, lit it with a match from my pocket, and stepped out into the darkness.

Zeke Jr., tall as I, was nearly in tears, standing in the front doorway to keep everyone out. "Mother asked you to wait out here," he said to them. "She is busy and doesn't want you inside."

I put my hand on his shoulder. "You should go back to bed."

"No. Mother asked me to watch the door." He wouldn't move. I pushed past him into the front yard.

All the men and women stared at me. Still about three hours until sunrise and no one had plans to return to bed. The men held their hats and spoke in low voices. I wanted to number them, see who hadn't come up, but my head was swimming. I wished God would mark the killer's face with a sign, as he had done to Cain, who killed his brother Abel. But this sign should be a blazing red, a florid light all could see.

I searched the faces of my neighbors. They all looked worried, anxious, on the edge of anger. I could not discern that anyone was especially overwrought, someone with a recent killing on his soul.

"Horrible," said Sister Pritchard, a tall woman with a thick braid of golden hair. "I can't believe she's dead." She had long arms, nearly as strong as a man's. I imagined her swinging a shovel at Sophia's face. She had been apprenticed to a midwife in New York State before joining the Mormons. She had delivered every baby in town that I knew about. She had long hair, blond, which she braided and coiled. Once I had seen her with it free, and she looked like she wore a huge, hooded, golden cloak, one that went to the backs of her knees. I bit down on my own lip, feeling foolish that I suspected her.

If I could tell who had seen Sophia and who had not, I could ask them details about the cut, see who knew too much. As soon as I thought it I realized that the killer would have struck in the dark and maybe not known the damage he had done. Also, everyone had probably crowded into the house, a few at a time, to look down at the body and shake their heads. They all knew by now Sophia had been hit with a shovel blade.

I peered at the faces of the men, hardly able to see them in the sliver of moonlight. Brother Peterson—a man as round as he was tall—was absent. His fields, opposite J.D.'s, were the greenest in town. Could he have slipped water back down the west ditch after I had taken it the evening before? Had Sophia caught him at it? It was not likely. He was calm and intelligent, loved to read poetry. He even wrote some in imitation of Tennyson—careful, sometimes awkward explorations of the nature of God. It was more likely that his fields were green due to the fact that he laid out a complex of small ditches across his property and carefully lined each one with clay.

Brother Jenkins had dunked Brother Pritchard's son in the ditch. He would easily be violent enough to do this. But it had to be someone who Sophia caught stealing water, so that was probably someone on our side of the ditch. Brother Turner was still the most likely suspect.

The bishop sat on the stairs of the porch. His property lay west of the lane across from the Turners'. "Ach, my Rachel." He laid his chubby hand on my shoulder. "How can we stand this grievous trial?" I wondered why he was outside instead of inside ministering to Abigail. Did he feel guilty? Was he unable to abide being in the same room with the woman he had killed?

It was impossible he was the killer, this short, round, soft-spoken man. He wept easily, was a man of historic kindness to everyone in town. His own ground was dry because he was always late to take the water and early to let it go. He had shared water with everyone on the west side of the lane. Could he have come on Sophia in the dark as she wandered the ditches and thought she was stealing water? Could he have been angry enough at this supposed thief that he had struck her down? Unlikely. It was more likely that I had struck her down in my sleep.

"J.D. said she was down in the weir," said Brother Swensen, the water master. He stepped forward out of the shadow of a Russian olive tree. His beard stretched nearly to his belly. A man as firm and upright as J.D., he was in charge of the distribution of water. I knew that he walked the ditches day and night with his pocket watch in his palm, making sure people took the water on time, not early or late. Had he come on her as she bent over our own weir and thought she was someone else? I shook my head. All of it was impossible, impossible that she was dead.

"Rachel." Someone laid his hand on my shoulder, and I realized that Brother Swensen was still speaking to me. "That is perplexing."

"She'd been set up in the water gate. Somebody bashed her across the face with a shovel and set her up in the water gate."

Brother Swensen stared at me. "Why would someone do this?" His hands twitched. "Why would someone shove a woman he'd just killed into the water? It's a desecration." I knew he had a powerful sense of justice—also no sense of humor whatever. Time and time again his wife, Lizzie, had to explain to him why something was funny.

"J.D. said a Gentile slept in your barn," said Brother Bensen, a nervous, suspicious man. He had once accused the bishop of stealing water from him. "He told me before he left that he thought the killer put her in the ditch to make it *look* like a water killing." He was from somewhere in the East and was one of the few people in town who didn't have some kind of Old World accent.

"Gentile?" I said.

"Damn Gentiles," said Brother Franklin, who lived kitty-corner to Ezekiel's house. He had four wives, each poorer than the next, and his long face always looked weary. He worked harder than any man in town but was such a poor manager that he never could get ahead. He was extremely clever with carving wood and made doll heads for his daughters that I had coveted when I was eleven and new in town.

I wiped my palms down across my face. It was hardly likely that he would steal my water. He'd wait until it was someone's turn that was closer to him.

The bishop looked up. "Rachel, is it a sure thing this Gentile is the killer?"

"J.D. thinks so. He found that blanket in the barn. It may be that Sophia found the stranger there and he chased her to the weir, where I found her body." Every word felt like a nail in my brain.

"So it's settled," said Sister Pritchard. "It's small comfort that it wasn't one of us, but it's a comfort nonetheless." She turned and strode down the lane toward her house.

"Could have been one of us," I said. "Could have been any one of us."

The others turned their faces away as soon as I stopped talking. Several shook their heads, clearly not interested in believing that the killer was one of the Fold of God.

Brother Jenkins stood directly in front of me. "But he *was* a Gentile." Brother Jenkins was the tallest and thinnest man in town. Years before, I had been told, his fifteen-year-old daughter had run away with a soldier from the mining camp at the north end of Rush Valley where General Connor was prospecting. "He probably was a soldier." He pointed to the blanket, which I had left draped over the picket fence.

I walked forward and took it down. Returning to the house, I opened the door of the kitchen and threw it past Zeke Jr. inside. Then I turned back to face the people in the yard.

"Not one of the Saints. Couldn't have been one of the Saints." Sister Jenkins was so short that the top of her head was well below her husband's shoulder. She was an unstable woman, weeping and sometimes screaming without apparent reason.

"Someone *has* been stealing water," said Brother Swensen. He glared at the fence where Brother and Sister Jenkins and Sister Turner stood.

"She was set up in the gate like a warning," I said.

"We must take care not to judge unrighteously," said the bishop.

I shook my head once, sharply. Talking about it did no good. I thrust my knuckle into my mouth and bit down, grateful for the distracting pain.

I thought about the men who lived on the east side of the ditch, from top down—Brother Olson, Brother Turner, then our house, Brothers Ault, Nebeker, and Johnson. On the other side Pritchard, Jenkins, the bishop, Swensen, Franklin, Peterson, and J.D. Almost all stood in my yard, except for Brother Turner, J.D., and the three who had ridden with him. I counted a few more who were absent: Brother Olson, who had roused the telegraph operator, Brother Jenkins' oldest son; and Brother Franklin, who said he was going to try to go back to sleep.

Brother Turner was the only man who hadn't come up at all. He was the only one I thought capable of killing an innocent woman. I had never trusted him. I told myself that I should rely on my own good sense, which could be telling me that he was the killer. He was a small man, boasted that he had worked before his conversion as a racing horse jockey in England. When I was a girl and he was new in town, I had seen him scoop beans from a barrel into his pocket, all the while talking across the store to Brother Olson, who had been owner of the Merc before Ezekiel took it over.

"Her babies," said Sister Franklin, sniffling into a handkerchief. "Her two waifs." She was nearly forty but had just the previous month borne a tiny girl.

"Judgment of God," said Sister Jenkins, stoop-shouldered, sunk into the mire of her bitterness. She had the dourest face of any woman I knew.

"Emily," said Brother Jenkins. "You don't know this. You don't know." I found myself examining the feet of the men gathered, something I'd never had the occasion or motivation to do before. All had round-toed boots. They all had been purchased at Ezekiel's store, and we had purchased them through Zion's Cooperative Mercantile Institution. Brigham Young and the prophets since then had made it clear that Mormons should not purchase Gentile shoes.

"You must leave this matter in the hands of J.D. Rockwood," said the bishop, his voice booming. He was a small man and his feet were small. Standing, he always seemed ready to topple over. "He will find the killer. He told me it was not a Saint did this killing."

Brother Turner had larger feet. I itched to slink away and look at the tracks.

"Letting those Gentiles into the valley," said Sister Jenkins. "Buying from Gentile stores. First the drought and now this. Judgment of God. Blood has soiled the ground, ran in the water and stained our fields."

I looked at this wild-eyed woman who, like Sophia, had found evil everywhere. I examined the ground in my yard, a confused tangle of tracks, made even more confusing by the shifting light from the lanterns.

"Emily," said Brother Jenkins, bending down toward her. I estimated that his feet were larger than the prints I'd seen. "You're all worked up. You need some rest." Sister Jenkins pulled herself out of his arms. She held her arms tight around her own body.

I watched the crowd, peering at every face. Sister Turner stood at the back weeping. "Soph come down nearly ever' week and give me eggs."

Brother Swensen turned at her words. His face was still angry above his long, white beard. "Let's hope J.D. finds this man who is not of our faith. Let's pray that God will hasten his pursuit and hinder this Gentile's escape."

He was a small, compact man. He walked with a swagger, maybe because he was so conscious of his size. His face was stern, judgmental of Matthew. I had little hope that anyone in town would believe anything but that Matthew, a heathen Gentile, was a killer. They wouldn't even see contrary evidence.

But then the contrary evidence was too scant for even me to have much hope.

Leaving my neighbors talking in our yard, I brushed past Zeke Jr. and walked straight through the kitchen, ignoring Abigail and the two other women who sat at the table. I continued straight through the house and out the front door. I doused the lantern and walked up the lane in front of the house.

Most of the group was behind the house, so they couldn't see me. I guess it wouldn't have mattered if they had. In fact, if the killer was not Matthew and he saw me messing in his yard, he might get anxious, maybe anxious enough to strike at me. I told myself I had to be ready for that. If it happened, I would know who killed Sophia. But that wouldn't be much consolation if I was dead. I walked past the church and past the Turners' place and up to Brother Olson's house. His light was still on and I heard his voice inside. "My Sven," I heard through the front window, but the rest was a mutter.

I walked on until I came to the weir at the top of town. I smelled moisture and heard the gurgle of water above in the creek, before it entered the weir. From there the water could channel down the west ditch to irrigate the fields and gardens on that side of town or into the ditch that watered those on the east side. That night the water had flowed through the gate into the east ditch. There was a wooden dam in the west gate, with a canvas laid across. Brother Swensen had switched the water over the day before yesterday. In this weather that was long enough to dry the surface of the ground.

I didn't want to light the lantern yet, so I got down in the west ditch and laid my palm against the dirt. Bone dry. Water had run down that ditch for the past week, and the bottom of the ditch was still wet underneath, but only when I dug down with my fingers. I found moist dirt only at a depth of three or four inches. No one had run the water down that direction anytime recently, certainly not a couple of hours earlier when Sophia had been killed. I stepped up out of the dry ditch and walked down along the flowing water in the east ditch, keeping to the side of the path in the weeds, which pricked my bare ankles. I stepped on a rock, but I refused to shift to the path and ruin tracks, which I could see better in the daylight. I had to gather my skirt in one hand to clamber over a pole fence into Brother Olson's yard. For the hundredth time in my life, I wished for trousers.

A few yards down was Olson's own water gate, with the wooden dam in place as it should be. His turn had been the night before, the same time frame as my own, from six in the evening to six in the morning. I stepped down into his ditch behind the dam and found the bottom of his ditch in nearly the same condition as the west ditch; the surface was powder dry from a whole day of direct sunlight, but when I dug I found moist dirt. No water had come down Brother Olson's ditch in the past few hours. I would bet my soul on it.

I crept past the barn from which Matthew had stolen Brother

Olson's horse, and continued down to the pole fence that marked the boundary between Brother Olson's yard and the Turners'. I wanted to be triple sure not to ruin tracks, so I lit the lantern. I checked the ground carefully before I put one foot down, then another. I could see no evidence in the path of the round-toed boots with the bad heel. After about ten minutes of laborious motion, I came to the Turners' water gate. I got down in the ditch that led to his garden, set the lantern on the bank, and bent to my hands and knees. Immediately I felt mud coating my palms and muddying my dress. Sticky, recent mud and water standing. I thought, *Damn Turner's dishonest hide!* The ground should be damp because the water had been taken the evening before, but this ditch had had water flow down much more recently than that. A drumbeat started in my head, and I knew I'd have to calm myself before talking to Turner; otherwise, I'd say or do something stupid.

I wiped my hands on my skirt, pulled out my watch, and checked the time. Three twenty. The bottom of the ditch should have been ten hours' dry. The bottom would still be moist, muddy even, but not the fresh and slimy mud I felt under my knees and against my palms. Just then I felt something behind me and I jumped to my feet, jerking toward whatever it was. A face thrust out of the darkness.

"What the hell are you doing snooping in my ditch?"

Brother Turner.

Calm and steady, I told myself. *One, two, three, four, five.* "I was discovering that water has come down this ditch after I took it from you last evening."

He snorted. "You are determined to have me locked up again." He took a step forward and I grabbed the handle of my lantern, ready to swing it against his face if he came any closer. "That is mud from when I watered my garden last night. Any fool can see that."

"Any fool can see that this is fresh mud." I took a step toward him and he backed away one step. "Made this past hour."

"Get off my property before I lose my temper. Damn your Rockwood hide, snooping around my ditches and garden." He grabbed at my sleeve and I thrust the hot lantern toward him until he backed away.

"I'm going," I said. "I discovered what I needed to."

He walked behind me around his house. "You know you only harm my children and my Susan, when they have to take up the work I could be doing if I wasn't locked up." By the time he finished he was shouting at me.

"You should have thought of that before you stole the water."

He held his hands out, palms down. "Rachel, you have the power to harm me."

I didn't turn or answer him, I was so angry. When I entered the lane, I heard him open the door to his house and close it quietly behind him.I stood in the lane and watched his house, but he didn't come out again, didn't light a lantern or candle inside, at least not that I could see.

I thought about telling the bishop and Brother Swensen what I had discovered in the bottom of Turners' ditch. I decided to wait, because stealing water was not the problem that night. Murder was. I needed tracks to link the stealing to the killing.

I breathed and breathed, trying to work down my fury. I would bet my entire stake of two hundred dollars in gold coins that Turner had killed Sophia. He may have come down to our weir, waiting there for me to change the water. When I came out, he would run back up the ditch and fix his dam again. But somehow Sophia surprised him hiding there, and he hit her with his shovel.

Standing in the lane, I turned and looked toward Rockwood Creek Pass, toward which Matthew had fled. The wide, low pass, only four miles away, seemed impossibly far; J.D. wouldn't have had time to catch up to Matthew, who foolishly thought the sand dunes as a place where a man could lose any tracker. J.D. was not any tracker. If a wind didn't come up even I could see where a man had walked across the dunes.

Hopefully he was far past the dunes and on his way back to Lookout Station. My husband. Running away through the dark.

Did he regret stepping into the traces with a Mormon woman?

Still brim full of anger at Brother Turner, I stood near our black orchard, leaving my lantern still unlit. While Matthew ran, I was safe in Rockwood town. I staggered as I tried to walk toward Ezekiel's house.

Chapter Fourteen

I had entered the lane when I heard a horse behind me. J.D. Alone. He should have been miles away at the sand dunes, following the tracks of a rider-less horse. I turned and blocked his way.

"Rachel?"

"Yes."

The huge black horse pranced in place. After an hour of hard riding, he was still ready to go. My heart rose to my mouth. I grabbed at J.D.'s hand, high above me in the dark. "Did you shoot him already?"

His voice burst out of the darkness. "No."

Matthew had gotten away.

He stared at me. "Why are you so worried about this Gentile?"

"I—I don't want anyone dead."

I couldn't say, "I knew him in Nevada." I couldn't say, "He is my husband."

"It's good you don't have to kill then," said J.D.

I followed King down the street to J.D.'s house. He dismounted and together we went inside. J.D. strode into the kitchen and lit a lantern. I sat at the table. Soon Mary's head appeared in the doorway to the back room. "It's all right," he said to her. "Just go back to bed."

He peered inside the breadbox. "I have figured how to head him off." He pulled out half a loaf and took it to the table to cut.

My soul sank again, as he sliced two thick slabs of bread.

"Follow this thinking with me, Rachel. I don't have much time, but your head may be clearer than mine. Maybe my sixty-four years has dulled my brain."

He grinned like a kid, obviously not thinking his brain was less than it had ever been. What he wanted was to brag about his cleverness. For sure and certain I didn't feel like grinning with him.

"As I was following the tracks I went over what I know about him. He came from the west, and we know from the blanket that he's probably a soldier from Paiute Hell Station."

He stood to take butter and a crock of jam out of the cabinet. "So we're left with a few mysteries." He sat again and spread one piece of bread with the butter. He held one finger in front of my face. "The first: Why was Sophia a threat to him?" Two fingers. "Why did he have no gear?" Three. "And why was he confused about where to run?"

"Wait a minute! You're going too fast."

J.D. looked at me. "Too fast for you, Rachel? I've never heard that before." His eyes were alight with pure pleasure at figuring something out that I couldn't. I dreaded what he would say next. He touched my hand. "This night has been too much for you. The terrible strain shows in your face."

Lucky for me he had an explanation for everything.

"I walked up the ditch and looked at the tracks. Brother Turner's boots. Water in the Turners' ditch."

"You think he would kill?"

I nodded.

"I think you are set against him. Now let me get back to what I was saying. You can be a help to me if you tell me where I am going wrong."

"That's what I was trying to do. The tracks…"

"Rachel!" he shouted. "Just let me finish. For once don't be so bull-headed. Now let me explain."

He folded his hands in front of him, watching his hands instead of my face. I thought about leaving him to his stupid ideas, but I couldn't afford that kind of tantrum. I had to calm myself, had to engage with him. Had to.

"Because I thought he was a deserter, because of the blanket, I had an idea so firmly in my mind that I could see no other."

I carefully nodded my head. The cords in my neck were

tight enough to give me a headache. "You cannot see it could be someone else doing the killing."

"No!" J.D.'s voice exploded. "That part is sure. He ran toward her and she is dead. Listen to me, Rachel. This Gentile went into the barn, I thought, so that he could have a soft bed on the hay."

I couldn't afford to let even the smallest sign escape my face. I felt like holding my breath, hiding my face.

"Sophia discovered him." He pointed the butter knife at me. "Desperate to keep himself hidden, I thought, he ran toward her, grabbing the closest weapon to hand and bashing her head as she turned. What had she said to him that so incited his fear and anger?" He spread the other piece of bread with jam. Despite myself, my mouth started watering. "Perhaps nothing. Perhaps the fear of discovery was great enough that he would have attacked anyone. While I rode with the brethren, I had time to think over what I had thought. At the bottom of it, all we know is that Sophia threatened him somehow. Maybe because he was a deserter, but maybe for some other reason. So I let myself imagine other reasons."

"Pass me that knife." I was sure he could see the blood pounding in my neck.

He offered me the butter knife.

"No," I said. "The sharp one." He handed me the knife and somehow instead of plunging it into his hand, I slowed and calmed myself enough that I could cut two thick slices from the loaf.

Somehow I kept my hand from shaking as I spread butter and jam on the soft bread. As I took a large bite, the bread and jam drew my saliva so sharply that it hurt. I wanted to take the bread and use it to stop J.D.'s mouth before he accused me, but at the same time I hung on every word.

"The second mystery…where was the rest of the killer's gear?"

I stopped chewing. "You haven't revealed the first mystery,"

I said before I could stop myself. I sure didn't want to know the answer. "The rest of what gear?"

"His food, cooking gear, gun? What might have caused him to abandon his western home so quickly that he'd had no time to grab anything but a single blanket? He had not come a great distance. No one could survive crossing the western desert—Paiute Hell—without equipment. No horse, no food, or water."

I feared where J.D. was headed with his beastly logic.

He continued. "But what doesn't make sense is why he started westward when he first ran from here."

"What do you mean?"

"Remember, above the barn on the hillside? The first tracks started back toward the way he came from. So the third mystery is this... Why did he waver when deciding where to run?"

I opened my mouth but shut it again. If I tried to lead J.D. off the track he would know I was up to something. And so far he was dead on Matthew's mental trail.

"The killer's first instinct was to go west to safety." J.D. paused. "This is not something a deserter would think for a moment. West would not be safe to him." He slapped the table and I nearly jumped out of my frock. "Then he started north—Rush Lake Station and the freight route. Hamblin City and the railroad. Salt Lake City. Then he turned back, traveling straight south. Possibly a rational plan had replaced the first impulses or perhaps he was just confused and terrified."

It wouldn't take long for J.D. to come to the idea that the mystery man had come to town not because he was a deserter but for a woman. Would he then know that the woman was me, and then that the man was Matthew? I took bite after bite of food until my mouth was too full to chew. Then I stood and spit it out in the chicken bucket.

J.D. stared at me. "I've never seen you throw away food before."

"I bit off more than I could chew."

J.D. laughed. "Brother Nebeker continues to think the man is a deserter. He said that kind of man would do almost anything to keep from being discovered. Sophia gets him caught and he's facing a firing squad. Possible. But I realized as soon as I started thinking about these mysteries about the tracks, that a deserter would not have come to Rockwood at all. He would know that the best place to lose trackers is at the sand dunes and he would have headed straight for there. Why would a deserter leave Paiute Hell Station and run seven miles along the freight route past Lookout Station and four more miles to Rockwood town and then three or four more miles back to the sand dunes, when he could head straight for the dunes from Paiute Station, a distance of only four or five miles total? The answer is that he wouldn't. He'd take the shortest route." He sat back in his chair, a smug look pasted on his face.

I shook my head. "What are you saying, J.D.? I don't understand."

"He's not a deserter, but a fornicator."

Because I had expected it, the shock was not as great as I thought it would be. "Maybe he was as distracted as you claim."

J.D. shook his head. "Listen and don't interrupt me. Then when I'm finished, you tell me if I'm speculating too much or not." He leaned forward. "This is a reason for a soldier to walk eleven miles to Rockwood. The first impulse of such a man, if he is a soldier, would be to return home."

I wanted to say, "Not Sophia. Sophia would never go out to meet a man at midnight," but I didn't. There was one other woman out in the night that J.D. hadn't thought about. I trembled in fear that his next words would be, "And thou art the woman."

J.D. went on. "This woman was surely not Sophia, who always has a word of extreme piety in her mouth."

Unable to think clearly, I cut another piece of bread. Set it aside. Held my hands clasped in front of me.

J.D. thought again, his fingers tracing a circle on his

crown. There was a tumult in my gut and I wanted to slap his beastly hand, stop its eternal circling. "They could be one of the unmarried girls in town, seduced by a soldier's clothing, agreeing to lie with him in the night."

I cleared my throat, but he didn't pause in his rush of words.

"Who can fathom the mysteries of a woman's soul? I've never understood why Eve, with full knowledge, took the forbidden fruit. I do think I know Sophia's soul, though. She was the same on the surface as she was to her core. So he didn't come to try to seduce her from the path of righteousness." He chuckled at the idea. "But Sophia was always walking about at night. She may have stumbled across this man and his woman in the barn. She would immediately call down heaven's fire on them. The man would anger and hit her with the closest weapon to hand. Then he would be scared. If he tried to run, we and the army both would be after him, but if he could confuse his tracks and get back to his bed before sunrise, he would be safe. I now believe this was his thinking. I believe the tracks have let me inhabit his head."

Maybe Matthew was right and J.D. did have devilish powers that made him see visions in the tracks. I could hardly breathe.

J.D. leaned forward. "If he gets back in time, no one will believe that he was involved with a killing. Or maybe he wouldn't need to hide. Captain Jardine is assigned to protect the freight and telegraph routes, but he has never hidden his hatred of Mormons. Perhaps he would think it a joke that a Mormon woman is butchered."

I opened my mouth, but no words came to my tongue, which felt as if it had swollen in my mouth.

"It's crazy. I admit it freely. Only a man possessed by lust would try to run barefoot from Paiute Hell Station to Rockwood and back in one night, twenty-two miles."

"Maybe—maybe he didn't run. Maybe he has a horse tethered just west of town."

J.D. glared at me. "Why would he steal Olson's horse then? Use your head, Rachel. But what I've been thinking is that, if this speculation is true, the distance back to Paiute Station going by way of the sand dunes would give him a chance to get back to Paiute Hell, protected by a known Mormon-hater." He shook his head. "All this is guesswork, but following the tracks, I had a strong feeling that I was thinking the way the killer was. If he's a deserter, he'll head south from the sand dunes and those three brethren will probably catch up to him, but if he's a whoremonger, he will head back to Paiute Station. Once inside that station, the killer will be difficult to pry out and take to a court of law, just on the evidence of tracks. Hatred can make people capable of any atrocity, can make them blind to justice."

"But you have left his tracks. You could have followed him straight from the dunes to Paiute Hell Station."

"But we were only halfway to the dunes when I turned back. The tracks before us were so clear that even a child could follow them, let alone three experienced men. I knew that the worst I could lose by playing my hunch was to put myself several hours behind those three capable men. I might learn from Jardine or my brother Ambrose a name and description to go with the tracks. But, if I'm right, by riding quickly on the road while the killer is still struggling across eight miles of sand and then desert, I can get Jardine's ear before the killer does. Or if Jardine won't listen, I can position myself between Paiute Station and the dunes. If I push my horse, a better mount than the one the killer stole from Brother Olson, I might arrive at Paiute Hell Station before him."

"It's crazy thinking."

I knew I should just tell him right then who Matthew was, but I couldn't do it. It seemed physically impossible. I rationalized that if J.D. was headed toward Paiute Hell, he'd pass quickly through Lookout Station, which was Matthew's real destination. Matthew might already be there in bed, before J.D. passed through. For sure he would make it there before J.D. discovered his error farther west at Paiute Hell Station.

"But I'm sure I'm right." He clutched my shoulder. "You could help me by thinking who the woman could be. Try to discover her. That would be very important in my efforts to convince Jardine that this theory is right. You can telegraph me at both Lookout and Paiute Hell Stations."

"If you're right about Jardine, that knowledge wouldn't change his mind." For sure, knowledge didn't change a man's mind. I had tried to turn J.D.'s head from the hunt to evidence in Rockwood town and I couldn't do it. "Don't shoot him."

J.D. glared at me and strode out the door. I stood on the stoop and watched him remount his horse and head northwest toward the road that led to Lookout Pass. Except for his few mistakes, I could have believed the legends were right and he had some sight from God or the devil that enabled him to read Matthew's mind. Nothing would stop him except for the identity of the real killer.

For the hundredth time, it seemed, I found my watch in my pocket and felt the dial. Just past three-thirty. Two hours until dawn. I prayed for the ability to read tracks in the dark.

Chapter Fifteen

When I came to the top of Ezekiel's orchard, I lit my lantern again and tipped the light at an angle so that I could see the ground. In a few minutes, I found the round-toed boot prints, shadowy but distinct. I looked for a while, moving the lantern in a slow circle, and I could see that J.D. was right two hours earlier when he had glanced at the pathway. On top of all the other tracks, on top of my track going up and down, someone had come down the ditch and gone back up. *Damn J.D. for not taking ten minutes to look at these tracks.* He had seen them more clearly than I had, but he had refused to discern their significance.

Walking to one side of the path, I followed the tracks a few yards up along the dusty bank. I found a boot print going up the ditch laid over a boot print coming down, proving my theory about the person's movement. As I continued following the tracks, I moved slower than J.D. would have, partly because I had to constantly tip the light back and forth. The base of the lamp made a big shadow, but when I tipped it far enough to cast light directly on the ground, smoke blacked the glass chimney. The shifting shadows made it difficult to see. Luckily, feet passing through the summer had ground the bank to powdered dust, so the round-toed prints were on top of all the others—very distinct. Noticing that the prints pointed inward at the toes, I frowned. I hadn't remembered that Brother Turner was pigeon-toed. The tracks continued to follow the bank of the ditch around the curve of the hill below the church. I crossed back onto the Turners' property, but this time from the bottom coming up. I found a clear track where one of the prints turned in at the toe. I shook my head, wishing again for J.D.'s ability to see the person from the track.

I came to the same place I had been an hour earlier. At the water gate, the footsteps crossed a muddy patch, leaving prints as clear as plaster casts. The left heel was normal but worn; the right had been repaired with a slightly larger heel. The toes clearly pointed toward each other.

Suddenly a woman wailed, a high, rising cry, something like the call of a despairing coyote. The sound was below me, past our property along the ditch. Running back down around the hill, I saw a light in the Aults' yard. I glanced toward my own house. Brother Swensen was first out the gate; the others followed, running.

I moved quickly across our property and climbed the pole fence into the Aults' back garden. I soon came face to face with a woman dressed in white—Sophia? I dropped the lantern. "Oh!" My breath went out of me as if I'd been slugged. "Sister Ault." I quickly righted my lantern, which had smoked the chimney.

"Rachel," said the woman in a voice as thin as a child's. "What are you doing on my lot? Did you turn the water down the ditch early? I wasn't ready for it. It made a flood through my garden." She looked as if she wanted to swing a shovel at me. Then she wailed. "It's ruined. All my labor lost."

Soon the others had arrived, men and women of town rushing up from my yard.

"My potatoes," Sister Ault said to them. "Someone flooded them and ruined them. What are we going to eat this fall?"

I turned and walked fifty feet down the side ditch to her potato patch. Sister Jenkins followed, and then several others crowded past to see the damage. It still seemed strange to have nearly the whole town up in the middle of the night.

"Someone flooded your garden?" said Brother Swensen.

"Ach," said the bishop. "All this in one night."

"It's either too much water or not enough," said Sister Pritchard.

"Look at it," said Sister Ault. "I couldn't sleep after my Thomas left with J.D. So I finally decided to come up and get my small ditches ready so I could take the water at six this morning.

I already had my dam across the main ditch, but I wasn't ready except for that. I wasn't ready, so now my garden is ruined. How could this have happened? Who would have done this?"

I joined the others at the garden. The water forced down the ditch by Sophia's body had rushed across the Aults' potato patch, carrying away the soft soil. A swath six feet wide ran through the whole patch. The upper roots and half-grown potatoes were exposed. Uncovered in this manner, they would be ruined by sun and soon by frost.

"Why?" She turned her angry face into my lantern light. "Ruined."

I pointed back toward my dam. "Sophia's body forced the water downstream. Whoever killed her did this to your garden."

Sister Ault turned to me. "What are you doing spying in my backyard when you should be helping Abigail?"

"J.D. and Brother Ault have gone after this terrible killer," said the bishop. "You good sisters just leave it to them." I turned from the group in the garden and walked back up the ditch. I understood Sister Ault's anguish and confused anger, lashing out at the closest person. All her work ruined.

Had Sophia discovered Brother Ault stealing water so he killed her? He was a small man, with a narrow, dark face. I knew him to be a man of violent temper, but I couldn't imagine him striking down a woman. There was a little ticking in the back of my head—something I wasn't seeing.

I wished I had more time. As I paused, I wondered whether J.D. going one way or the other three men going the other way would get to Matthew first. I pictured the party of three closing in on him in the cedars above the dunes, cornering him like I'd seen J.D. and his sons cornering a cougar once. The animal hid until it was too late and then leaped out of the tree, landing running. The dogs were on him but he outran them and leaped into another tree, where one of the men walked up and shot him. Brother Ault might be the first to shoot. Matthew might fall with a soft thud to the ground, just as the cougar had. With the obvious killer dead, why would anyone look for another?

Into my head came the image of Matthew, half-covered with a sheet of canvas, lying on the ground next to a hole—his own grave. I touched his stiffened body, laid my palm on his cold and grimacing face.

Opening my eyes, I shook myself. *Just your out-of-control imagination,* I said to myself.

Then I realized what had lingered in the shadows of my mind. Someone in town might strike out with his shovel when surprised in the act of stealing water, but hardly anyone was capable of killing and then being calm enough to carefully put Sophia in the ditch as a dam—not even sour-faced Brother Ault. He would have been driven mad by his act, unable to think what to do next. And he certainly wouldn't have ruined his own garden.

J.D.'s claim that Matthew had set her up this way also seemed ridiculous to me, but more likely him than one of the innocent town folk. Any of them would run with horror from what they had done.

I wiped one hand down my face, trying to think clearly. In the heat of killing, Brother Ault might have forgotten to get his own garden ready for the flood of water. Or had he ruined his garden to direct attention elsewhere? I shook my head. Brother Ault, I believed, was incapable of that kind of deviousness. He was always in trouble with someone because his mouth said directly what was in his head. Once he had let spill that he coveted Brother Bensen's lone wife. I believed him incapable of dissembling.

Fifty yards away from me, Sister Ault and the others stared at the ruined garden. I turned away and continued up the main ditch. I followed again the prints with the odd heels as they went up toward Turner's water gate. All up and down the ditch were other tracks underneath the tracks I followed. I wished again for J.D.'s ability. The tracks might be either the water master's or the bishop's; either one of those two men would have reason to go up and down the ditch, checking on violators of their plan to have twelve-hour water turns. But neither was likely to have these worn-out, patched shoes, and neither had feet quite this large. I then noticed that some of the ones going up were pigeon-toed, and some were not. *Bewildering!* I looked more carefully and saw the same print side-to-side with another, one pigeon-toed, the other not. Both had the distinctive worn heel. One set of tracks went down the ditch, but two sets had gone up, all wearing the same boots. I couldn't imagine a scenario that fit this impossibility.

I walked back up to the pole fence at the edge of the Turners' property. I swung myself over, following the doubled tracks, which led straight into the barnyard. Another set of tracks mingled with the ones I had been following, another set of round-toed prints—but these had new heels and were as small as the bishop's. Apparently the bishop or Brother Swensen, who had almost the same size feet, had also walked through the Turners' yard. The round-toed tracks with the worn left heel passed through the garden. The track changed to a toe-only print that showed he was running. The prints crossed the garden and went up to the back door. Why would Brother Turner run to his own home?

I looked into the dark toward Lookout Pass, where J.D. and Matthew moved toward each other, Matthew from the south, along the mountain range, J.D. from the east, along the road. I strode around to the front of the small building. Seeing a light on inside, I beat on the door and a child opened—a frightened child, about eleven. Behind him I could see a small girl sit up in bed, her eyes wide. I had waked her.

"Your father."

"Not here."

"Mother."

"Not here."

"Where?"

Quick shrug of shoulders.

I turned and walked through the dusty yard, around the cedar tree between our house and the road. Suddenly I bumped into Brother Turner. I gave a little shriek before I could stop myself.

"What the hell you doing here?" he said, belligerent as ever. "I tolt you to stay offn' my property. Seems like this whole town has gone crazy tonight."

I had once seen him tear into Brother Nebeker. Brother Nebeker had accused him of cheating in the trade of two heifers for a horse. Said that neither heifer would take, even after he had left them with a bull all summer. Brother Turner knocked Brother Nebeker down with a broken ax handle and beat him until the bishop pulled him off.

In the dark yard, Brother Turner took a step toward me. I took a step backward. He said, "I heard about Sophia. I'm sorry."

I stepped around him into the road, where I could shout or run from him. Down the street, Brother Swensen emerged from the Aults' yard step in step with the bishop. They both turned back into my yard, where a group of men and women still clustered. "I followed tracks coming from where Sophia's body lay, straight to here." I stepped even farther into the street in case he came after me.

"What? I get suspected of ever' thing in this damned town. Just because I ain't regular at church."

"I have no idea who killed her. I just want to know what you saw."

Brother Turner's face showed shock; then he smiled, a sly smile.

"I walked down there last night to make sure you weren't skulking around, trying to take the water early."

"Something I've never in my life done. And these prints were made in the night, after I had already taken the water." He was clearly lying about something. Why lie when someone had been killed? The act of murder crowded out every other consideration.

He went on. "Everybody up the line steals from those down the line. The water master's never called to get after them." I knew that he still hated me for having him locked up before.

"Brother Swensen would notice a big patch of mud in *anybody's* garden or field. Or do you suspect Brother Olson of stealing from you?" Brother Olson, next yard up, would still have wet fields when the Turners took the water.

He turned away. "Another couple of weeks and the creek'll dry up completely. I guess I'll be blamed for that, too."

"Did you know the water running down from Sophia's body ruined the Aults' garden?"

"Ruined?"

He seemed surprised. I wished I could see his face better.

"I…everything looked normal when I walked down last evening."

"Of course it was normal. Sophia wasn't dead in the water gate." His words made no sense and I wondered what he was hiding. "*Your* garden's still wet, too. When did you walk down?"

He ignored my last question. "I watered it until you took what little there was at five last evening. An hour early. How can I water my garden when you always take the water early? And Swensen always agreeing with you." He walked toward me, fierce as a badger. "Just what you saying I done? I'm sorry about Sophia, but I didn't have *nothing* to do with her death. Or with stealing your precious water."

He walked past me into the house. "Brother Turner. I believe that J.D.'s gone after an innocent man."

Brother Turner turned. "He's gone after someone?" He almost smiled, visibly relieved.

"You didn't hear? Someone was in our barn. J.D.'s tracking him."

"Someone was in your barn?" he said. "Yes. J.D. will bring

him back. J.D. will bring back Sophia's killer." He walked toward his house. "My children are frightened. I'm sorry I got no way to help you." He closed the door behind him.

I leaned forward, hands down against my knees, until my heart slowed.

I turned and examined the ground where he had stepped just now. Same worn left heel, same large new right heel. I followed the tracks backward across his dusty barnyard, tracks he had made only moments before while he walked away from me toward his house. For sure the toe didn't turn in—no longer pigeon-toed. I stopped in the road, thinking; then I walked back to bang on the door again.

"What the blazes do you want now?" He stepped forward until his face nearly touched mine.

"Where is your wife, Brother Turner?"

"You leave my wife alone! Just leave her alone!"

"Probably up at my house."

"She's trying to give comfort to them poor children. What are you doing? She's up there giving them comfort when you're running around in the dark accusing innocent people."

"I've accused no one." Knowing I'd get nothing else out of him, I turned and walked back up the lane. I was certain the round-toed and pigeon-toed tracks with the odd heels were Sister Turner's.

I had no doubt they had stolen water again.

Chapter Sixteen

As I strode up the lane, Brother Peterson left his doorway and walked out to his front gate, staring sadly. "Hard times."

Across the street, Brother Pritchard led his white horse back down to his yard. "Damn thing climbs fences like they was ladders." Brother Pritchard's pants had a dozen patches; he was nearly the stingiest man in a very poor town. His children, now mostly grown, had been my age when we all went to the small academy in the back of the church house. They came to school with only an apple or carrot or a potato for lunch. That was mostly what his family lived on. When they had meat in the pot it was a special occasion for them. But now he fed the apples and carrots to his horse. After spending a year in the cellar, they were wizened and smelled of dank earth, not pleasant to eat. The horse nuzzled at his pockets and he handed him a small apple. I thought of the horse wandering the town, seeing everything, but registering nothing with his animal brain. I wished I could see through his eyes, know what he had seen at my dam.

Sister Turner, her head held low, walked up the street toward me. Apparently she had held back, talking to Sister Jenkins or perhaps walking in to see the body of the woman who'd given her cream and eggs, before returning home from Ezekiel's house. I knew that with only four children Sister Turner must be thirty or younger, but walking down the lane in the dark, she looked like an ancient woman. Her shoulders bowed forward, her feet shuffled, and she muttered to herself in the dark. When we came closer, I said loudly, "We can remember Sophia with kindness."

Sister Turner's head jerked up; her eyes bulged as if surprised. But her eyes always bulged as if surprised.

"She did many acts of secret charity." I took Sister Turner's arm and held her from walking on. "I need to talk to you."

Sister Turner pulled free, surprisingly strong.

"Why did you walk down the ditch last night? When you came back to your house, you were running."

Sister Turner, barefoot just like me, looked down at her hand, which twisted in her dress. "Why do you say that? I think William checked the water yesterday early in the evening. If it wasn't him, it was nobody. What, you think you're a tracker like J.D., another conscience for this town?" Her husband's belligerence came into her voice.

I pointed down at Sister Turner's feet, turned in so far that the big toes touched. "They were your husband's shoes, but the person who walked up the ditch and ran back was pigeon-toed. Your husband would fall on his face making those prints." I held the lantern high and pointed at the prints behind her in the dusty road.

Sister Turner stared at the tracks. "Why would I wear his boots? I'm just fine barefoot. You go barefoot too." Sister Turner pointed at my feet. "Nothing wrong with being too poor to afford shoes."

"Do you go barefoot to change the water?"

"Yes. Yes, I do."

I stepped forward. "Listen. I don't think for an instant you're capable of swinging that shovel at Sophia. But somebody did. J.D. could be chasing a man who had nothing to do with this. Then the killer would go on living in the middle of Rockwood town. In the middle of the Saints."

"Until God harrows up his conscience and he confesses."

"That might never happen."

"You got even less faith than me."

"How do we know it is a *man* who killed her? Look. I know you walked down the ditch last night."

"You don't know. Probably the person J.D.'s chasing. You don't know nothing."

"I don't care, not even a pinch, why you came down. I just want to know if you saw anything."

"Ask William. I was taking care of my babe."

"So you were awake?"

"Might have been. I don't know exactly when he went down."

"Your husband told you what story to tell. Tell me the truth. What were you doing down at my weir last night?"

She frowned. "I'm sure my children's going to starve this winter." She walked quickly up the lane toward her house. She pointed toward Brother Pritchard's white horse. "We'll have to eat what that horse passes over."

I pushed her too hard, I thought. I should have tempered my tongue, had more patience. I turned on my heel and walked up to the back door of my house. I wasn't in the mood to talk to Abigail or anyone still gossiping in the front yard. I imagined Matthew riding Brother Olson's horse, a nag that even I could beat in a foot race.

Ahead I saw lanterns still shone in my yard, the whole town roused as if for Sunday meeting. Sister Ault came up from her house just as I tried to enter my gate. She looked up at me. "Some of it is all right. I'll have to dig the potatoes early."

"Or shovel dirt back over them."

"Won't do," said Sister Ault. "It'd just turn to adobe. They're ruined unless we dig them before they're full grown. Shame to lose all that growth. Silly, wasteful shame."

"Maybe straw would cover them enough."

She stared at me. "That just might work. Thank you, Rachel."

At my front door I paused, my hand on the handle of the screen door. I glanced southeastward toward Rockwood Creek Pass; the sky was slightly paler than the range. I wished I could ride Babe fast enough to catch J.D. and tell him what I'd found.

But what *had* I found? I knew that the Turners were both lying, that Sister Turner had walked down the ditch in the night. I stood at the back door, still caught by my own thinking, like a cow struggling in a mire. Even if I did follow J.D., I would never catch up. All I could do was pray that he would talk to Matthew before shooting him. In Rockwood, I could keep pushing to find out what the Turners knew.

The bishop might be at my house or he might have gone home. Although the Turners had ignored me, they couldn't ignore him.

I looked into the sky at the Big Dipper and judged that it was probably not long until daylight. I checked my watch to make sure. Just after five o'clock. About right.

I found the bishop inside the kitchen. Abigail sat slumped at the table, and he was patting her small hand with his plump one. No children were around. They both turned to stare at me.

"Where you been?" said Abigail. "You left when we was in the middle of it. She's lying in there cleaned and dressed now. We finally got my kids back to bed. Where in heaven's name you been?"

"Bishop, J.D. and I found a set of tracks along the west ditch. The prints are from Brother Turner's shoes but it wasn't Brother Turner." They looked at me, puzzled. "Come with me and talk to them. They'll listen to you when they won't listen to me."

"What are you talking about?" said Abigail. "I've never seen you like this."

"Listen," I said, angry that they couldn't understand plain language. "These tracks go from where Sophia was killed straight to the Turners."

"When could J.D. have followed the tracks with you?"

I took a breath. "I followed the tracks. They go straight from the water gates to the Turners' house. They were Brother Turner's boots, but he's not pigeon-toed. She was wearing his boots."

"What? Who was wearing his boots?"

"Sister Turner!"

"Slow down. I canna understand you when you talk so fast. Sister Turner in her husband's boots? Why is that of any importance?"

I took a breath. "I don't know. The prints go up from my dam where I found Sophia."

"They may lead away from the weir, but so do a dozen others." He laid his hand on my arm. "My young Rachel, I know you are all worked up."

"J.D.'s gone after the killer," said Abigail. "He wouldn't go after somebody he wasn't sure of."

"You accusing the Turners of killing Sophia?" asked the bishop.

"What if they were stealing water again and Sophia caught Sister Turner putting a board across the ditch to turn the water back onto her garden? What if Sophia used her sharp tongue on Sister Turner? She might swing her shovel in anger."

"I think you're carrying a grudge too far. They stole your water once but I donna think they've done it since we locked William up."

Abigail frowned. "Sophia would give them the water. That foolish woman was sharp with everyone, but not with their small children. They wouldn't have to kill her for it. She was always giving them people cream and eggs."

"All you know is that someone walked down the ditch and back," said the bishop. "You don't know they've done any wrong."

I walked out of the kitchen and back up to the water gate at the top of my field. I could see nothing, so I ran down to the house for the lantern, where I must have left it. I could see its light against the wall of our house, glowing as if it were afire. I had set it next to the door when I had gone inside.

Calm down, woman, I said to myself. *Next you'll burn the house down.* Both the bishop and J.D. were right, the tracks alone proved nothing. I breathed and breathed, calming myself and walked back to the weir with the lantern.

I stood on the ditch bank and wished for light. There was a white line along the horizon and light had begun to spread upward, a hand's breadth of paleness. I looked down at the ground, at the shadows cast by the lantern, shifting deceiving shadows that I wasn't good enough to see past. I was not as good as J.D., able to follow tracks in the dark, see every detail without complete light. He had spent his life looking at tracks in shadow, under snow, after rain, in every condition, and he could see the ground like a seer could see the fabric of time. His eyes were of the highest order. This was true, despite the fact that he said he couldn't see as well as he used to. It felt silly to say it, but he possessed eyes so refined that they were nearly spiritual eyes. It wasn't a mystical idea for me, that J.D. could work his flesh toward the Celestial. I believed it in my gut that I could do the same. J.D.'s gift was to see the ground; mine was to see the mind of my fellow being with clarity. When I was young, I thought everyone had this sense, but even J.D., who I admired with my life, didn't have my gift, just as I didn't have his.

Still I was in a position where my sight into souls was not enough, and my inferior tracking eyes had to wait for daylight to see. I started to walk up the bank, but the tangle of tracks would reveal nothing new to me, so I sat on the water gate in despair.

With any luck, or with the blessing of God, Matthew would be safe in bed by now. But I didn't trust luck, and I wasn't sure God wanted to bless my husband. Matthew had plenty of time to run across the foothills southwest of where I sat. He would have crossed the last low mountain and dropped into the valley of Lookout Station. Libby's dogs might bark but quiet themselves once they smelled Matthew. Hopefully he now slept inside his shack, which leaned against the main station building.

Ambrose had settled in that valley, which was watered by a spring. The Pony Express had used his place as one of their stations, and later the telegraph and the Wells Fargo stage and freight route followed the same road westward. Now Ambrose was well off, despite the fact that his herds of sheep, cattle, and horses were not as large as his brother J.D.'s.

If only I knew for sure Matthew was safe. I could wake Brother Peterson, the telegraph operator, and send a telegram to

Ambrose. "Wells Fargo driver in bed?" But that question would ruin everything if Matthew was there, and would help nothing if he wasn't. I was still stymied, unable to do anything to prevent my husband's death.

When I reentered the kitchen, I found that the bishop and the two other women had gone home. Abigail sat at the table, staring at a lone moth, which brushed against the lantern chimney. The moth flew above the lantern and fell to the table, dead. I sat across from her and she took my two hands in her own. I wanted to pull my hands away, but didn't dare.

"Going to be different now," Abigail said. "Just the two of us."

I touched her hand. "I still can't believe it."

"I keep thinking about poor Marianne."

"At least she'll remember Sophia. Stephen won't even remember her."

"I'm going to miss her," said Abigail.

"We'll raise those kids as if they were our own." Then I remembered I wouldn't be there to help her. Regret took me, like a flood takes a field. None of my choices seemed to have been good ones.

"The kids will be all right. I just hope somebody's holding onto Sophia's spirit body right now. It would be one awful shock to be knocked out of this world like that. I hope somebody has their arms wrapped tight around her. She's the one I feel bad for—right now weeping up in heaven because she's just figuring out that she's had to leave those good kids behind. All she can do is watch them. She can't never touch them." Abigail looked at me. "I feel bad for us, too. What are we going to do without her?"

"You'll get along somehow."

She looked at me, stern and bewildered at the same time.

"I mean, one of us will have to learn how to weave." The lie burned on my tongue.

"I don't mean that. Sure, it'll be harder now. But I mean I don't know what we're going to do without *her*. When light comes I'll expect her to walk into the kitchen, proclaiming someone's sins. Then she'll go into the weaving room and start rocking back and forward with the loom, quoting herself the word of God."

"We won't have her to tell us what's right."

Abigail smiled. "I can hear her voice now. Railing on every Saint in the kingdom."

"Last week I walked up to her while she worked on the loom. 'We're all whited sepulchers,' she told me. I never knew what she was talking about."

"She had a way, didn't she?"

"'Who can find a virtuous woman?' I think she said that to me and you and herself a hundred times. She didn't just rail on other people with the scriptures. She railed on herself worst of all."

"Her price is far above rubies." Abigail said, examining my face. "You been rushing all around in the dark. Why?"

"I think J.D.'s going after a man who didn't kill her."

"What makes you think that?"

"Intuition. I just feel it." I needed to be back up at the ditch at the first light, little more than an hour away.

"I don't believe in intuition," said Abigail. "Hard facts for me. I'm going to lie down a bit. This is a goin' to be a real hard day."

I watched as the stout woman pushed against the table and stood. Time was when I had no affection for Ezekiel's first wife. Now I felt differently. I went into Sophia's room and sat on the bed next the body. She and I had not been friends; we thought too differently. But we had gone through such difficult experiences together that I had felt married to my sister-wife. It felt remarkable that after half a year of fighting, which began immediately after Ezekiel left for England, the three of us—

Abigail, Sophia, and I—had formed a community of women. Now the community was broken.

I sat on my bed, my arms wrapped around my legs, and I rocked back and forth. The devil had spoken to me out of the orchard, tempting me away from a husband who would lead me to a glorious kingdom in heaven. Why was I searching tracks to prove Matthew innocent? I stood from my bed, more confused than ever.

Chapter Seventeen

Everyone in the house seemed to be asleep as I left again. The people in our yard had gone home. I walked up to the barn, tangling further the already confused tracks that led up through the field. The rim of white at the east had widened and brightened a little. I walked into the barn, smelling the hay, cow and horse manure—dusty, comfortable barn-smell. I wanted so much to turn time back that I almost believed nothing had happened. Sophia was not lying cold as ditchwater in Abigail's bed but was sleeping peacefully in her own. I had just changed the water and would in a moment climb the ladder to Matthew, who would be warm, waiting on a pad of horse blankets, his brown arms wide. I almost heard the rustle of hay above me.

Babe nickered, her head thrust over the board fence of her pen. I climbed over and lay on her bare back, my cheek on her rump, legs hooked around her neck. I wanted that contact. Babe walked out of the barn and drank from her bucket, the bucket Matthew must have refilled, because it was nearly empty the evening before when I'd greeted Babe after changing the water. "I'll be back at midnight," I had said to her then. "I will greet him with a holy kiss."

Now I lay on Babe's back and was straightway possessed by the horrific memory of what actually happened. I remembered getting down on my knees and putting my hands on Sophia's cold arm, cold body. I had wrestled her out of the ditch and dumped her on the muddy bank. I wanted to wash myself, wash my own mind of what I had done. I shook my head and tried to regain the vision of a raven, flying above the pattern of tracks. Unfortunately, I couldn't see anything clearly; the tracks swirled like water in my head.

Sophia walked up to the water gate and then to the barn and was killed back at the ditch. Someone—I suspected Sister

Turner—wearing Brother Turner's boots, had walked down the ditch. Why? If she was stealing water, why would she walk down to check our dam when she could just open her own gate to steal a little water? Who might have swung the shovel? I could easily picture sour-minded Brother Turner striking Sophia after she called down the powers of heaven against him, swearing him up and down in pious language. But Sister Turner, I believed, was incapable of such an act. Who had set Sophia's body up like a dam? And why?

I was still missing some detail, some fact that would make sense out of the tracks and events. Even after I did make sense of the tangle, I knew I'd have trouble convincing anyone, especially J.D. Every person believed the comfortable story that a Gentile stranger had killed Sophia.

Second by second, minute by minute, the eastern sky would grow brighter. Still, in an hour it would be light enough to see well. I prayed ardently for that light to come suddenly so that I could learn something new from the tracks. Every degree of brightness in the east brought Matthew closer to safety, but also brought J.D. closer to Matthew and brought me closer to being able to see. I wanted time to slow down, give Matthew time to get safe, and to speed up, give me ability to find the real killer. What I wanted was rivers and pools of time, Matthew moving like a rapid stream across the countryside, while J.D. was caught in an eddy, moving slow. I wanted the sun to rise on the tracks I tried to read, but not on those Matthew made now. I wanted impossible paradoxes.

I didn't have the faith to move a mountain or change the rotation of the earth. I didn't even have enough faith to purify my stolid flesh. But I wished for enough faith to make the moon shine more brightly. I knew I couldn't manage that. I only had enough faith to marry Matthew against the law of the Church, doing what my gut said was right, in the face of all opposition.

The night seemed interminable. At the same time, it seemed as if only a minute had passed since I had discovered Sophia's body. It seemed that my own body had slipped outside time, so that time was at once fast and slow. Maybe the earth had stopped turning and our lives were all suspended. Had so much really happened in the space of four hours, since I had awakened late and discovered Sophia's body?

Was time like a stream? Joseph Smith had written what Abraham had known—that time was different for God than for man. God lived on a planet so massive, and that rotated so slowly, that a day for God is like a thousand years for man on earth, which rotates faster. All the planets, ranging from greatest to least in their spheres, created time and the laws that governed the lives of each resident of each planet. "The earth rolls upon her wings, and the sun giveth his light by day, and the moon giveth her light by night, and the stars also give their light, as they roll upon their wings in their glory, in the midst of the power of God.... And they give light to each other in their times and in their seasons. In their minutes, in their hours, in their days, in their weeks, in their months, in their years. . . "

Lying on Babe's back, I was transported by the beauty of the stars and moon and the scant light I had to see by. All these rolling in order through the universe. "And thus there shall be the reckoning of the time of one planet above another, until thou come nigh unto Kolob, which Kolob is after the reckoning of the Lord's time; which Kolob is set nigh unto the throne of God, to govern all those planets which belong to the same order as that upon which thou standest. If two things exist, and there be one above the other, there shall be greater things above them; therefore, Kolob is the greatest of all the Kokaubeam that thou hast seen, because it is nearest unto me."

I had once looked through a large telescope, on a trip with J.D. to Salt Lake City. It had been like traveling through the universe in a vision, seeing the moon as a landscape, not as a smooth object hanging as if a decoration on the wall of space. The universe had texture and depth, was a domain to explore as if it were a great ocean. I longed for the vehicle that would take me there, maybe the wings of an angel, maybe one day, after I had lived a full life on my planet, I could go there on my own wings. Mormons didn't believe that angels really had wings, but I knew they could move through space.

And right then I prayed to God either to give Matthew wings or to loan them to me so that I could fly across the mountains in an instant and protect him, to enable me to ward danger away from this man who had become truly flesh of my flesh, so much so that when I dreamed, I dreamed his reality. I saw myself as a blazing angel of light, standing between Matthew and J.D., both men I loved beyond any love I'd experienced for anyone else. I knew that light drove the universe, like the steam of a steam engine or the pull of a magnet or the attraction of an object toward the earth, its gravity. God was connected to that light, a bond between physical and spiritual that I couldn't understand. How could I stand as light between two good men?

In similar manner, I didn't understand how Joseph Smith could be the avenue through which this light had come to earth, this understanding of the way the universe was—extraordinary, beautiful, simple, and elegant. And the same man, I believed, had brought plural marriage into the world. I had tried to embrace it and had proved to myself that it was a corrupt system. Mary and J.D. had made it work through the sheer force of their goodness, but it didn't work in general. How could one man see the universe so clearly and still believe he was acting for God when he encouraged men to bed multiple women?

I shook myself out of my useless speculations about the nature of the universe. If nothing had gone wrong (and something always went wrong), Matthew would have already crept back into his bed at Lookout. If J.D. had reason to accuse

Matthew, had reason to examine his feet, he would find sand and mountain dust and a vestige of mud from the ditch bank that I stood above. J.D. rode hard toward Paiute Hell Station, but his intent was to ride straight through Lookout Pass. I hoped he would miss Matthew's tracks coming into the station.

Babe walked to her feed bin and lipped grass hay into her mouth. My ear against Babe's wide butt, I felt in the bones of my head the grinding of the stems. Outside town a coyote yelped. A cow lowed farther down in J.D.'s or Brother Olson's barnyard. I let my arms and legs swing loose, heavy as lead.

My mother's face had been cold to the touch the morning I found her. God smiled from the top of a lupine-covered ridge. My mother, smiling as she never had in life, walked up the curve of the ridge. Sand whirled in a cloud and Matthew struggled up the side of a dune, large as the world. Three men dropped to their knees. I heard the crack of their rifles fired as one. I dug Matthew's grave. The dune, sandy on top, was hard as brick underneath—hard and choked with rocks of every size—as stony as J.D.'s soul. I had no gloves, and my hands were red and sore. Blisters rose on my palms. I dug hard until the blisters broke. The sun was hot on my forearms and on the top of my head. I scooped the dirt—all I could manage with the boulders, some small as my fist, some large as my head. Matthew, half-covered with a sheet of canvas, lay on the ground next to the hole. I touched his stiffened body, laid my palm on his cold and grimacing face.

Then the dream changed, and Matthew was alive.

Even in my sleep, I knew that what came next wasn't a dream. It felt too real. I was like a small bird flying above Matthew's head, sometimes in his head, this love of my soul, as he trotted along a deer trail that angled around the flank of the range. The trail was smooth and level, interrupted by only occasional boulders. Below him was the black pit of a canyon, above him the peak of one of the mountains in the Rockwood range. The air was laced with pine.

It was a higher communion than I had felt with Matthew ever before, a sacrament weaving my soul to his. God had given me the gift of seeing him alive. In my sleep, I felt tears of gratitude slip across my face and into my ears. The universe felt suddenly more wonderful than my imagination could contain. I felt like Moses or Abraham, able to see into the very fabric of the universe, into Matthew's precious mind.

We looked behind and saw the dunes, which glowed white far behind us, wondrous as a vision of heaven. To the west the pale desert bluffs of Paiute Hell. Even though he was in the western shadow of a peak, he could see a glimmer of light in the east. I felt his exultation: careful thinking and the ability to run long distances, both characteristics he'd inherited from his mother's Goshute people, had enabled him to beat J.D. Rockwood. Still running, he laid his head back and laughed upward at the stars.

As he looked up, a fist-sized rock rolled under his foot and his right ankle popped outward. He dropped to the ground. His foot felt as if it had been twisted off. He rolled on his back, clutching his ankle and howling with anger and pain. He clawed at the dirt, trying to stand. Curled on the ground, he waited for the pain to diminish. Finally he tried to move his ankle to test the damage, but even a small motion was excruciating. When the pain was less, he stood, but the foot would take no weight.

Soon he forced himself to stand and take one step and then another on his weak foot. He hobbled forward, wincing at the pain that came every step. His foot was unsteady, as if hardly a bone or sinew was left to bear his weight. *Damn,* I said to him, *you should watch your feet, not stare at the sky.*

He broke a branch off a dead pine and hobbled forward again. The foot would take no weight at all, so he had to hop on the good foot. I worried that he would soon twist that one as well.

I was Matthew in the dream, I was myself. I hated J.D., loved him. I floated above Matthew, who hobbled down a hillside. The duality felt right, but I remember thinking that when I woke, I would be bloody confused.

Chapter Eighteen

"Rachel!" I opened my eyes. My hair clung to my sweaty cheeks. The dream had come with the force of vision. "Rachel!" Abigail's oldest daughter, Sarah, stood outside the corral fence. "Mama needs you to help." I sat up on Babe's back. It was not full light but it was gray enough to see. It would get brighter minute by minute and soon the sun would rise. My face was damp, my eyes blurred with tears. I had overslept again, twice in one night. How I could stay asleep for nearly an hour while lying on Babe's back was beyond me. Then the knowledge from my dream—had it been just a dream?—came back to me full force. Matthew would never make it to Lookout Station in time. He might twist his other ankle and fall prey to any hunter, whether man or bear or coyote.

"I'll be down soon. I've been waiting for light to look at the tracks along the ditch and at Brother Turner's water gate."

Sarah stayed by the fence. "She really needs you, she said. She wants you to come now."

"Sarie, you tell her I'll be down as soon as I can." I could barely see the child's face between the split poles of the corral, but I could see that she had strict injunction to bring me down with her—as if she were my older sister and I needed scolding. "Go on now."

"You're just sitting on that old horse." She finally turned and walked back through the orchard.

I slid off Babe's back. Once again, I wished Matthew had taken her instead of Brother Olson's worthless nag.

I thought about my dream that was not a dream. Stranger things had happened to women, gifts from God, pictures of those on whom their hearts meditated. A year after arriving in the Salt Lake Valley, Mary had been shucking corn when some spirit lifted her from her chair and sent her running toward the half-dug well. She found David, her youngest son, teetering on the edge. His sister, who had been watching him, had gone inside for a drink of water and he had crawled fifty yards from the front yard to the well in half a minute.

Mary thought Isaac—the son lost in the North Platte River—had come to her and lifted her out of her chair. I thought that her constant brooding on Isaac, her unending pain, had focused her mind on influences many people do not feel. Mary told me the story of another mother who walked straight to where her lost child lay sleeping under a sagebrush. Another saw her daughter, who had died as a child, smiling, busy at some kind of heavenly labor.

I assumed that some men had this order of vision, but in my experience it was women who, focused by love, saw what no man would normally perceive.

So I had seen Matthew twist his ankle. His plan was in ruins; his identity would be uncovered. I knew in my beating heart, all along my veins, that this was true. Our secret marriage would come out. But all that didn't matter if he lived.

At last it was light enough to see, so I moved out of the corral. I followed Matthew's prints across the barnyard; they were soon joined by the prints that were smaller than my own, Sophia walking to her death. I walked toward the weir, stepping to the side of the track of my dead sister-wife. I could imagine no reason to leave them unspoiled now, but J.D. had made it the Eleventh Commandment: "Thou shalt not spoil a track."

I could see the valley, Lookout Pass, Rockwood Creek Pass, the knife-blade range of mountains, all the houses in town. Brother Swensen stood on his porch and, shielding his eyes from the sun, stared at me. Finally, he raised his hand in a short wave and I gave him an identical wave back. I felt suddenly naked, and it wasn't just that I had a frock with no slip under it. I felt that he could look into my soul and see my sin. And what was my sin? Was it adultery? I didn't think so. It was lying to J.D., hiding my marriage when it was clear that I should let my community know what I had done.I also felt naked because Matthew could be seen now, if he hadn't already gotten to his bed at Lookout Pass. I knew he had twisted his ankle, but when had that happened? He either was safe or he was still on his way. I felt a great urgency to know who had killed Sophia. Only firm, clear information would stop J.D.

The water still flowed into the field. In less than half an hour, at six, one of Brother Ault's wives or children would walk up the ditch and remove my dam. They would conveniently ignore the water that had come down most of the night. I passed the weir and kept going, walking to one side of the pigeon-toed, round-toed prints, made by Sister Turner, and the straight-toed round-toed prints, and the dozens of old prints, barefoot and shod, that daily went up and down the ditch. I bent low, peering at the prints in the shadowy light of dawn.

Suddenly I saw a bare print, just smaller than my own, then another and another, underneath the round-toed print of the work boots but on top of all the older tracks. The pattern of toes, shape of print, and length matched Sophia's print. I stopped, puzzled. Sophia couldn't lie dead and walk away from her death. I searched for any print coming back. I saw only old prints and Sophia's going up toward Turners' property, none of hers coming back down. I shook my head. Her tracks to the barn showed her going up to the door, then walking back down to the ditch, where J.D. thought she had been killed. But these tracks only went up. I hadn't seen them when I followed the boot tracks before. But that had been in the dark and I had been walking quickly, not looking for tracks made by a body walking away from her own death.

Obviously, they had been made before she was killed, but I could see no hint of her track returning down the bank.

I got on my hands and knees in the dry grass to the side of the path and examined every inch in a six-foot stretch of the path.

There was a tangle of old tracks, and there were my long, thin tracks going up and down. I found a place where Sophia's track going up lay over one of my own tracks. So she had walked up the ditch sometime between six in the evening and whenever she was killed, sometime before twelve-thirty when I found her body. On top of both our tracks were the round-toed boots going up and down, sometimes pigeon-toed, sometimes not. In several places a round-toed track was laid on the edge of another round-toed track going up. I sat back and considered: pigeon-toed went down and up. Straight-toed had gone only up. Both wearing the same boots. Pigeon-toed was Sister Turner. Straight-toed had to be Brother Turner, who had come down some other way and then gone back up—after his wife had gone down. I looked again and found plenty of Sophia's tracks going up but not a vestige of them coming back down. I spent fifteen more minutes staring at the tangle on the ground, covering each inch, hoping to see a pattern. So how far up did Sophia's tracks go? That was the next thing to discover.

I also realized that if she had walked up and not walked back down, she might not have been murdered at the weir on our property. Had she been murdered above, on the Turners' property maybe, and had someone carried her body back down?

Abigail was waiting for me, needed my help, but I ran up along the ditch, not certain I was seeing Sophia's tracks at all, but finding here and again the curve of a bare foot. As I passed around the hill below the church, I saw Brother Swensen across the lane in his orchard, picking up apples from the ground under his trees.

I nodded to him.

"Most years I'd just let them lie."

"What?" I was searching the ground for Sophia's next print.

"Sad day. Tragic." He lifted a bucket of apples. "For your pigs. I've got all I can give to mine, these small worm-eaten falls. I know your pigs could use some."

"Thank you. I'll get them later." I moved on without stopping.

"You were to the Turners' last night," he called.

"Yes."

"I think they've been stealing water from you." I turned to stare at him and he looked at me but his eyes moved on. He seemed to be looking past me.

He said, "I think Sophia may have caught them stealing water."

I thought about Sister Turner's frightened face. "I don't know."

"I just hope J.D. isn't running after the wrong person. I just hope it wasn't a viper in our midst."

"Did you see something last night?"

"No, no." He spoke quickly. "I didn't see anything. I'm just telling you my suspicions. I shouldn't do that...say anything without firm proof."

I stared at him and he turned back to the apple tree. For sure he was lying about something, which didn't seem like him. He was clear in his accusations against people who stole water. If he had seen something in the night, why was he hesitating to tell?

I passed on, examining the barefoot prints going up, but none coming back down. Then to one side of the ditch, half buried in mud, I found the embroidered fringe of a nightgown. I picked it up and examined the pattern, which was doubtless Sophia's work. On one edge there seemed to be a clump of mud. But when I took it between my fingers and rubbed, it showed reddish brown—a clot of blood. I hurried on through the thistle and rabbitbrush that grew to the side of the path.

Soon I came to the edge of the Turners' property. The bishop lived immediately opposite them, across the lane. Like Brother Swensen, he was up. He walked toward his barn with his milk bucket, frowning and looking down. He didn't see me, so I crossed the pole fence again. In the mud at the edge of the ditch were Sophia's prints, clear—her whole foot. The prints went down through the Turners' garden and then returned to the ditch. I went down on all fours, muddying again my hands and skirt, to examine the tracks. The tracks I had noticed in the night, the ones with two good heels, were very clear here. I had decided they were the bishop's. He often spent his evenings talking with one or another of his flock. His tracks would be omnipresent in town. Then, caught on a raspberry stalk, I found a small tuft of blond hair. A particle of bloody flesh clung to the hair. I noticed that the ground all around the edge of the raspberries was wet. It was not where the irrigation water naturally went. I decided that the mud looked as if water had been poured across it.

I put my hand against a post in the yard fence. If one of the Turners had struck Sophia down, they would certainly move the body out of their yard. But the only prints that went up the ditch and returned were Sister Turner's pigeon-toed boot tracks. Then another straight-toed set going up.

I stood and then strode down the ditch bank. I examined the prints that went up and down. All seemed the same depth. I looked at them again and distinguished the first track that was pigeon-toed and the second that was not. I damned myself again for not being a good enough tracker to ascertain from the tracks whether the person walking down had been carrying a body. Brother Turner was strong enough to carry Sophia, but Sister Turner, the one who had made the tracks, certainly wasn't. Maybe a tremendous fear had given her strength. I stood and ran for the bishop's house.

I came up suddenly to the bishop's barn and his cow jumped, kicking over the half-filled bucket. The bishop pulled his stool back, looking sadly down at the white froth soaking into the manure. "My bonnie Rachel," he said. "I do wish that you'd come on softer feet."

"I want you to see something new." I took his arm and led him across the lane to the eastern ditch. "Look. These are the tracks I told you about. The boots Brother Turner was wearing when I talked to him this morning make the same prints." I pointed. "The same broken nail, the same large heel. But he isn't pigeon-toed."

"Ach, you said all this earlier. So what if Sister Turner wears her husband's boots?" He thought. "When did you say the prints were made?"

"Recently, last night possibly. Whoever wore these boots walked down to my weir where Sophia's body was."

"I still have my doubts that either one of them is capable of killing."

I took a breath. "Someone was capable."

"Yes. And J.D.'s after him. These tracks may lead to the place of killing, but so do a dozen others. I know you're all excited."

"Sophia was killed in the Turners' yard. I found her tracks going up the ditch to their yard, but no tracks coming back down." I held the piece of fabric flat on my palm. "I found this and I found something else."

The bishop stood, holding his empty bucket and frowning at me.

"There's blood on this edge of Sophia's nightdress. And I found it halfway between my weir and the Turners'. She may not have been killed near my barn where the Gentile was hiding."

"That does not prove that this Gentile was not the killer."

"Just look, please." I climbed the fence and waited for him to follow. He looked toward the Turners' house, back at his own. "Please. It will take only a moment." He climbed over, and we walked across the lane and around the Turners' house. I thought I saw a face in the window as we passed.

I showed him the tuft of bloody hair.

"Could be Sophia's," he said. "Could be a rabbit's."

"This is no animal. Just talk to them with me."

"Ach, but what will you say to them? 'You killed Sophia'?"

"Talk to them with me. I promise I'll temper my tongue."

"I won't come unless you have more to base your suspicions

on. Those poor souls are blamed for every last wrong in this town. But they are both of them very tender. I hear many people in town shouting at their children, but I've never heard either one of them do that."

"So because they don't shout at their children, they couldn't get angry over water? Neither one of them could swing a shovel at someone who surprised them stealing water?" I took his sleeve. "Please."

He ducked his head. "I'll talk to them with you, but you must be civil."

I nodded and we walked together back toward the house.

We seemed to walk so slowly. I tried to picture Matthew walking or running but couldn't. I knew he had a broken or sprained ankle. I knew it as well as I breathed. Was he lying under a cedar? If so, he would be safe from J.D., but not from thirst and pain. How would I find him? If he was still moving, hop-walking on one foot, or with a cedar limb as a crutch, he was still moving toward danger. How would he get over the last mountain above the Lookout Station? It had cliffs and manzanita and slides of shale.

"Please hurry," I said to the bishop. "I have run out of time."

Chapter Nineteen

I strode around the corner of the Turners' house. The sun was just rising over the eastern hills. My hand made a fist, ready to pound on the door. But then I thought better of it. Anger would only breed anger. I opened my hand, shut it again, and tapped on the panel. Brother Turner opened the door. Behind him I saw Sister Turner with a pot in her hands, a cluster of children eating breakfast. The aroma of cedar smoke and cracked wheat came to me through the door.

"What do you want?" said Brother Turner. He nodded. "Bishop."

"Talk," I said. "We want to talk."

"I'm sorry about Sophia. But we're in the middle of eating. You could have some, but I'm sure you're both used to better." He started to shut the door but I put my shoulder against it.

"Please."

He opened the door again and put one hand on each of my shoulders, pushing me back from his doorway. It took all my focus to keep from raising my knee hard to strike him. I told myself that a man doubled over in pain would not likely want to answer my questions.

The bishop stepped forward. "And she just wants to talk to you. She wants an account of tracks that go down the ditch to her property."

"I already gave her my explanation."

"You're not pigeon-toed," I said. "The person who made tracks with your boots was pigeon-toed."

Sister Turner came up behind her husband. "William." I saw her eyes were puffy from crying.

"No." He started to shut the door again, but I put my foot in it and the bishop put one hand out to stop it.

"Ach, Brother Turner, but you can at least talk."

Brother Turner continued to shut the door on my foot, pushing against the bishop's hand.

Despite the pain in my bare foot, I kept talking. "You're trying to protect her. I thought it was you who came down to where Sophia's body was set up in our weir, but it was your wife. I don't think either one of you is capable of killing under normal circumstances." I pushed with both arms straight against the door, forcing it open again. I was inside now; the small windows and curtains made it seem dark as a cave. "Please." I stepped forward, face to face with Brother Turner, who stepped back.

The three children, seated at a plank table, looked up from their steaming mush. A kerosene lantern still burned on the table.

"You see, I know J.D.'s after the wrong person. And that person will die if I don't find out what happened. J.D. will kill him." I looked down at Sister Turner's bare feet. I remembered a picnic years earlier, a buzzing in the bushes and a cowering, petrified woman. "Rattlesnakes."

Sister Turner jumped. "Did you see a snake in our garden? I hope you killed it."

"Rattlesnakes get in the ditch and their rattles get wet and you can't even hear them."

She shuddered.

"You wore his boots?" said the bishop, standing in the doorway.

"That's why you wear his boots to irrigate, don't you?"

Sister Turner pushed through the door and pulled me outside. All the children were watching. Brother Turner came out and shut the door behind him. He folded his arms and stood with his back to the door. His face was defiant, I thought, or frightened.

"Sophia gave me eggs," said Sister Turner to her husband. "Eggs and cream every week. I just can't keep quiet."

"Why?" said Brother Turner, thrusting his face toward me. "Why can't you leave us alone?"

Sister Turner looked at the door. "William says they'll lay the murder at my feet if I tell."

"You know something you haven't come forward with?" The bishop laid his hand on Sister Turner's shoulder.

"A man running," I said, "and J.D. after him. The wrong man running. I don't know why he ran." I wanted to grab the woman by her shoulders and shake her until she said what she knew.

"Tell them," said Brother Turner, his voice hard. "Now that you've told some, tell all."

"A rush of water came down our garden ditch."

"A rush of water?" said the bishop.

I waited but she said nothing more. "Like a gift from God," I said finally.

"Yes," said Sister Turner, "just like that."

"Wait," I said. "You heard it? Saw it? What made you go out of your house in the middle of the night and find water rushing down your ditch?"

"I was up. Up with my child."

"Your child," I said. "You were up walking the ditch because of a colicky child?"

"You are not a Rockwood by blood," said Brother Turner, "but you come to their snobbery as if you were born to it. You talk civil to my wife."

"Don't make me tell why I was up and about," said Sister Turner. "I'm sure my children's going to starve this winter." She glanced at the bishop, who was in charge of distributing the fast offering to the poor.

"I just want you to speak the truth!" I shouted.

"Rachel," said the bishop.

"Listen," said Brother Turner, taking a step toward me. "Do you want to hear what she's got to say or not?" The bishop moved between us.

"Yes. I want to hear sense." I glared at him over the bishop's shoulder. "J.D.'s riding after an innocent man. I need to hear good sense and I need to hear it quickly."

"The water came rushing down, so I walked up through our garden past that row of big sagebrush at the top, all the way up to the main ditch, and saw our water gate was wide open." Sister Turner's hands twisted against each other, as if her small hands were cloths that she tried to wring out. "That's why the water was rushing down our garden ditch."

"When?"

"You know I don't have no timepiece. Not like them Rockwoods."

"By the stars."

"Some time before midnight."

"A couple of hours before midnight." I held myself from grabbing her and making her answer faster.

Sister Turner nodded. "So I ran, down the stream, William's boots a clomping, and hoped she was still there."

"Who was still where?"

Sister Turner said nothing.

"Susan walked down to your weir to thank Sophia," said Brother Turner.

"And?" said the bishop.

Sister Turner started weeping. "She wasn't there. I'd just barely..."

Her story was so implausible I hardly knew what to ask. "Why did you think Sophia had given you a gift of water?"

"That's all she has to say," said Brother Turner. "And that's too much. I *told* her you'd think for sure we done it."

"You're not telling me all of it," I shouted. "Please tell me everything. What you've told me makes no sense."

"Now, Rachel," said the bishop again. "You promised you would not lose your temper. Calm your soul."

"That's enough," said Brother Turner. "We will tell you no more. Can't you see you've plagued her enough?"

"I found blood and hair right behind your house in *your*

garden." That turned them both around. "Now tell the truth. Did she catch you stealing water and did you strike her down in anger? Did you carry her down to my weir?"

"My Lord," said Brother Turner. "If you think Susan could strike anyone down..."

"I didn't do nothing to her," said Sister Turner.

"If she was killed here on your property, then that's proof positive that J.D.'s after the wrong man. The man he's after left no tracks up here."

The bishop stared stolidly at whoever spoke.

"I heard something, so I come out." Sister Turner glared at me. "We've got these lilac bushes below our garden as well as those tall sage above, so I couldn't see clear. There was a trickle of water running down my row of carrots." She put her hands flat against her own cheeks. "I walked up a little farther and there was someone talking to herself. That's the part I left out."

"Sophia." I almost heard her quiet voice, speaking the judgment of God.

"I..." Sister Turner worked her hands in front of her.

"So you let a trickle of water into your garden during our water turn, which is another part you left out, and she came up to see who was taking water."

"I hid behind this serviceberry bush next to the ditch. I could see her easy because of the white nightdress she had on. She was standing on the bank of the ditch looking down at my water gate."

"At the water running into your garden."

"Do you think you're God Himself," said Sister Turner, "that you got to sniff out every sin?" She stared at me. "Yes. The water was running into our garden. The barest trickle."

"From the rock you put in the gate."

"My kids are going to starve this winter."

"Go on."

"So anyways she didn't shut the trickle of water off. It was the smallest trickle. Then she turned and walked toward me but I didn't think she saw me yet, so I backed up plenty fast, keeping the bush between me and her, and then I turned and ran. I came down the path toward our house, and I slipped around the corner before she could see me. I looked at my dark house, and I thought she'd come banging on my door right then. But instead she turned around herself and marched up through our garden toward the ditch."

"You saw her walk back toward the main ditch?" asked the bishop.

"I don't know. I went inside so quickly. I was frightened."

I stepped even closer to her, until our noses were almost touching. "A moment ago you said a rush of water came down. Now you say it was the smallest trickle."

"I shouldn't have gone inside. I should have run after her right then. She might be alive now."

"Or you'd be dead with her," said Brother Turner.

"The first water was just a trickle. This was before I heard her and saw her white nightdress. After she walked toward me and scairt me inside, I set on my bed worrying that she'd tell on me and they'd lock Will up again, thinking he was the one who slipped a little water back to water my poor garden. Finally I couldn't stand it anymore. I started after her, but I barely got to the garden when the water came down. A big rush of water. I just stood there frozen and stared at that flood of water. I watched it fill every row. I thought, thank you, Sophia; this is the first time this summer my garden'll get a real soaking."

"You really think she let the water down?"

"I don't know now." She wouldn't look at me. "For a while I thought it was a gift. But after a time I thought I'd better walk up to shut it off."

"You knew there'd be water standing in your garden today. Proclaiming to anyone who looked that you'd stolen water."

"Rachel," said the bishop. "My Rachel. How does this anger

help?"

Sister Turner faced me. "I decided that maybe I'd mis-thought. That maybe instead of a gift, she was making me out worse than I am. She was going to fill my garden with water and then blame me for it. I doubted what had at first seemed to be an act of kindness."

"Not Sophia," I said. "Sophia would play no trick."

"So I started up to put the water gate back in and send all the water down to your fields. And I turned around that serviceberry bush and there she was, right by my water gate, half in the ditch and blood was still running down her face. I thought she might be alive but then when I rolled her out of the ditch and took her head acrost my lap, I knew she was dead. Her face bashed in. Her head all loose, like her neck was broke. I tried to listen for breath but I could tell she was dead. But she was still warm. She had spoke to herself only a few minutes before. Then I was scairt because whoever kilt her might still be around. I slid out from under her and ran back to my house."

I waited but no one spoke. "So how did she get back down to our place where I found her? Did she fly?"

Sister Turner glanced toward her husband.

"The killer must have come back and carried her down to your place," he said.

"Leaving no tracks."

"You think you're another damn J.D.," said Brother Turner. "We don't know no more. That's it, then, Susan." He turned toward the door.

"How did Sophia's body get down to my water gate?"

"How could you put her back in that water?" said Sister Turner. "How could you do it?"

Brother Turner didn't move. His head was still down. "Susan."

"There were none of your tracks going down," I said to Brother Turner. "Only the pigeon-toed ones of your wife."

The bishop also turned toward Brother Turner, who slumped

against the side of his house.

"My good brother," the bishop said.

Turner held his hand palm up in the bishop's face. He spoke to his wife. "Susan. I was scared. When I saw all that water coming down and her body there, I knowed that we'd be blamed for the killing."

I said, "Whoever killed her let the rush of water down into your garden."

"That's what I think," said Brother Turner. "Or Sophia could have opened our water gate wide and somebody else could have killed her."

"I keep thinkin' of poor Soph down in that ditch," said Sister Turner.

"You carried her down the ditch?" I asked Brother Turner.

"I wasn't thinking clear. I just knew I had to get her away from our place. I knowed J.D. would come and read my tracks, so I carried her down the bottom of the ditch. I waded in the water and carried her. It was a trick hoisting her over the fence, but I done it. When I come to your weir, I remembered that Susan had worn my boots down the ditch."

"Which you couldn't explain away."

"So, like I was trying to say," said Brother Turner. "After Sophia was kilt and I carried her down the ditch, I was going to lay her on the bank, but then remembered about Susan's tracks down there. She told me what she'd done and I knew her tracks everywhere from walking back and forth would make J.D. suspicious. So I..."

The bishop nodded. "So you..."

"So I thought, Sophia's dead. She can't feel nothing no more.' I wanted the water to flood all over those tracks. I thought that if I stuck her up in your gate like a sign people would think that somebody had killed her over water and stuck her up for a warning."

"I thought it," I said. "Still think it."

"I didn't kill her. I did carry her down the bottom of the ditch and walked back up the bottom of the ditch. I knowed for sure what you'd all think, finding a body in my garden. Nobody in this damn town would believe I didn't kill her." He looked up at his wife. "Look, would I tell you I carried her down if I killed her?"

I strode forward until I stood nose to nose with him. "You stuck her in my water gate and the water went over the main gate and down to Aults' place. You wanted people to believe that he killed her because she caught him stealing water. But all the water did was ruin their garden. It didn't properly cover your wife's tracks."

"William!" said Sister Turner.

"I wanted to protect you."

His wife stared at him. "You think I done it?"

"No. Nobody could think that." He turned to the bishop. "Look. I'm 'shamed of what I done. All I could think was everybody would judge us, and the only way anyone would think either one of us killed her was the water coming down. So I shut the water off going to my garden, and I carried her down the bottom of the ditch and put her in the water gate so that the pool would cover all the tracks and I took out the top board so the water wouldn't just wear a ditch in the bank. I knew some water would go down to Aults' place, but I didn't know it would ruin their garden."

"So who killed Sophia in your yard?"

"I don't know. But it wasn't either of us." Brother Turner was desperate. "You got to believe me."

"Ach," said the bishop. "You have done evil. But I believe you're no killer."

I thought. "Nobody could make this up. It's too tangled."

"J.D.'s after a stranger?" said Brother Turner.

"Yes. Tracks all around our ditch."

"There's one more thing I haven't spoke clear about," said

Sister Turner. "My walking down was after I found the body. After I seen her I told my husband what I'd seen and I got into bed. Then he went out and carried her down. Then he came back into the house and got into bed. Then I started thinking about Sophia down in your gate, sitting dead in that cold water, and I asked William to go down and take her out, but he refused. So I walked down there wanting to pull her out." She leaned against the house, weeping. "But I remembered about the tracks, so I walked off to the side this time, in the brush. When I came close, somebody was there. I thought that maybe it was the killer come back. Maybe it was J.D. And there was nothing more I could do for her."

"Or for yourself."

"Right, or for myself. I hid behint that big sagebrush and watched this man pick her up as if he was sorry for killing her, but then he put her back down. He stood in the water staring right at me so I crouched down and moved back away from him. I didn't say nothing because I knew the people of this town would believe I done it. They'd judge me quick. I hate what we done, William putting her there, and me not running to Bishop when I seen her killer standing above her. He was nobody I knew. Nobody from this town. Now that's all of it. Please go away. Our children are scairt out of their minds."

"Thank you," said the bishop. "I believe you."

"What will happen to us?" Brother Turner asked the bishop.

"I'll get with Brother Swensen and we'll decide."

"Please. Just you. I swear we'll never take water again. We've harmed only the Rockwoods, and them not much. I guess the Aults. We'll do anything you say. Just don't get that strick-thinking man Swensen in on it."

"The most important thing is finding Sophia's killer," I said. "The man who slept in our barn didn't come up the ditch. He left no tracks anywhere but near the barn, in the orchard, and going up the hill. He couldn't have killed her if she was killed up here in your garden."

"The man J.D.'s following," said Sister Turner. "I'm sure the man I saw standing above her was a stranger. Even in the dark I'd have recognized anybody in town. I was lucky he never seen me. I thought I was standing in plain sight."

I stood. "This man saw her in the ditch and lifted her to see if she was still alive. She was already dead when you saw all this. What you saw doesn't help *me* know who killed her."

I looked at the sun and at my watch. Well after six and still no idea of who had lifted the shovel against Sophia.

When J.D. and I had solved the crime in Centre Town, the murder of two anti-polygamous federal deputies, he had followed the tracks, believing that the physical evidence would allow him to determine who was the killer. He found talking to people frustrating because clearly most people in that town thought that the killing was not murder but an act of war against the federal government, which was trying to stomp out the fire of polygamy. His approach of looking at the evidence failed because snow had covered all the tracks and because of what contradictory evidence there was—a fire that burned through a snowstorm, the position of the pools of blood, the fact that the dead deputies had been hauled from where they were killed to the floor of the one store in town. So that crime had J.D. pulling out his hair.

My approach had been to look at the people, trying to figure out who had reason to kill. My approach failed because everyone in Centre had reason to want the federal deputies dead. Everyone we talked to seemed guilty. What happened was that the killing was done for a reason no one thought of, a paradoxical reason. What led to the conclusion was belief that both the physical evidence, and the evidence of people's motives and character could solve the crime—that and reliance on the good sense of a meddling old woman in town, a woman J.D. had not respected.

This case was much clearer: either Matthew had killed because Sophia discovered him or someone else had killed over water. Again, J.D. and I were at odds over the case. Either he was right or I was right or, I had to admit, just as in the other case, there was something I wasn't thinking about, something I wasn't seeing. Here both of us were the trackers and the motive seekers. J.D. had made a decision based on what he knew of the killer to abandon the tracks and to try to guess what Matthew would do. He had been remarkably accurate, so far as I could tell. I had been the one left following the tracks. I had to be both me and J.D., using both our propensities to discover. Still I was stymied, unable to make the last step, the last connection.

Chapter Twenty

I stood in the high window of the barn watching westward with the spyglass J.D. had given me when he got his new one. I had used it to locate cattle and look at the stars or the moon. I examined Lookout Pass, which J.D. had hopefully passed through already and which was Matthew's destination. I could see the canyon, dark with willows, stretches of the pale road, the cedared hills to either side, but nothing else. No rider, freight wagon, or man walking. I swept the glass southward across the knife-blade mountain range. I saw only the tall gray peaks, the scattering of aspens and pines. Still nothing.

Because I believed my dream, I thought it improbable that Matthew was at Lookout Station, sitting down to breakfast with Ambrose, Libby, and the dogs when J.D. rode through. Had Ambrose told J.D. that the freight driver was missing? It was hell not knowing where either Matthew or J.D. was.

I remembered my dream of touching Matthew's cold face. He wouldn't give up, would go on hands and knees if he had to. Stubborn man. He would move forward tenaciously to where J.D. might be waiting for him, rifle raised. He'd crawl to his own death.

I dragged my attention back to the ditch and the tracks along it. Was Sister Turner still lying? Had she swung the shovel against Sophia in tremendous anger? She had stolen water to feed her children; she might do much worse if threatened with an imprisonment that would take her from them. But the pattern of tracks, tracks that the Turners couldn't have easily examined until morning, fit her final story.

Someone else had killed Sophia in the Turners' yard. It felt as if I was starting over.

I looked out over the town as I had often before, generally a peaceful place, with green trees and fertile fields—at least in good years. Across town on the western rim of the valley, Brother Olson and his two sons were digging Sophia's grave. I felt with fresh shock my sister-wife's death.

I breathed in the mingled smell of hay and horse, an aroma that usually comforted me. The wretched smell of the pigs in a pen a distance away from the barn was not a comfort ever. Now I only wanted sleep. I saw Brother Pritchard's horse push its nose under the top bar of the gate and lift it loose. The long-legged beast simply walked over the other two bars and ambled down the ditch, cropping grass. Despite myself, I smiled. The old beast knew how to take care of himself.

Then Brother Swensen walked up the ditch. The horse turned toward him, nosing the front of his shirt. Brother Swensen took an apple out of his pocket and gave it to the horse. He took a string out of his pocket and made a hackamore, then swung himself up and rode back to the Pritchards' house.

I climbed down from the loft and walked through my fields to the house in a daze. I hadn't slept except for about an hour the previous night. Entering the kitchen, I started cleaning away the breakfast. I didn't know where the children were.

Before long, Brother Olson brought to Ezekiel's household a telegram from Ambrose. Abigail read it, frowning. I asked to see the message, and Abigail handed it to me. "J.D. here 5 a.m. Gone to Paiute. Freight driver missing 6 a.m. A. R."

I stared at the paper, which helped confirm my dream of a twisted ankle. Otherwise, he would have had time to ride and run ten miles in five or six hours. Why had Ambrose directed the telegram to our house instead of J.D.'s? Did he think that J.D. and I were working together on this manhunt? Or did he suspect that Matthew meant more to me than he should?

Whatever Ambrose suspected and whatever the extent of his charity toward me, soon everything would be uncovered—my "sinful" relation. It was still in the balance whether Matthew and I could get away together or whether disaster would happen.

It would take J.D. an hour and a half on a good horse to get from Lookout to Paiute Station. Same on the way back, longer if his horse was tired. It was seven now, so he might not get back to Lookout Station for another hour. I could get there in forty-five minutes, if I left right away.

I knew I had to find Matthew or J.D. before they found each other. J.D. was Matthew's danger; I believed Matthew could outrun or outsmart anyone else. If I could hold J.D. back, talk him into some kind of moderation, Matthew would be safe. Waiting behind had become unbearable.

As I saddled Babe, I pictured J.D. riding up to Paiute Station. He would be in a frenzy, but Jardine wouldn't let anybody rush him. J.D. would insist that Jardine tell him who the deserter was. "What deserter?" Jardine would say. I smiled. Jardine had married Matthew and me and was a sharp-eyed, quick-thinking Vermonter. It would take him about a second to understand who J.D. was after, and only another second to understand that J.D. didn't know he hunted my husband. I knew from Matthew and others that Jardine had little love for J.D. Jardine would probably keep our secret, but if he said one word about marrying us, J.D. would believe he knew Matthew's motive for killing.

I put my foot in the stirrup and swung myself up. I urged Babe out of the barn but then hesitated. I looped Babe's reins around the bar of the corral and turned to walk the ditch one more time. I saw Sister Turner's tracks, Sophia's walking up to get killed, no other footprints except for old tracks and the prints of Brother Pritchard's horse.

Suddenly I remembered Brother Swensen feeding his windfall apples to the horse. Both wandered the town at will. Had Brother Swensen found Sophia in the Turners' garden and struck her with the shovel? He might have rushed up to her in the dark, furious that water was being stolen again, and thought that she was Sister Turner. He might have struck her before she could even call out. I remembered the other tracks in the Turners' garden—tracks I'd assumed were the bishop's.

Brother Swensen worried his hair white, trying to keep the town alive, distributing shares of water, administering with justice the lifeblood of the town. He thought of it as the Lord's water. Two months earlier, when I had accused Brother Turner, Brother Swensen had been hysterical from anger. He'd said in church that he'd rather see the Saints dead than stealing from each other.

A willfully dishonest act performed by a member of the Church would disturb the order of his universe.

Then I shook my head. I had no firm proof.

I ran across the lane to the southern boundary of Brother Swensen's property, a pole fence that crossed the ditch and extended down toward his field. I found prints in the dust, new heels, short feet, the same print that I had seen in the Turners' garden and along their ditch, tracks I'd foolishly assumed were the bishop's. The tracks continued toward Brother Swensen's barn.

Rushing toward the back door of his house, I stopped at the pump above his well. There was a water trough about six feet long under the spigot. I pumped the handle once and water rushed into his trough. I glanced at the window to his house but could see no one's face peering out to catch me snooping. All around the trough was a splash where water had been poured. On the bottom of the step I found droplets of almost dry mud, as if someone had sat on a higher step and washed his feet. I touched my finger in the mud, sandy, like that at the bottom of the ditch. Next to the water pump on the ground was the sideways curve of a shovel blade. None of this was unusual, except the splashing of water all around the trough. In this drought year, the water master wouldn't use that much water to wash mud off his boots and his shovel.

I examined the ground around the trough, finding the same boot prints. Still, this proved nothing. I walked to the shed where

I knew Brother Swensen kept his tools, which I had occasionally borrowed. I picked up his shovel and examined it. Clean. Not even a particle of dirt clung to the surface. Everything in his shed was precisely arranged.

Desperate, I rushed back to the watering trough, casting my eyes back and forth across the ground and the trough. I saw drops of mud on the side of the trough, white splotches where sandy mud had dried. I got down on my hands and knees in the dirt and looked at the side of the trough. Up near the top, almost covered by the lip of the trough, I found a dark spot, a few blond hairs sticking from a clot of blood.

I thrust my fisted hands up against my cheekbones, wondering about my own mind, which screened out the most significant information because it didn't fit what I'd thought happened. I hadn't seen Sophia's tracks walking up from my weir, because they couldn't have been there. I hadn't worried about Brother Swensen's tracks in the garden because I believed one of the Turners had struck Sophia down.

I ran through the Swensens' barnyard and banged on his back door. The oldest Sister Swensen answered. "Where is your husband?" I asked.

"Back in the field cutting hay. Is something else wrong?"

Returning to the shed, I grabbed his shovel, the weapon I believed he used to kill Sophia. Soon I saw he had two horses pulling the cutter. The long mower blade with its triangular, vibrating teeth stuck out to one side. The clatter of the mower sounded like a huge mechanical insect.

I walked straight toward his horses. When I was still fifteen feet away, Brother Swensen pulled them to a stop. "What is it, Rachel?" He sat on the mower, holding the reins. He smiled, just as he had smiled countless times at church. As first counselor to the bishop, Brother Swensen sat on the stand or shook the hands of members, always looking like a kind grandfather, except when angry about the water. I walked close to the cutter on the opposite side of the blade. I reared back and swung the shovel at his face, stopping it just short of hitting him. He jerked his hands up and the two horses backed, swinging their heads up, jawing at their bits. The teeth of the mower clacked with each motion. I stepped away from him, the shovel ready. He let his hands fall but didn't look at me."It was an accident," I said. "You struck her in a fit of anger."

He said nothing.

"J.D. is riding after an innocent man."

He stepped off and laid the reins on the seat.

I backed up in the field. "Come with me to the telegraph. He's going to Paiute Station. You can send a message and tell him to stop."

"No." He looped the reins around the gear handle. "I couldn't do that. I couldn't do that."

He walked toward me. I held the shovel in front of me, blade toward him. I had broken the necks of badgers running at my legs out of dark, water-filled holes in my field. But could I find the strength—and the will—to strike a man, a brother in the gospel? He took another step forward and I took another step back. I slipped my right palm over the rounded end of the handle, ready to thrust the shovel at his face.

"I'm not the one you need fear." He turned and walked toward his house, leaving the team untended. They moved a few feet nervously, dragging the cutter knife sideways across the end of the row. It clacked and clattered, and they held their ears back toward it, uncertain what to do.

I ran after him. "Please. We can telegraph and prevent another death."

"No. No. It's not good people we need to fear. It's liars and Gentiles and water thieves." He crossed the dry ditch and walked through his yard. He seemed to be a man walking asleep. I believed that in his dazed state he might do harm to the Turners or to himself. He entered his back door, and I ran for the bishop's house.

I found the bishop outside his shed, turning a great white whetstone with one foot, sharpening a scythe. "It was Brother Swensen. I believe he killed Sophia. I know he killed her." The bishop stared at me, his face incredulous. The stone still turned and caught the sharp edge of the scythe, twisting it out of his hands. He glanced sadly at the tool lying on the ground.

"When he struck her down, he thought she was Sister Turner. There was ditch mud splashed against his trough. And a small speck of blood and hair."

"Rachel, Rachel, Rachel," he said. "You have come to me three times and each time the story is more unintelligible and more extravagant. I canna believe you anymore."

"Listen. I don't give a holy blasted bloody damn whether you understand or believe or not. Just watch Brother Swensen. He seems very strange. Just go talk to him. He's so distracted right now that he doesn't seem to care what he does. I'm worried that he might do harm to the Turners, he hates them so bad. Maybe you can stop him. Just go."

I turned and ran toward home and Babe. I didn't look back to see whether he'd moved from staring after me.

Abigail came out of the back doorway as I ran past. "I—I need..."

"I cannot help you."

"Rachel." She hefted my damp quilt up from the bench on the back porch. I had been too distracted to see it sitting there. "Zeke Jr. found your quilt in the cold cellar, sopping wet. Can you explain this?"

"Not now!" I shouted as I ran up to the barn. I had left both the bishop and Abigail staring after me, but I couldn't afford even the time it would take to change out of my dress. And I had no explanation for Abigail's question anyway.

If Matthew was frightened enough to run, he would be too frightened to talk to J.D. He was a man, so he'd do something stupid, and J.D. would kill him. I had no doubt about either the danger of Matthew's pride or my stepfather's steadiness with a rifle.

I jumped Babe across the creek. I turned at the lane and rode up toward the bishop in his yard. "Please do me a favor. Get Brother Peterson to send a telegraph to both Paiute Station and Lookout saying that the Gentile didn't kill Sophia. I'll pay for it later." I trotted Babe back down the street, passing the bishop as he walked down toward Brother Swensen's house.

"I am going against all my instincts and doing what you say," he said. "I will find Brother Swensen."

"Thank you. I'm riding after J.D. I'm anxious he will shoot and ask questions later."

"Why do you think this Gentile ran?"

"Wouldn't you run if you found a dead woman and you were a Gentile in J.D. Rockwood's town?"

The bishop nodded. I could see no sign of Brother Swensen, and I hoped he was in his house, instead of walking toward his shed where he could find an ax, scythe, or some other weapon. I hoped he wasn't already on his way toward the Turners' house. If he was, I had made a mistake in dashing off toward Lookout. Something else to feel guilty about.

I crossed the bridge over the west irrigation ditch and started along the road toward Lookout Pass. I glanced at the spot where J.D. had found the prints showing that Matthew had run barefoot but put his boots back on to walk into town. I gave my horse her head and then pulled her back to a walk, counting to a hundred, limbering her legs as both J.D. and Matthew had taught me. Then I trotted for a hundred counts, loped a hundred, trotted a hundred—all the while wishing I was riding a train, which would take me in minutes to Lookout Station.

The flat outside Rockwood was covered with gray sagebrush and yellowed grass. Ahead lay the dry farm wheat fields. I was four miles from Lookout Station, eleven from Paiute. If I pushed

Babe, trotting and running her, pushing her as hard as I could, I'd get to Lookout in less than an hour, unless Babe gave out or stepped into a hole. I moved into a rhythm, lifting myself in the stirrups every other step, just as J.D. had taught me. It kept my spine from breaking at Babe's bone-jarring trot.

Chapter Twenty-one

Babe was lathered; the dust she kicked up in the dry farm fields turned her neck and flanks gray with dark rivulets of mud where the sweat ran. The fields with their stunted wheat seemed impossibly wide, stretching to the foothills. Far ahead opened Lookout Pass. The creek that flowed out of the cleft was marked by the green of poplar trees, lighter than the cedars and pines on the hillside. The sun was warm and I wished I had remembered my hat. I started feeling light-headed and parched from the heat, but Babe seemed strong, striding forward in her tireless trot.

The dry farm fields stretched from near Rockwood almost to the mountains. Some fields lay fallow—dry, plowed ground. They were planted every other year; on the off year they preserved moisture. But this year even the planted fields looked fallow, the wheat sparse and short. Ezekiel's field lay to the south. Samuel Pritchard and a few other brothers helped me farm it. Soon they would drag the harvester up from Rockwood and see what they would get—certainly a scanty harvest.

I thought about Wyoming. I had pictured shipping my cattle northward; Matthew and I would follow in style on a passenger train. At first we had talked about unloading in Cheyenne and trailing the cattle farther north until we found an empty valley with a river running through it. Grass would be as tall as a horse's belly and the air would be moist. Pine trees would cover the hillsides surrounding the valley. Everything would be brown or a shade of green—no more deathlike gray and white. We would build a cabin on a low hill, so that from our windows we could overlook the valley. We might have trouble from wolves or bears, but we both were good shots and we could either use the pelts from those animals for winter blankets or coats, or sell them for cash money.

Soon we realized that the dream was impractical because

most of the land had already been taken up. We started to look into actual properties. Matthew traveled through Salt Lake City and Sacramento regularly, and he had heard news of the cattle boom in Wyoming, which had just been made a state. The cattle industry there had been facilitated by the building of railroads, and Matthew said there was no end of growth in sight. When I asked J.D. about this, being careful to make clear it was just my curiosity that made me ask, he had told me that the boom there was over, that the place to raise cattle was in Utah, where the economy was more stable. Still Matthew and I talked about Wyoming or Montana as our new home.

Two of Matthew's horses were of Morgan stock, stout enough to plow the thick sod. The first year we'd work the land together—plowing, cutting timber for house and fences, digging ditches, harrowing, planting, irrigating, harvesting grass until we could get a stand of lucerne to grow. A tent would seem like a palace. We would be wealthy in our farm and in each other.

Thinking about it made me ache with a permanent hunger. I had grown to think of Abigail and Sophia with charity, but I yearned to be my own agent, without a tangle of wives to work through in every decision, with a husband present, by my side, one I could reach out and touch and who clearly loved me. Ah, it seemed more than a dream. It was heaven on earth. No difficulty from hard work could tarnish that.

The second year I would be with child—a small boy or girl in the image of Matthew and me. Our lovemaking would be slower and more luxurious than the urgent, haphazard work Ezekiel had performed, trying to get me with child. I thought of settling myself in the tent with Matthew, of taking my time, a month, half a year, whatever it took to start our child.

I nearly smelled the green grass, nearly heard the sound of our cattle and horses feeding, nearly felt the touch of Matthew's hand on my bare skin. I knew God loved community, a people who bound together every Sunday, and whose affairs were laced together, just as my marriage with my wives was, but I also had to think that if God was a man and a woman, like Adam and Eve, and then children—a family—that He might forgive me for making a divine community of my own, might forgive me not being in Church every Sunday. After my life in Nevada and Utah, the dream seemed like a vision of Eden, a fantasy of freedom.

Then the vision changed suddenly. Despite the fact that I trotted Babe across a wide desert, I imagined a shot sounding, pictured Matthew's head swinging back, his eyes staring. I laid my palm against his slack face. J.D. walked forward, rifle still held at the ready. I shook my head. I would never forgive him if he shot Matthew, never forgive myself for not being more forthright or more careful. More something.

Looking ahead at the mouth of the canyon, I found tears springing to my eyes, not just because I might lose Matthew, but because I had lost J.D. already, who had been a complete father to me, tender and intelligent. That man was dead. He was replaced by a savage man, one who wouldn't consider any truth he didn't want to see. He had decided Matthew was guilty before he looked at all the evidence.

If I had told him Matthew was my husband, he would still have gone after him.

I rose and fell in the saddle, endless rhythmic motion. I kicked Babe up again, alternating between her steady trot and a faster lope. My powerful horse gave whatever I asked. Patches of foam gathered on Babe's neck, flecked my tan dress and bare arms, slid down her legs to the ground.

At the mouth of the canyon, I smelled water and saw the fan of green grass. Then I saw the willows, a darker green winding up the bottom of the canyon. Lookout Springs made only a trickle compared to Rockwood Creek, and it soaked into the ground before a hundred yards from the canyon. Ambrose rode down a couple of times a week to move the water to a new location on the small delta of good soil. Each fall he cut a healthy crop of grass hay to feed the freight horses and his own through the winter. The canyon was a narrow notch, cedars on the foothills, willows and cottonwoods along the bottom near the water. The road led along the stream, passing under the overarching cottonwood branches. I was within fifteen minutes of Ambrose's valley. I began to have hope that I could get there before J.D. came back from Paiute Station. Ahead, the canyon ascended steeply; the creek fell in a series of short waterfalls.

The road left the creek, becoming rocky, weaving back and forth like a snake up the dry, brushy hillside. From the hillside I looked back on Rockwood. I had pushed Babe hard and had made excellent time. I topped the hillside and trotted Babe around the curve of the road. Ahead and above us, still out of sight, was the edge of the valley where Lookout Station squatted. In wet years, J.D. had told me, before Ambrose confined the stream in red, brick-baked pipe, the valley had yearly become a shallow lake.

I pushed Babe up the road. Powdered dust rose from her hooves. I didn't want to kill my horse saving Matthew, but I didn't want to save Babe if I could get to the station in time.

As I set Babe to the last slope, the stream gurgled beside me. Babe wanted to walk up the last hill—the first time she had ever been slow about attacking any climb. "I know I've worn you out, but we're not there yet." I kicked Babe and she clambered up in a series of jumps that nearly took me out of the saddle.

As I crested the hill and saw the valley, the house and outbuildings spread before me, I heard the boom of a rifle. All blood seemed to rush from my body. I kicked Babe forward, forcing her to run across the meadow toward Ambrose's station.

The universe seemed to darken with only a tunnel of light in front of me. As I pushed my horse hard across the flat, Ambrose's house and outbuildings lay to the right. To my left was a sagebrushy hill. I saw a man walking forward, his rifle raised, just as I had imagined it. J.D. I scanned the hillside but could see nothing. I wanted to lift my hand and smash that small man, so little in the distance. Opposite me, another man entered the valley, loping his horse and shouting something at J.D. Probably Ambrose. I was too late, everlastingly too late. Just as I had been the night before, when I had slept in and rose too late to prevent any of this tragedy from happening.

As I drew closer I saw J.D.'s rifle trained on something on the ground. My blood beat in my throat. I shouted, "J.D., don't shoot again." I bunched my dress up around my thighs. Someone was screaming, a loud keen of anguish and anger, and I realized it was me.

When I rode closer, J.D. turned. He walked forward as Babe slowed, stiff-legged, and stopped.

I wondered how I had ever seen kindness in that man. He was a devil, his face that of a pious, heartless demon.

He said, "You're going to kill that horse."

"Where is he?" I searched the ground but could not see Matthew.

"Where is who?"

"Matthew," I screamed. "Where is he?"

"Matthew?" he said. "Who is Matthew. I shot Sophia's killer."

I called out, an inhuman cry like I had heard dying deer make. "Where is he, you evil bastard?"

He pointed toward the ground. I saw Matthew lying face down on the far side of a sagebrush clump. He was unmoving, and I shrieked again.

I flung myself off Babe and ran forward. Matthew's thigh was bloody and a circle of blood soaked the dust under him. I saw where the shot had exploded from the far side of his leg. The wound still seeped blood. I turned him and clutched at his shirt. Ripping it open, I laid my ear against his chest, hearing only the thudding of blood in my own ears. I thrust my fingers up under his chin. His throat was still warm, but I could feel no pulse. I smelled the dark, heavy odor of his blood. Dogs howled inside the house.

"Rachel," said J.D. again.

I felt his free hand on my shoulder, but I just thrust my face against Matthew's throat, laced my fingers in his hair. His eyes were closed and his body was still warm. Sophia's had been cold.

"Rachel."

The blood on Matthew's leg was bright, not yet thickened. I had missed saving him by minutes. "No," I whispered. "Oh, no, oh, no. Don't take him from me." God could raise the dead, I knew. Especially the newly dead.

"Let's lay him flat," J.D. said. He laid his rifle carefully across a boulder and helped me move Matthew's shoulders until they lay straight, spreading Matthew's legs slightly.

Matthew groaned and flung one arm up across his face.

My breath caught in my throat. "He's alive."

I pushed J.D. away and knelt at Matthew's side. The bullet had gone through the outside of his thigh and exited on the inside midway between his groin and his knee. He must have been running or the slug would have gone through both legs. A little higher and he would have been dead for sure. The slug had burst through the cloth of Matthew's trousers; all around the hole the cloth was red with blood. J.D. took out his knife and handed it to me. I cut the tattered cloth back farther. The flesh of Matthew's inner thigh was open like a wide, irregular sponge, oozing blood. I tore off the lower part of my dress and wadded it against the wound.

J.D. took his shirt off and folded it, pressing it into the flowing blood. "Hold this." He removed his belt and cinched it above the wound, slowing the flow. Then he tore Matthew's shirt and handed the cloth to me. I put it over the wound and continued to push down. Blood still flowed.

I said, "I hope you roast in hell for this. I'll never forgive you."

"You were the woman he came to meet," said J.D. "Not an unmarried woman at all."

My voice wouldn't work again.

"Rachel, have you committed adultery with this murderer?"

Ambrose rode up and dismounted. "Shit, J.D., you don't even know he done it."

"He killed Sophia," said J.D. "I called out to him but he reached down for a gun. Into his boot. He wouldn't stop to talk."

"He's not wearing boots," I said.

"What the hell did you expect?" said Ambrose. "Why did you shoot him? Where was he going to run?"

"He had no gun. He doesn't even have boots on." I reached and touched his swollen foot and he groaned again. "Sprained. Probably hurt to run."

I pushed against the wound. "Go get a wagon," I shouted to Ambrose. "We need to get him inside." Ambrose mounted and trotted his horse toward the house.

I lifted my face to J.D. "He didn't kill Sophia."

"You don't know that."

"I do know it." Blood seeped from between my fingers.

Ambrose came running, pulling a handcart. The three of us lifted Matthew inside. I climbed in with him and pressed down on the cloth over the wound.

By the time we reached the house, Matthew was limp again—whether dead or alive I couldn't tell. We laid him on the front porch of the house. J.D. squatted and looked at Matthew's leg. I kept pressure on the wound, which still bled, although not as severely as before.

The dogs were raising a hellish ruckus at the smell of blood, yapping and barking and howling. Libby came out and saw Matthew. "Get him away from my babies," she shrieked. I realized she was talking about her dogs.

So J.D. and Ambrose lifted Matthew again while I kept the bandage in place, and we carried him back to the lean-to. With their help, I laid him on his bed.

"If only he'd stayed here," said Ambrose.

With one hand, I held pressure on the wound, which started flowing again whenever I took my hand away. I glared at J.D. "If you're not going to help, go get Libby." I grabbed a shirt that hung near the window, folded it, and pressed it onto the old bloody pad. Ambrose bent low, trying to hear Matthew's breath. He ripped his own shirt, folded part, and tied the cloth cord around Matthew's leg and twisted the tourniquet tight. He rested the fingers of his free hand on Matthew's arm, trying to feel for heartbeat. J.D. stood in the doorway.

"Don't leave me, Matthew," I called. "Don't leave me." I turned my face toward J.D. "You have shot an innocent man."

"You don't know this."

I nodded. "I know this man and he is not a killer. I know him because he is my husband."

"Husband?" said J.D. "Husband?"

"Yes, Jardine married us."

His mouth opened and shut several times before he could get the words out. "What have you done, my Rachel. Oh, what have you done?"

"My husband left, I took another."

He shook his head and turned from my face.

Chapter Twenty-two

After J.D. left the lean-to, Ambrose stayed to help me. Sitting on the bed, I bore down on the wound on Matthew's thigh. The shirt soaked through, red spreading through the cloth. I knelt, still pressing hard with my hand, and laid my ear against his chest. "I think he's gone. Oh, I think he's gone." Then I felt the slight motion of Matthew's breath—his miraculous breath. Tears ran down my face; I couldn't stop them.

"Give him room." Ambrose laid his hand on my shoulder. "You're going to suffocate him."

"He's still breathing. He's still breathing."

"For now," said Ambrose. He left the lean-to.

I forced my palm against the wound. When blood showed again, I lifted a shirt from Matthew's open bag on the floor. I folded it with my free hand and placed it over the bloody bandage. Blood had soaked into the blanket on his cot. His face and body were still as death. The veil was so thin, he could easily slip across into the unseen world. "Please," I prayed. "Don't take him twice." The inside of the lean-to seemed dark as a cave.

The door opened and J.D. stepped inside. I couldn't see his face. "I don't understand." His voice quivered as if he would weep. But he didn't weep. "You married this man?"

"Yes."

"I don't understand."

I glared at him. "If you're not going to help me, get out of here."

He shook his head and stepped forward.

"He may still die," I shouted. "You may still have killed him."

"You married Ezekiel." He was obviously perplexed. He shifted his weight back and forth, straightening one leg, then the other.

"Ezekiel has enough wives."

Libby came inside and set a basket of clean rags beside Matthew. She sat at the foot of the bed and began folding them into pads for me to use.

"You should have said something last night," J.D. said.

I wanted to shove him out the door. But I didn't dare lift my hand from the bandage.

"Would have saved us all a lot of trouble," said J.D.

Libby stood without speaking and left the lean-to.

I shook my head once, hard. I focused on keeping a firm, even pressure on the wound. J.D. seemed a stranger to me. "What could I have said to make you stop going after him? Once you believed he was the killer, nothing could pull you back. There was nothing I could have said."

"You could have tried."

The bandage became moist. "Can you help?"

He thrust his fist against Matthew's thigh above the wound. He reached for a spoon on the windowsill and twisted it into the cloth tourniquet.

"Matthew didn't kill Sophia."

"Did he tell you that?" J.D. shook his head. "Did you believe all of this man's lies? Sophia discovered him and started to run for help. He became frightened that your evil secret had been revealed, so he killed her. The tracks show that I'm telling the truth. He ran after her and hit her with the shovel. All night I wondered why he should do something so savage. Now I know. He had adultery on his mind." He bound the spoon in place and stepped back. "Sin begets sin."

I had one hand on Matthew's wound and the other on his chest. I still could feel the slight motion of his breathing. Surprised at my own calmness, I said, "Brother Swensen killed Sophia. He mistook her for Sister Turner and swung at her in the dark. He thought she was stealing water."

"No," J.D. said, standing from the bed. "You're mistaken, Rachel. You're seeing what you want to see because the truth is unbearable."

I watched him struggling with himself. "You hunted down the wrong man. Last night I went up the ditch three times. The first time I found tracks—pigeon-toed Sister Turner wearing her husband's shoes. They were the tracks you wouldn't follow. She'd put a rock under her dam to slip water to her garden. Until I had more evidence, both she and Brother Turner denied taking water or seeing Sophia at the gate. The next time I went up I found Sophia's tracks. She'd walked up but didn't return. I also found a piece of trim off her dress in the Turners' garden. Bloody. Then at dawn, also in Turners' garden, I found a tuft of blond hair and blood."

I pressed on the wound, my eyes on J.D.'s face, which was the face of an old man. I couldn't physically make him go away and leave Matthew alone. Only words could do it. "I took the bishop to their house and finally Sister Turner said she had seen Sophia talking to herself in their garden and she hid. When she went back out, she found Sophia dead. Brother Turner carried her down the ditch and put her in our water gate. They both swore that they hadn't harmed her. The third time I walked the ditch, I found ditch-bottom mud on Brother Swensen's trough. I saw where he had washed his shovel off."

J.D.'s face was angry. "None of this is proof he was the killer."

"No," I said sharply. "I'm not stupid. I found a spot of blood and blond hair on the trough."

J.D. looked at me. "Still not conclusive proof."

Ambrose came in with a can of black gunpowder. "Couldn't find the damn thing," he said. "He could have died while I was finding it." He held a dry pad of cloth above the wound. I moved my hands, Ambrose pressed down on the pad. Soon blood soaked through it.

I folded another cloth. "I confronted Brother Swensen in his field. He denied nothing. He looked and talked like a man wandering in a dream. He was so distracted that he left his team in the field with the cutter still attached to them. He said, `It's not good people who need to be punished.'"

"No. Until he confesses I won't believe. You must have confused the tracks." He turned to the door. "Likely as not firing that gunpowder won't stop the bleeding. You'll just tear the flesh more. Do like you did with that mare, Ambrose." He left the lean-to. Soon I heard the thud of hooves.

I had always idolized him; now he seemed merely a pathetic man, driven by his own stupidity.

Ambrose spoke. "He's still bleeding steadily." He took out his pocketknife and slit Matthew's trousers from the wound down to the cuff and then up to the waist. He laid the material back from Matthew's white leg. All this time I still pressed down on the wound as if I could stop the bleeding with my hands and my will. I wanted Matthew to move, to groan and fling his arm across his chest—any movement to calm my fear. But he didn't twitch or sigh; his eyes still didn't open.

"Slower but steady," Ambrose said. "I don't understand how he can still be alive. We'd better do what J.D. suggested."

He left, and I heard him moving in the blacksmith shop near the barn. Soon I smelled the heavy smoke of a coal fire. Suddenly, I noticed Libby standing in the corner of the dark room. My hand became once again wet with blood, and I covered the soaked bandage with a new pad. I bore down again. Finally, Ambrose entered with a short iron poker, glowing red on the end.

I stood, my hand still pressing on the bandage. "What are you going to do?"

"Cauterize the wound."

"No. You'll just kill him."

"Like J.D. said, I saved a horse this way once. Best mare I ever had. Shoulder and lower neck clawed to pieces by a cougar. Decided not to shoot her and was right. She bore five good colts after she got better." He looked down at me. "You say."

I looked at the thick bandage. I felt blood soaking through the top pad. I nodded.

Libby lit a lantern and held it high. I peeled back the thick red wad of bandages. Ambrose peered at the bullet hole, which was already filling with blood, and touched the glowing tip to the edge of the wound. Matthew twitched and a thread of acrid smoke rose. Libby held her free hand across her mouth and nose against the bitter, eye-watering smoke. The flesh was black and charred on one side but on the other, a smaller stream of blood entered the bullet hole. Ambrose touched the iron to the wound again then lifted the iron away, waving his hand at the smoke. He touched the wound once more and then left the lean-to.

I covered the wound with a clean cloth, bound it down with strips torn from an old shirt. No red showed through the bandage. Soon Ambrose returned. Still no red showed. "Looks like that stopped it. Looks like you did it." I touched Ambrose on the hand.

I knelt next to the bed. I stroked Matthew's forehead, tangled my fingers in his hair. "With luck, the cure won't kill him."

"We need to undo that tourniquet," Ambrose said. He untwisted the spoon one slow turn at a time. Libby held the lantern and I peered at the bandage that covered the bullet hole. "Still all right. No sign of blood."

Ambrose unwound the cloth of the tourniquet. He took a small jar from his pocket—consecrated olive oil—used for blessing the sick and wounded. He laid his hands on Matthew's bandage. Libby walked forward and placed her hands over his, and I put my hands over hers.

Ambrose pronounced the blessing: "I say unto you, Matthew Harker, that the bleeding in your upper thigh will remain staunched. You will not lose your leg. You will not die at this time. The time of your death is hidden from you, but your Savior doesn't require your presence at this time."

Libby smiled at me and walked outside again. I stroked Matthew's forehead, his cheeks.

"I telegraphed for the doctor in Hamblin," said Ambrose. "I got a telegraph back saying that the Wells Fargo manager in Hamblin has loaned the doctor his own horse, the best he owns. The doctor should be here this afternoon."

"Will Matthew live that long?"

"Course he will. You shouldn't even think that." Ambrose smiled. "You know with Matthew down, I had to get somebody to drive the freight until Wells Fargo can send out a new driver. So I telegraphed Captain Jardine."

"He's the one who married us."

"I know. He told me. He got someone to drive, but then he offered to send one of his soldiers who was a first-rate horse doctor."

"I like Jardine," I said. "But he sure hates J.D."

"I told him we already had a first-rate horse doctor," Ambrose said. I smiled and he grinned back. "Matthew will make it now."

Libby entered the lean-to with a plate of hotcakes, which I placed on the bed next to Matthew's head.

"For you," she said. "But maybe the smell will waft over and wake him."

"Thanks. He would have died but for you and Ambrose."

"Might still die. But I hope you don't lose him. I know what it is like to lose a loved one." I frowned. Libby was childless, had no close relatives that I knew about. Then I remembered a story I'd heard. I did not know if it was true or not. Two years earlier, Josephine, a border-collie black-Labrador cross, had fallen sick. Libby made Ambrose telegraph the doctor in Hamblin. "Josephine dying, come quick." The doctor whipped his horse through the mud, nearly a full-day trip. When he drove up to the station and discovered that Josephine was a dog, he injected the animal with strychnine and charged Ambrose 200 dollars in gold. No one ever told Libby what he'd done. I had never dared ask Ambrose if the strange story was true.

I laid my hand across Libby's. The older woman leaned

forward and hugged me. Suddenly I sobbed, my arms tight around her. Then she stood and left the lean-to. She did everything in a herky-jerky manner. I knew she was not right in her head, but she was a kind woman.

"I'm worried about this doctor," said Ambrose. "She's new, only been a doctor for a short while. But she's all we've got other than me and Jardine's vet. So I went ahead and sent for her."

"Can't be worse than the last one," I said, and he nodded grimly.

I ate the hotcakes, then felt so weary that I could hardly lift my hand from my lap. I leaned back against the wall and slept.

Chapter Twenty-three

It seemed that the small shack had become my whole world. Through the middle of the day and into the afternoon, I slept, then woke and leaned across to make sure Matthew was still breathing. I ate the bread and tea Abby brought me. Then I slept some more. Late in the afternoon when I wiped Matthew's grimy face with a rag, his eyes opened. "How did I get here?"

I laid my fingers across his lips. "Don't talk." My hand on his chest, I pushed him back down on his bed. "Don't try to do anything."

"How did *you* get here? Did I die? I'm so weary." He shut his eyes and was out again. But this time his breathing seemed more like sleep than a swoon.

I heard voices outside—Ambrose and others I couldn't recognize. Walking to the window, I saw the three men, haggard-faced, who had ridden with J.D. He should never have left them, should never have ridden across the dark flat alone, following his blind impulse—even if his impulse was correct, according to his own light.

They gestured and their voices grumbled at Ambrose. Clearly, they were upset about their wild chase. I worried that they might try to come after Matthew, so I looked around the room for a weapon. There was nothing but the chair I sat on. I picked it up so I could bring it down on their heads if they tried to come in.

"Damn his hide," shouted Brother Pritchard. "He just ran off and left us to follow the tracks." I relaxed a little. It was good their anger had a channel—J.D.

Then Ambrose led them into his house. I lay down next to Matthew, who still slept. It was good to see his chest rise and fall, to hear the sigh of his breath. Soon I heard the door to the house open. The Rockwood men walked across the lane to their horses, smiling and joking with Ambrose. They mounted their horses and headed toward Rockwood. I don't know what Ambrose had told them about Matthew, since they had followed his tracks right to Ambrose's door, but whatever he said, it worked. They didn't bother us.

Later Matthew woke but was still weak. He didn't seem to know where he was, and I wondered if he would ever come back to himself.

In the evening, while I was eating Libby's stew. I heard noise outside again. I stepped to the window as the doctor drove up in her buggy. She climbed down immediately, a tall, thin, dark-haired woman. She lifted her black bag from the buggy. I stepped outside and motioned to her.

Inside the lean-to, she uncovered the wound and examined it. "What is all this black?" she asked. "He's been shot and burned."

"We stopped the bleeding," Ambrose said.

"I can hardly see in here," the doctor said. She opened the door and pulled the bed, with Ambrose's help, closer to the doorway.

She bent over the wound again. "Brother Rockwood, you took a great chance." She pointed into the wound. "If you had burned through that vein, he would be dead now."

"If I hadn't tried, he'd be dead now."

She asked for a basin of water. She opened her bag and removed a jar of cotton and another jar with an amber liquid in it. She washed her hands with the amber liquid and rinsed them in the basin. Removing a set of tongs from her bag, she dipped the cotton in the amber liquid and carefully cleaned the wound. Matthew woke. "Ow," he said. "That hurts like hell. Rachel?" He seemed more aware than when he had woken earlier.

"No," said the doctor. "Not Rachel. Violet."

He tried to pull the blanket back across himself, which was the most dramatic action he had achieved since he had been shot.

She slapped his hand away. "Hold still."

He groaned and looked around. "Is this hell?"

"Close enough," the doctor said. "But don't tell Ambrose. He thinks it is fairest heaven." She removed another jar from her bag, this one filled with a yellow powder. "Now, don't move even one muscle," she said to Matthew. "Or I'll ask Ambrose to bring back his hot iron."

"What is that?" I asked.

"Carbolic acid." She dumped some in the wound and Matthew winced. "Don't be such a baby." She poked his other leg. "Were you shot anywhere else?"

"One shot," said Ambrose.

"My foot," said Matthew.

"You were shot in the foot?"

"Just look at my foot."

The doctor probed his swollen and purple foot with her fingers.

"Damn," Matthew said. "Now I feel it."

"No bones broken," she said. "At least I think not."

"Feels like it's broken off."

"Torn ligaments. You won't be able to walk on that for a long time." She took a roll of cloth out of her bag and unwound a long strip. She wrapped his foot in a crisscross, figure-eight pattern. "Don't get up, not even when you feel better. You need several weeks' rest."

The doctor motioned to me and the two of us dragged the bed back into place. She handed the jar of powder to me. "Put some on his wound once a day. If he gets a high fever, start digging a grave." She repacked her black bag and turned to me. "Fifty dollars."

"I have it in Rockwood."

She frowned at me.

"I have the money," said Ambrose.

He stepped outside.

"I'd never tell him this," the doctor said, "but he saved this man's life. Your husband?"

I nodded.

Ambrose returned with Libby right behind him. He opened his hand and the doctor plucked the coins off his palm.

"Until you can pay me back," he said to me.

I nodded and she put the gold into a purse she had attached to the belt of her dress.

"Would you please stay for dinner?"

"Thank you," she said. "But we'll have to hurry. I need to get down to Centre before midnight. Matilda Hansen is sick as a dog." Libby stared at the doctor but then motioned her to follow. I remained in the lean-to, sharing with Matthew the plate Libby brought me. He ate a few bites of mashed potato when I insisted. Before long I heard voices and stepped out. The doctor mounted her buggy, whipped up her horse and was gone. She had come, done her business, and left as suddenly as if she was one of the Three Nephites, who wandered the earth doing good to people.

"You won't get there before midnight," said Ambrose. "Not even with that good of a horse."

"I'll sleep on the way," she called back.

I returned inside and sat on the bed next to Matthew.

"Shit," said Matthew, "I'm so weak that I…" Then he shut his eyes and slept again.

Libby and Ambrose brought in another cot, and I bedded down next to Matthew. Before dawn, I woke. His breathing had changed, shallower and more rapid.

"Matthew," I said.

"I'm here," he said.

The inside of the lean-to was as black as inside the stomach of a cow. I reached to touch his face.

"Ow. Poked me right in the eye."

"I thought you were dead."

"Is that the test, poke a man in the eye and if he flinches he's not dead?"

"I meant earlier. I didn't think you were dead just now." I laid my fingers on his throat. "I heard you breathing."

"Am I really alive?"

"Yes, yes, yes, alive, my Matthew, you are alive."

"Did you figure out who killed that woman, your, ah…"

"Sister-wife."

"Abominable."

"It was the water master. He thought Sophia was stealing water."

"Harsh punishment for a water thief."

"He lost control. Someone else really was stealing water and Sophia just was in the wrong place at the wrong time."

"Tell me."

So being an obedient wife, I told him all about my night's adventures. When I finished, I thought he was asleep. "Matthew?"

He opened his eyes. "I was a fool to run. I could have saved us all a passel of trouble if I'd just stayed. Nobody would have suspected me if I had raised the alarm over the murder."

"I thought that at first, but who knows what J.D. would have done if you had stayed? He might not have believed you didn't kill her."

"Not even J.D. would dare contradict you."

"You sweet talker. It's not even true. He listens to nobody, not even God. I thought you would die and that I was going to have to go back to Ezekiel."

"No. You wouldn't have done that."

"Right, I wouldn't."

He said, "I thought you were dead."

I patted his cheek. "Same with me. I thought I had lost you."

"I thought it was you."

I frowned at him. "You thought who was me?"

"Down in the water gate. By the barn where you were to meet me." My face must have still showed my puzzlement. "Sweet dummy. Your barn. The dead woman. I thought it was you in that ditch. From the barn window I saw something white down in the weir. I thought he'd killed you for marrying me. I thought that fanatical, murderous Danite had killed you for lying with a Gentile and left you there for a sign."

"He wouldn't do that. Won't do that. He knows now."

"We won't give him a chance. We're going to have no more of this living apart."

"When I found her, she was cold. You left her in that cold water."

"I tipped her face up, saw she wasn't you. I felt like singing for joy. I closed her eyes—poor, staring woman—and then I was scared that I had run to my own death, that she was a trap to lure me out of the barn. I thought J.D. was going to shoot me any second."

"You were a fool to think that. You don't know J.D."

"You don't know him. He did shoot me. Just not then."

I pursed my lips. "He was a fool also. Is a fool."

"She was still warm when I got to her. I knew she was one of the women who lived in the same house as you—another polygamist wife. Because I thought any second a bullet would hit me, I got back away from her. I wanted to sneak through the orchard and beat on your door. Tell you, 'There's a woman dead in your ditch.' I was worried you might not believe I had nothing to do with it."

I laid my hand on his chest. "I believed you without you beating on my door." At least I eventually believed that. I would never tell him my early suspicions. "We could have figured some plan that would have kept you from harming your fool self."

"Some other fool harmed my fool self. How could I stay? I was a Gentile in a Mormon town, and I knew they'd blame me without asking questions. Probably would have lynched me with the first rope."

"They blamed you without you being there. You couldn't

have done worse with me there to defend you."

"I wasn't sure you'd stand forth and say, 'This man is my husband.' And even if you did, why would they believe that I hadn't killed her?"

Tears came to my eyes. "You are right. I didn't dare say, 'This man is my husband.' I didn't dare say it."

Matthew watched me. "Not even now?"

"Yes, now I'll declare it to the world, now that everyone knows anyway. I'm not proud of my cowardice."

"You told me that they'd think our marriage was adultery. I thought that they might kill an adulterous woman. You did what you thought right. And suppose you said it, "This man is my husband." Why wouldn't they leap to thinking I'd murder, too?"

Most people in town would not have made that leap. But some would, I knew. Some were ready to blame Gentiles for every bad thing, J.D. among them.

"It was so odd finding her body in that water gate, as if she was a dam. I thought maybe if I left her there, they'd think it was a water killing."

"I did think that."

"I'd just started back from her body when I heard someone coming."

"Sister Turner."

"No. Wasn't a person. Nearly killed me from fright. It was an old swaybacked, grizzle-faced horse, cropping grass as if nothing was wrong."

"Brother Pritchard's horse."

"Anyway I knew I was in a world of trouble, but I couldn't decide where to run. I thought of running to Jardine or Salt Lake City. Then I had the idea of getting back to my bed before anybody knew."

"Foolish man."

"From the look of the stars I thought I had five, maybe even six hours. Then I had this brainy idea. I'd borrow a horse. But by that time I couldn't see the loose horse anymore."

"Borrow. Men have been hung for less. You should have taken my horse."

"If I'd done that you would have had no mount to ride to save my life."

"If you'd taken her, you would have outdistanced any followers. I wouldn't have had to ride to save your fool of a life."

He shrugged. "Anyway, I planned to push that poor old horse that I stole for an hour and a half and leave him at the dunes for J.D. to find. I thought about how shocked he'd be when he found that horse and I wasn't on it." Matthew cackled like an old man. "I'd get to the dunes all rested, make it so nobody could track me, and just run on over to Lookout Station."

"I figured all this out. So did J.D. You are as transparent as a baby, you triply vain and foolish man." I wondered whether I should tell him that really it was guesswork and what I saw in my dream. What would Matthew think if I told him I was a visionary woman?

"Do you want to hear my story or not?"

I lay against him, careful not to jostle his leg.

"Tell on, precious husband of mine."

"I got to the dunes in about an hour after leaving Rockwood town. I rode the horse down through the cedars toward the sand. I felt not even the slightest breeze on my cheek and I knew there would be no wind to blow and cover my tracks. I tried to figure how I could confuse my tracks enough that J.D. couldn't follow them."

"Which I told you was impossible."

"So this is what I did. That old nag sank past its hocks every step. I saw a lone cedar tree right on the edge of the dunes, so I rode the horse under a low branch and, caught on, lifting myself out of the saddle. I hoped the horse would just keep going."

"But he wouldn't."

"Right. The horse stopped, turning in the sand, confused."

"It did not want to keep going without a rider."

"You guessed it. I broke dead branches and flung them at that beast. He finally moved out onto the sand—this dark creature struggling across the moonlit dunes. I watched him and he tried to go up the edge of a dune. He made it halfway up and slipped, rolling once. He clambered up, standing shaking at the bottom of the dune. He tried to climb up again but finally stood, quivering, in the valley.

"'I used you up,' I called to the horse. 'The others will be along in a couple of hours, and they'll help you.' Then I became frightened, thinking about J.D. coming steadily after me. I dropped out of the tree and started walking backward across the dunes."

"Such a silly ruse. Any other tracker might be bewildered when he found the horse and no rider and found tracks leading up to a tree. But a tracker like J.D. would figure it out. It wouldn't even delay him for more than a couple of minutes."

"Still I had to try. Finally, I climbed to the rocks above the dunes. I tied my boots around my neck. I ran along the rocky ridges up the westward side of this range. I began to think I might make it, and I would have done it except I sprained my ankle."

"Except." I laid my face against his cheek.

"And except for that damn J.D."

"Yes," I said. "A pair of silly, bumbling fools. I saw you sprain your ankle."

"What?"

"You stepped on a fist-sized rock that rolled and your ankle popped to one side. You took a cedar branch and used it as a crutch. This was on a slope of oak brush, cedars, and a few piñons."

"Right," he said. "How did you know that?"

"I had a dream vision."

He frowned at me and then touched fingertips to my cheek,

my lips. "I don't believe in dream visions."

"It happened. I saw you."

"I do believe in you." He laid his hand on my arm.

I smiled and kissed his fingertips. "Well, that's enough."

"Crawling across the mountain, I told myself that if I allowed myself to be captured or shot, I would be separated from you. That's all that kept me going."

"All that kept me going was the thought of losing you through a mistake."

"There's more to tell," Matthew said.

"I've heard enough. Enough for now. Don't want to tire you out in our first conversation."

"What now?"

"Don't worry," I scooted closer to him and he winced. "Sorry."

"I am worried. We are discovered. We need to leave here. Wyoming. Tomorrow, when I'm back to full strength. Or Montana."

"You lost too much blood. It'll take weeks for you to get back on your feet."

"I lost less than what would fill a glass fruit jar."

"Months. Maybe years. We don't have enough money to ship our cattle after I pay Ambrose back for the doctor. Fifty dollars."

"I wasn't worth it."

"Almost worth it. I would have paid thirty and not thought twice about it."

"I want to light out of here. I can't stand Utah Territory for one more day. Remember, in Wyoming the mountains are twice as tall as those in Utah. The smallest creek is bigger than any Utah river. Plenty of space."

"I'm telling you, Matthew, we don't have enough money to ship our cattle. And I can't go back to Rockwood, can't wait any longer. Yes. I'm ready to have our own place, but it has to be somewhere not so far away. Nevada would be close. Good, too. I've heard that the Ruby Valley is beautiful, with some land still open for homesteading."

"*Too* close. California."

"Colorado."

The next morning I heard the church bell, faint and distant, calling the Rockwood Saints to Sophia's funeral. From the edge of the valley, I peered across at the town of Rockwood. Ambrose had lent me his own spyglass, and with it, I watched them gather. At first I wanted to go down, see Sophia in her coffin laid across the sacrament table in the chapel. But Matthew was still not out of danger. I had seen Sophia buried in water; I had no need of seeing my sister-wife committed to earth.

I couldn't see figures clearly through the glass, but I imagined J.D. walking up to the church house. I was baptized in the ditch just below there, in the same spot I had found Sophia's body. The best part of my childhood and the first part of my adult life had been spent in that town.

When I was a girl and we walked into Rockwood town with our belongings on our backs, J.D. was the biggest man I had ever seen. His beard went to his chest. He spoke kindly to me. I saw through his shirt collar the hair on his neck; even the backs of his hands were hairy. I had slunk back to hide behind my mother.

When I was twelve he caught me up on the flat where I had gone after "borrowing" his small-bore rifle, the one he used for shooting jack rabbits that came into his garden. I was flat on my belly, getting ready to fire it at a rock I set up on an anthill. He showed me how to sight and hold the gun steady while I squeezed the trigger. He taught me to fire the rifle kneeling on one knee and also how to shoot while standing. On my thirteenth birthday he gave me a heifer and my own rifle. No other man had treated me the same as the boys. I had free access to his library, and many evenings we sat and talked about what I had been reading. I rode after cattle with him, getting to know every canyon, water hole, and meadow in the mountains to the south and west of Rockwood town. He taught me to rope, helped me shoot my first buck. Mary, his wife, chided him in my presence. "Where will this lead?" He didn't listen to her. On my fourteenth birthday he gave me Babe, a cross got by breeding a mustang stud and a thoroughbred mare. She had a stride that outstripped smaller horses and she could go all day and never tire.

When I was seventeen everything changed. He decided I should get married, started feeling guilty about having taught me everything he knew about manly activities. He worried he had ruined me for life, but he hadn't. I learned everything I needed to know about being a woman from my mother and from Mary. He kept after me until I gave up and married Ezekiel, mostly so I could stay in Rockwood close to this man whom I considered my true father.

Now he had shot and nearly killed my husband. The father I had loved seemed gone, the one who held the barrel of the rifle steady across his forearm while I sighted and shot. I didn't know how to bring him back. One morning when we had worked together irrigating his fields, I had asked him when he would send my mother and us children on our way. This was before he married my mother, and I couldn't imagine anyone paying for our keep longer than he needed to.

"Never. You never have to leave." Not long after that he let Mary convince him to marry my mother.

I had believed him. That one of us would never have to leave the other. Now I would soon leave him, and I would be glad for it. He was violent, stubborn, and pious. He would always see Matthew and me as sinners.

Still, I missed the days when his face brightened every time he saw me. "You are like the sun dawning to me," he had told me.

That man had died to me just as surely as my blood father had died in Osceola.

That night I dreamed I was walking up and down the lane in Rockwood town. My body was heavy and I moved with lumbering steps. I discovered myself to be J.D., beard and all. "This can't look good," I thought to myself. Walking to the bottom of town, I turned and returned to the top. Was I walking sentry or walking because my conscience bothered me? In a way it was both. I walked sentry on myself. Then everything changed and I stood in front of Ambrose's house and saw the man I had been hunting coming down the hill. I raised my rifle to my shoulder and shot. The man tumbled down the hillside.

I woke in the darkness and grabbed at Matthew, my hands gripping his shoulders, until he groaned and tried to roll out of my grasp. When I knew he was still alive, I let him go and lay back on my cot near the door. But I couldn't go back to sleep. I had been J.D. shooting at Matthew. That was awful enough, but it also brought something to my mind. J.D. must have been only a hundred and fifty yards from Matthew when he shot. At the very farthest he couldn't have been more than two hundred. He could shoot a jack rabbit from that distance. Not a standing jack, one flat-out running. How had he missed shooting Matthew in the head or full in the body? I was forced to conclude that he hadn't shot to kill. He had shot to take Matthew's legs out from under him. That Matthew had nearly died had probably not been his intention. I wanted to feel better about the whole thing, but the problem was that J.D. had still shot my husband, who had nearly died. How was I supposed to convince myself that was a good thing he had done? I couldn't forgive J.D. simply because he hadn't shot to kill.

Chapter Twenty-four

By the second evening I noticed that the lean-to smelled like my father's cabin in Nevada. More particularly I noticed that Matthew smelled like my father. "You are filthy."

I carried a large pot of steaming water and set it on the floor of the lean-to. Matthew tried to sit up, but he fell back, his face alarmed. "No woman has bathed me since my mother. And that was nearly twenty years ago."

"Well, it's time you had it done right. No man has the wits to bathe himself." I unbuttoned his shirt, soiled from his run through the mountains. I removed one sleeve, then the other. I dipped the rag in the steaming water and wiped his face. A white streak appeared. "Good heavens. It's going to take more than this one pot." I cleaned his face, ears, and bent his head forward to wash his neck.

He spoke through the steaming cloth that covered his face. "If I wasn't so laid up and weary, I wouldn't stand for this indignity."

"If you weren't so laid up and weary, I wouldn't have to do it." I dipped the rag and washed each arm, washed his chest and belly. "Can you roll over?" He winced as he tried to turn. I laid my hand on his shoulder. "Maybe we'll get your back later."

Then he rolled over. "Damn. That hurt."

While he lay on his stomach, I washed his back. I whipped back the blanket and washed his feet, calves, thighs, except for the wound, still covered with salve. Then I washed his lovely, firm buttocks, which were clenched tight. "Now. You're almost clean." I helped him turn back again. I washed his toes and moved up his legs. He yelped and covered himself with both hands, cupped.

I couldn't help laughing.

"Rachel!" His voice was much louder than it needed to be. "I can finish."

I grinned. "You're bashful. I've married a bashful man." He grimaced as he took the rag. He could hardly hold it in his hand, he was so weak.

I turned my back, just as Ambrose appeared in the doorway. "What the hell is going on in here? Why are you raising such a ruckus? Libby's dogs are all upset." He took one look at Matthew, stark naked with only a rag to cover his privates. "Holy hell, Matthew, a man in your condition should not be exposed to clean water. It may kill you, weak as you are." He stomped off toward his house.

I stood on the porch and stretched toward the hot sun. I felt happier than I had in what seemed like forever.

"I'm finished." I walked back inside and sat on the edge of the bed. He pulled me toward him. "Am I less offensive?"

"Slightly." I took an old shirt from the rags Libby had first given us. I rubbed his face and chest and back until he was dry. Then I laid the damp rag aside and kissed his hand, wrist, sternum, neck, and mouth.

He lay back on the bed, taking my hand. "Now where were we before all this started?"

"When you're better."

"I'm feeling better already."

"You are insane." He reached his arms around me and tried to pull me down. "You're weak as a baby." I stood and found clean clothing in the bag at the foot of his bed. I pulled clean underwear up his legs, helping him turn and pull them up in back. Working together we slipped one arm and then the other into a clean shirt. He lay down and buttoned it. There were no trousers in the bag, so I borrowed a pair from Ambrose. I thrust the trousers over both legs and he slithered into them. I pulled on socks I found, then walked out on the hillside to find his boots. I could put on one boot, but the other was hopeless. He sat on the stoop of the lean-to with one boot and one stocking.

"Now," I said. "You look almost like a human being."

"I feel like a half-dead coyote."

"At least you don't smell like one anymore."

Libby appeared with two plates of food. "Thank you," he said.

"Hearing you talk is thanks enough." Libby turned on her heel and left.

He looked at the food. "I'm not even hungry."

I slid toward him and forked a piece of potato into his mouth. He ate half a plate. I ate the rest of his and mine as well.

"How are we going to keep food on the table?" he said. "You and your appetite will do us in."

"I have always loved good food. And Libby is one of the best cooks in the whole west desert." I laughed out loud for the pleasure of having a full belly and having the horrible tension of the past couple of days over.

He stared at me, a slight smile on his lips. "My lord, you are a handsome woman. I can hardly believe you are my wife. I can hardly believe I stole you away from that damned lecher."

"Lecher doesn't really describe what he was. He was, by his own light, a good husband."

"You can't call him husband. I'm your husband."

I kissed his brow. "Yes, you are. Still, I married him before God, and I want a divorce from him."

"No law counts you as married to Ezekiel. That was not a real marriage."

I shook my head. Some things I couldn't make Matthew understand. So I grinned and buried my face in his neck. "I am grateful beyond words that I didn't lose you." I kissed his eyes, tasting the salt there. I kissed the lobe of his ear, his cheekbone, savored his lips, the sweet tip of his tongue. "You're alive. Not much else matters."

I stood and put a chair back against the doorknob. I pulled the curtains as tight together as I could.

What happened next was not conventional, but we managed.

After breakfast I made Matthew sit up and take a pencil in his hand. I found a newspaper we could write across, and a book—a King James Bible—for a flat surface. "Resources," I said. "Subheadings Matthew and Rachel."

"Why do we need subheadings?" he said.

"So we are in this together. So we know we are equal partners."

"We *are* in this together."

"Fifteen Hereford cattle. Write it under my name."

He wrote on the paper, and then said, "Two hundred dollars in gold." He started to write.

"No. I paid the doctor who saved your life fifty dollars."

"You and Ambrose saved my life."

"Maybe. I couldn't take chances. You weren't available to consult."

"Shouldn't have done it."

"Water under the bridge. A hundred and fifty dollars."

Matthew crossed out the figure and wrote the correct number. "Five horses."

Ambrose stuck his head in the doorway.

"This is a private meeting, Ambrose," I said. "Saddle, bridle, blankets. One quilt. Various dresses. One rope."

"A shirt."

"A bloody shirt."

Matthew wrote it down. "I don't even own a pair of damn trousers anymore."

I bent forward and laughed into my hands, which covered my face. "Some might say that is an advantage."

"Kid needs someone to watch out for his interests," Ambrose said. "Damn clear who wears the trousers in this family."

I said, "Good somebody does."

Ambrose grinned and went on about his chores.

"That's all," I said. "All our resources."

Matthew had been quiet since Ambrose left.

"What? What's eating you?"

He looked at the paper.

"Are you feeling sensitive because your list is shorter than mine?" At first I wanted to laugh. "J.D. gave me all of that. I've worked hard, but if I had been working hard for anybody else I would have nothing. Nobody expects a woman to want to have cattle."

"I wear the damn trousers," he said. "I will work just as hard as you and I will make the list equal."

I let my breath out. "These are our goods. Together. Maybe we should have just made one list."

"Doesn't matter."

"Does matter. Something else, Matthew. Sometimes, like right now when you're injured, I'm going to wear the damn trousers."

He glared at me and then his face softened. "What are we arguing about?" He seemed to dismiss the whole conflict, but I knew it would come up again.

He kept writing under Rachel. I turned the paper around. Beauty and brains, he had written.

I took the pencil and wrote under Matthew's name "Good teeth and one good leg."

"Can't make it to Wyoming, and certainly not to Montana," I said. "Not on a hundred and fifty dollars and our good looks."

"I've been thinking the same."

"I hate Nevada," I said.

"I hate Utah Territory."

"But I admit we've only seen one part of Nevada. I've heard same as you that the Ruby Valley…"

"Nevada is as dry as Utah, drier."

"Not every place," I said. "The Ruby Valley has grass, streams, mountains. It's like a little Wyoming."

Matthew frowned at me, and I stared at the paper as if my mental focus could change our circumstances. The words stayed just the same.

"We have no other choice."

"A hundred miles from here," he said. "We can trail the cattle there in a couple weeks."

"We can trail them to Wyoming in three times that."

"We'd never make it. And they'd be skin and bones."

"Right." I left the room and paced up and down in the barnyard.

Matthew appeared in the doorway.

"Lie back down," I said to him. "Get back in bed."

"You were thinking of leaving me."

I helped him back to bed. Sat next to him, holding his hand clasped in mine. "Not for a second. Just getting used to the idea of Nevada. My whole life it has been my vision of hell." I saw his face. "Except for you there was nothing good about it."

"Ranchers in Ruby Valley," he said. "Not miners."

"Ranchers are as bad as miners."

"No. They're set. They don't want to just get their stash and move on. Whole different thing."

"So we trail them to Nevada. I've got work to do." I turned on my heel and left him. Disappointment was still bitter in my mouth.

Chapter Twenty-five

With Matthew in the clear, I felt confident that I could leave him for a day. I wanted to find out how J.D. had dealt with Brother Swensen. Nothing had come across the telegraph, so I assumed that whatever he had done, it hadn't been violent. Despite Matthew's protests that those crazy Mormons would lynch me for adultery, I saddled Babe and rode to Rockwood. I wanted to savor my anger at J.D. for pursuing and shooting Matthew, but as I rode all his kindnesses rushed back at me—his face as he gave me Babe, as he sorrowed with me at my mother's death, as he rode with me in his buggy to my wedding to Ezekiel. I shook my head, unable to understand the contrary workings of his soul, of my own.

Then I started getting worried. What would the bishop say to me? He was a kind man, but would some hothead decide my sins could be wiped out only by the shedding of blood? I decided that even Brother Pritchard and Brother Ault were more concerned with water than with sin. If I diverted their water onto my field, I might be in danger. Not so much for bedding a man they wouldn't accept as my husband.

An hour and a half later I crossed the bridge and rode into town. Though the ditch this low was dry, I smelled water in the air—sweet liquid, not a good reason for killing.

After removing the saddle and brushing Babe, penning her in her old place, I walked toward the house. Abigail stood in the doorway. Her face was more haggard than I had ever seen her before. She touched my arm and the two of us sat inside at the table.

Abigail said, "I don't understand—"

"He's my husband."

"—but don't try to explain it to me. You have sold your birthright."

Abigail didn't take her hand away from my arm, but her head was down, her face closed to me.

The room was hot already, even though it wasn't noon. Even the thick adobe walls didn't keep out this kind of heat.

"We need to build a back building for cooking in the summer," I said. "*You* need to build a back building. I won't be here."

"Yes. But instead of you, a hard-working woman, it will be that child Ezekiel has married." Abigail's face turned even sadder. Despite myself, I again felt my newfound freedom.

"You want to eat?" said Abigail. "I can make some pan bread and I have cold mutton. I can fry it up."

I shook my head. Then I realized that I was hungry after all. "Yes. I would like some food."

Abigail laid the skillet on the stove, dropped in a dollop of grease and cut the meat. "It's going to be hard for me with Sophia's children, but—" She stopped. "Sophia's funeral was nice."

"I thought I would just be a distraction, but I wanted to come." I stood next to her. "We're leaving the valley. Matthew and I."

"That's smart. Make it right away. I was up late last night and the bishop came by, said he doesn't know how to avoid excommunicating a woman who took another husband when her first was still alive." She slid the meat onto a plate and laid it in front of me.

I opened my mouth and shut it again. My soul felt cold as stone. I didn't know how to convince the bishop to give me a divorce without excommunicating me at the same time. If he called a Church court, the brethren would want to do both at once. Efficient. I stood from the food.

"Oh, Rachel," said Abigail. "I said what I planned to say, but it feels real hard saying it."

"I'd rather hear it from you than from either J.D. or the bishop. Although I think the bishop's the kind who'd hardly see a court through to the end."

Abigail walked around the table and held her arms around me. "In the same breath he told me he'd help us through the winter. He's going to assign brethren to do the work you and Sophia were doing. He's set up a rotation of all the brethren, a different man to help every day of the week."

"Just like the water rotation."

"No, just like charity. I don't want to owe so many people for my survival."

Still standing, I forked a few bites of mutton into my mouth.

"I can't stay. I can't stay to help you."

"Wasn't asking you to. Wouldn't work for you to stay. I have written to Ezekiel and the bishop has also, asking him to just come home. But I'm not looking forward to having another child to teach and take care of. I don't want to have that girl, that baby in my house. Makes me want to bring a pot down on that damn Ezekiel's head." She turned away from me. "You say you can't stay, as if it's out of your hands. But you did make choices. We had a good household here. Your choices have broken that to bits."

"Brother Swensen's choices made it difficult."

She shrugged.

"If you—" She shook her head sharply. "I've had enough of ifs. What happened happened. Nothing to do now."

I looked at her strong back. How would she do it? She would have the work of three women, despite the offer of all the brethren in the world. I hadn't wanted to hurt her, but I certainly had. Didn't like the person I was, causing her trouble. "I'm sorry."

"Too late for that. No use talking about it. But you can do one thing. Both Brother Turner and Brother Swensen are locked in different rooms of the storehouse. Each claims the other did it. They fought each other, beating each other with their fists, so the bishop locked them up. J.D.'s solution was to hang them both, but the bishop held him back. It's all sorted out in your head, but it's still a mess for us. You clean up that mess."

I turned and walked toward Sophia's room. Sarah was inside playing with the little kids. She looked up and turned back to her playing. I walked up the stairs, entered my room, and sat on my bed, already nostalgic for the place I had left only two days earlier.

I gathered my stash of gold pieces, gifts each year from J.D. and money from my calves before I married. We had enough to get provisions from Ezekiel's store for our journey to Nevada, and enough for a down payment on land that Matthew would find as I drove the cattle west. We didn't have enough to go anywhere else and I wouldn't ask J.D. for help. So we were going with faith and not much else.

I cleaned out my drawers and called for Sarah to come up. I gave the child my few dresses, "for when you grow up." I was so thin that it wouldn't take her long to fill them. Then I stuffed what I needed into some flour sacks that Abigail brought up.

Sophia's two children came to me, and I sat on my bed and sang songs to them. "Lead Thou me on. The night is dark and I am far from home. Lead Thou me on." When Abigail called them downstairs for chores, I followed.

I left my belongings in the kitchen and walked up the ditch to the point of the hill just under the white wooden church. Instead of following the ditch up toward the Turners' place, I climbed the wooden stairs. I opened the door and stepped inside—polished oak floor, oak and black wrought-iron pews, white curtains in the windows. If I got up on my toes, I could look out the bottom of one of the windows and see all the way across town, all the way to Lookout Pass. I sat on a pew and looked at the sacrament table where Sophia's coffin had rested. "What unfortunate dream made you go out?" I whispered. "You should have stayed in bed." Outside the window, cottonwood leaves rustled. I breathed the faint intermingled scent of lucerne blossom and dust and a touch of Russian olive—the smell of Rockwood from high summer to early autumn. This is where I had first started to believe in the Mormon God, that the universe was endless, as was humanity, composed of raw material called intelligence, which was something like light. Sometimes the flesh dampened that brightness and made men stupid. The flesh seemed especially thick for Brother Swensen and for J.D., two such pious and even holy men. I shook my head at the irony.

I said a prayer for Matthew and me, that we would be fruitful and multiply, just as Adam and Eve had. I felt Eve's misery; both of us women were cast outs. Just as she and Adam had, Matthew and I would wander in the wilderness.

Nevada had been my home for five years, then Rockwood for nearly ten. *Where will the next decade find me?*

Sitting in the church, I had the feeling again that it was J.D., not Sophia, who had died. Unaccountably I found myself weeping.

I climbed down the hill and walked through the fields to Ezekiel's porch and found the bishop waiting there for me. He caught me by the elbow. "Rachel."

"You want to hold a court."

He flapped both hands in exasperation. "I'm not thinking about that. Brother Swensen wants to talk to you. I think he's ready to confess."

I drew back from him. "I don't want to hear his confession."

"I told him all about J.D. shooting Matthew because he thought Matthew had killed Sophia. That didn't soften him in the slightest. But now that you've come back, he wants to talk to you." He took me by the sleeve and tugged. "Please come."

I followed the bishop down to the storehouse. When I saw that J.D. was there, I wanted to turn away. He lifted his hand as if to touch me on the shoulder, but then he let his hand drop. The bishop unlocked the door to Brother Swensen's room and J.D. stepped inside. Brother Swensen sat in a chair at the window. He stared and the whites of his eyes showed. He glanced at J.D. but seemed to look through him. "You're not her." The hackles rose on the back of my neck.

J.D. stepped forward as if he would speak to Brother Swensen.

"Rachel," said Brother Swensen. "I must talk to Rachel, not you. I must tell her it was an accident." He moved his hand before his face as if he was brushing flies away.

I stepped into the room and moved from behind J.D. Brother Swensen looked up at me and pointed to J.D. "Not him. I don't want him anywhere near me."

I glanced at J.D. and he stepped back outside the building. I pulled the door shut. But then a knock came and the bishop stepped in. Brother Swensen didn't seem to notice. He sat with his hands clasped in front of him as if he was praying. He was stock still as he spoke.

"I didn't know it was Sophia. No one should be punished for an accident. The Turners are the ones who did willful evil." He turned to the bishop. "I don't want to be here another night. I need to get out before she comes back. I offered to shake Sophia's hand and she wouldn't. She just looked at me and quoted scripture to me. I know damn well my damnation slumbereth not. She doesn't need to tell me that again and again all night. I tried to talk to her but she wouldn't be quiet long enough to listen. I tried to tell her it was an accident. She was standing above the Turners' weir and I thought she was one of them stealing water. I swung the shovel without recognizing her." He looked up at me and the bishop. "That's all. That's all I have to say. Only just this. Don't leave me here another night. I can't stand another night of her talking and talking to me with no rest."

"I think wherever you are, she's going to talk," I said. "That's just her way."

He shook his head, and his mouth twisted in a profound frown. I almost felt sorry for him. Almost.

The bishop and I stepped out. He locked Brother Swensen's door and unlocked Brother Turner's.

As Brother Turner came out, the bishop said, "Never steal water again."

"Thank you," said Brother Turner. "My children thank you for coming to your senses." He scurried down the road toward his house.

J.D. stood in front of the building; he stepped toward me. "You did well finding who killed Sophia."

I shrugged and turned toward the bishop. "I'm leaving Rockwood town," I said. "I'll be gone in a day or two. You don't need to excommunicate me."

He frowned and then opened his mouth as if he was going to say something. Maybe to correct my misconception. Maybe he thought I needed to be excommunicated no matter where on this earth I was headed. Even if he thought all that, I'm grateful that he didn't say it.

"I don't know how to ask this. You can give me a divorce. I don't want to be married to Ezekiel, not before God or anybody."

He nodded. "I understand what you want. But it takes time to hold a court."

"Send me a letter."

"You want me to divorce you, but not excommunicate you."

I nodded. "Yes, that's what I want."

"Ach, and you want the world and all the stars." His face was sad and bitter.

I shook my head. "No, just my old marriage dissolved. Not my relation to God."

"I can make no promise."

I nodded. "But you can write a letter to Ruby Valley and tell me what you have done."

"Yes, my Rachel, I can do that."

When I returned to Ezekiel's house, Abigail was in the kitchen staring at the slab-board table in the light of a lantern. I leaned against the sink where Abigail, Sophia, and I had washed the dishes. "We fought all the time." The children called and laughed, playing in the yard.

"What?"

"This kitchen was the scene of a hundred arguments."

"Working out our salvation." She looked at me. "I don't believe you to be an evil woman. But I worry that you have left your faith."

"I don't feel like an evil woman."

"But gradually what you believe will change. You have to have a community of people to keep yourself firm."

I shrugged. "For me it's more personal than something I share with other people."

"Doesn't make sense to me." She shook her head. "But everyone has their own cross to bear. It's going to be all I can do to keep from throttling that girl he's bringing back. The simpering, lisping child."

I stared at Abigail. "I don't envy you that challenge." The two of us sat silent for a moment. "Why did Sophia go out?"

"Sophia?"

I nodded.

She rose. "I have something to show you." She labored up the stairs and soon returned, carrying a black book, which she handed to me. The cover of the book was labeled, "Sophia Nielsen Wainwright, My Diary." I opened it to the end and glanced through the last few entries. "My dreams are filled with faces twisted by carnality. What sin have I committed to deserve such poison in my head?" I turned the page. "Her room is empty. She took the water at midnight but hasn't returned since. It's nearly six in the morning. Should I count it lucky or unlucky that the dreams woke me? She has stayed out all night taking the water. I know she doesn't spend the time irrigating, and I know she can have no righteous purpose. The Lord can abide no measure of lasciviousness. When she takes the water next, I will wait for her near the barn." I looked back up at the date, August 15, 1891—

the day I married Matthew.

"But she found the ditch low and followed it up," I said. "Even to her, stealing water was a more immediate crime than adultery."

"If you hadn't..."

"Dozens of ifs. You said you were done with them."

Aunt Mary knocked at the window and came in. I stood and walked toward her. We hugged and joined Abigail at the table. "He's walking between our barn and house. Wearing a path. A word from you would help."

"And what word could that be?"

Mary folded her hands in her lap. "I can't think of one either." One cheek quivered and she wiped her nose on the back of her hand. "It's good that Christ is the one who must sort all this out. No one else is competent to do it."

I didn't know what to say, so I took each of their hands. We sat connected in that way, two women with a third whom they knew as a sinner but still loved.

The next morning at the Merc I bought a cooking pan, sugar, salt, coffee, flour, leavening, corned beef, and a second rifle. I stuffed a couple of dresses into one saddlebag. In the other I put underwear, my scriptures, and a framed picture of my mother. I gave to Abigail my other dresses, my books, and trinkets that were gifts to me at Christmas and on birthdays. Abigail leaned forward against the kitchen table laughing. "I won't fit into those dresses even in the Millennium."

"Sell them, give them away, save them for the child bride."

Abigail, Zeke Jr., and I drove the cattle up from the wiregrass pasture and corralled them. The boy wouldn't talk to me or look straight at me. We two women strode out into the corral and began dividing the herd. Abigail chose a brindle-backed cow with a large udder, and we put her into Babe's old pen. Zeke Jr. worked the gates. Then I picked a long-horned, white-eyed cow, wildest of the bunch. We cut her out onto the sage-brushy hillside. Abigail picked another, then I picked, until they were all divided. I felt like Abraham and Lot dividing the herds.

J.D. walked up as we were finishing. "Where you going?"

"Nevada. Ruby Valley."

"You'll kill them driving them across Paiute Hell. Last water for fifty miles is at Paiute Hell Station."

"You want me here?"

He just looked down at the pole he leaned over. I wanted like sin to walk over and hug him, tell him goodbye.

Finally he said, "I thank you for discovering the killer to be Brother Swensen. He might never in his whole lifetime have confessed. It would have cankered his soul beyond repair."

"You're welcome. Do you understand I still have difficulty forgiving you for shooting my husband?"

He seemed to be working over a puzzle in his head.

I strode down to the house, where I retrieved my saddlebag. By the time I came back he was gone.

Abigail handed me a map he had drawn of a spring twenty miles into the desert past Paiute Hell Station. "He said only the sheep men know about it."

I hugged Abigail and the children. Zeke Jr. stood stiffly, tears in his eyes. I didn't know what to say to the boy. I opened the gate to the corral and mounted Babe. I pushed my cattle across the creek just above the weir. Abigail was already walking with the children back to the house.

The cattle lined out on the road to Lookout. On the west edge of town I drove them up out of the long valley, leaving Rockwood town behind. Crossing the dry-farm flat toward Lookout Pass, the cattle ambled through the squat sagebrush, cropping the sparse, yellow grass that grew between. I rode back and forth behind the cattle. Suddenly King was there, with J.D. riding him. "I was wrong. So were you. We both made mistakes."

I found tears coming again. "You gave me my life, more even

than my own father. But I can't forgive you yet."

"Don't talk then." He took the left flank of the small herd, keeping them out of Brother Nebeker's wheat field. I watched King moving—a good horse, knowing what the cattle would do before they knew it. I watched the broad-shouldered man riding.

Suddenly there came into my mind a Pioneer Day celebration when I was about fourteen. The citizens of Rockwood town and all the ranches for ten miles in every direction gathered for the festivities—first, an early morning devotional where the bishop and each counselor expressed gratitude for their small community in the desert. Midmorning, boys rode with letter bags tied behind their saddles, dashing down the lane between the houses as if they were Pony Express riders. The old Pony Express route passed south of Rockwood, along the current freight and telegraph route. Young women on horseback carried banners that proclaimed Rockwood as the Rose of Zion in the desert. On that day, the town seemed as blessed and as congenial as the City of Enoch, which had been lifted to heaven for righteousness. God's ways were one eternal round, and his plans for his children would succeed. Men drove their wagons, harnesses oiled and horses washed. J.D. Rockwood appeared in his new buggy, his long gray-black beard carefully combed, his steel-gray eyes flashing. I swelled with pride, thinking J.D. was almost a god, so perfect a man, one who clearly was also proud of me.

That feeling was gone forever except as a distant memory. My anger was still like a rock inside, but I knew that after a long time even rocks wore down. After the herd passed the last of the dry farm fields, J.D. rode toward me. "Good luck. I wish with my life that it could have been different."

I touched his forearm. "I won't ever forget you." I would remember the best and the worst that man could be, all in J.D. Rockwood.

When the herd was in the mouth of Lookout Canyon, I turned

in the saddle and looked back. J.D. was out of sight. The black trees of Rockwood looked like a bruise on the gray flat. I didn't look back again.

Chapter Twenty-six

I arrived at Lookout Station by dusk. Matthew waved and hobbled out on the crutches Ambrose had made for him. Together we sat and watched our cattle eating the wiregrass around the spring. Ambrose soon joined us, a tray of coffee cups in his hand.

"Should I pen them?" I asked.

"They won't move in the dark," Ambrose said. "But you better be up before dawn."

Matthew and I ate dinner with Ambrose, Libby, and the dogs—nine total around the table. The table was set up not in the kitchen, as in most houses, but in a formal dining room. Ambrose had even built a chandelier out of broken windowpanes that held coal oil lanterns, four of them. It was bright as day and hotter than a crematorium inside that room.

"I'll bless the food," Ambrose said. We all bowed our heads. "Lord, we thank thee that this tangle involving J.D. and thy son Matthew and thy daughter Rachel has resolved itself as well as could be expected." I opened one eye to see if the dogs had bowed their heads and closed their eyes, maybe folded their paws. But they just sat, looking at the roast on the platter and at the heap of potatoes and bread, but not going for it. "We bless them on their journey toward a new life. Bless them with prosperity and bless them that they might remember the source of their prosperity. Bless these our do—I mean, our children with health and strength, so that they can chase after rabbits and not be weary, hunt coyotes and not faint. Thank thee for this our bounty, in the name of Jesus Christ, Amen."

"Amen," said Libby in a loud voice.

"Amen," said Matthew and I in quieter voices. The dogs said nothing.

Ambrose carved the roast, while Matthew and I took potatoes and bread. After the roast was sliced, Libby stood and took up the platter. The dogs were still polite, but there was an edge of excitement in the way they perked their ears and wagged their tails. She reached over their shoulders and laid a thick piece of meat on each plate. The dogs discreetly bit the edge of the slices of roast mutton. Then they lapped the potatoes and gravy. I caught Ambrose's eye and he smiled grimly.

Matthew cut his own meat and chewed, though I half expected him to imitate the dogs, he was so attentive to their every move.

"So Ambrose was neglectful," Libby said. "He should have blessed you with a fertile womb."

Matthew choked on a piece of meat and Ambrose had to stand and beat on his shoulders before he could get the meat to where he could chew it again.

"You're not the only one who has that prayer in her heart." I gave Matthew a grin that made his face turn bright red.

"I find that keeping mistletoe in the room where you're sleeping works well," she said. "I'm not sure Ambrose and I would have had any children at all without that help."

Matthew choked again and had to excuse himself. Out in the yard I heard him coughing and making a kind of grunting noise that was neither clearly laughter nor weeping.

That night I walked through the cedars with a lantern until I found a clump of mistletoe high in the branches of an old tree. I set the lantern on the ground and climbed high enough that I could break off a few rubbery twigs.

"Where you been?" asked Matthew when I returned.

I grinned at him. "Gathering material for potions." I hooked the mistletoe over a nail in the wall of the lean-to.

"That won't make any difference," he said.

"Worked for Libby." I blew out the lantern and started unbuttoning Matthew's shirt. "I want to give birth to a coyote, a wolf, and a bear."

"Why are you talking so crazy? It makes me real nervous to

have you talk like this."

I laid my hands flat against his chest. "Get used to it. I want to be just like Libby when I'm older. Make my children howl like wolves."

Before dawn I saddled Babe. A man's shirt hung from my shoulders, trousers were baggy around my waist and legs, but I might pass for an impoverished young man who couldn't afford a better fit. I didn't even need to bind my breasts with cloth as the young women in Shakespeare's plays were supposed to have done. I was not ample enough to need any such disguise.

Matthew and Libby and Ambrose waved from the stoop of their house. Matthew would follow on the freight wagon. He'd pass me in three or four days. The cattle were just lifting their heavy bodies from the ground, hindquarters first, then front. I drove them over the cedared hill to the west of the station and down the other side. The road led around a hill and across the white-hot prairie toward Paiute Hell Station. The alkali flats I would have to cross wavered in the sunlight and above them hung a white peak, nearly the same color as the sky. When I passed that peak, I'd be out of Utah Territory.

At Government Creek I found only a dry channel. By evening I came to the sandy flat below Paiute Hell Springs. While my cattle ate the dry bunch grass, I rode up to ask permission to water. When I turned, the cattle, having smelled the water, were trailing up behind me. Captain Jardine walked out of one of the buildings. He stared at me. "I thought you were a boy," he said. "You're the woman I married to that freight driver. Rachel Rockwood. J.D. said you'd been killed."

"Not yet."

"There was some confusion."

"Yes, a great mix-up."

"J.D. shot your husband."

"Fortunately, he didn't shoot well."

"You mean he missed on purpose. J.D. always shoots well."

I shrugged my shoulders. "That's what I've concluded myself, but it doesn't change anything."

"Maybe not."

After watering my cattle, I trailed them back down to the flat. Jardine rode down at dusk and asked me to have dinner with him and his men.

I looked up from my fire. "No thanks."

He smiled, watching me as I squatted next to my fire. "Will I bother you if I stay and chat for a while? I mean nothing about it, no insult, but it's rare we have any order of woman out here and I miss the talking."

He made me a little nervous, saying that, but I nodded anyway.

"Matthew will come through in a few days on the freight wagon."

"Where do you think you'll settle?"

"Probably Ruby Valley."

"Why there?"

"We heard it's a good place. Lots of water. Wide meadows."

"It's wetter than here, I'll admit, but it's no Eden—wide dry flats."

"Hell."

"There are streams coming out of the mountains. Mountains are wetter than here. Not many people there."

"Good."

"The Donner Party passed through there. Pony Express also. But the railroad went through far to the north, so a lot of people's hopes were for nothing. Hardly anybody stayed after the railroad went around them. It's also choked with Mormonites."

"Oh, hell. Don't tell Matthew."

He laughed. "No Mormonites until you get to the Carson Valley, clear on the other side of the state. I just wanted to see how you would react."

I glared at him.

Then it seemed as if we had nothing to say. He stood awhile and then said, "I'm married. I have a wife, back in Ohio, where we have a small farm. My son is working it while I'm gone. I don't know what's going to happen when I get out of the army, because that little spot of ground isn't nearly enough for more than one man to work."

It sounded as if he was talking to me about J.D., saying that there's rarely enough land for a man to share with all his children. At least that's how I took what he was saying.

"You're not nearly the Mormon hater you pretend to be," I said.

"Oh, I don't like the religion or the politics, but people are people. I'm more of a philosopher than a fighter." He shook my hand and said good night.

After he left, I ate my bread and warm mutton. If the wide world had a few people like him sprinkled across it, Matthew and I might do all right. Jardine was a courteous man. I thought about J.D. and all his contradictions—as if his long-bearded face swam and changed before my eyes. He was grim and fatherly, kind and violent, a saint and a devil. Then I thought about my future, finding land where I could build a ranch to run with my man. I would be isolated from my adopted people, the Mormons. Despite Abigail's fear that I would lose my faith, I still thought of myself as one of God's children. Still, Mormons always come in communities. It would seem strange to any Mormon, not just Abigail, to worship God as a solitary woman. I would have to find a way. Maybe like my mother found a way toward her new life. Like Eve before her.

The ground was sandy, and I laid all my clothing over the blanket, but cold came up out of the ground and I spent a nearly sleepless night. The only comfort was the sound of my cattle breathing around me, the sound of Babe stamping her feet.

The next morning—a cool morning—while my cattle grazed,

I cooked breakfast and stared across the white, forbidding plain.

Letting my cattle drift out onto the flat, I felt light, disembodied, as Babe moved strong and vigorous beneath me. At one stroke I had been stripped of home and family, but not of husband. The freight wagon would soon pass me, with Matthew inside. Soon he would be strong as ever.

Behind my cattle, I rode free and grateful across the face of God's tumultuous earth.

FICTION

Put simply, we publish great stories. Whether it's literary or popular, a gentle tale or a pulsating thriller, the connecting theme in all Roundfire fiction titles is that once you pick them up you won't want to put them down.

If you have enjoyed this book, why not tell other readers by posting a review on your preferred book site.

Recent bestsellers from Roundfire are:

The Bookseller's Sonnets

Andi Rosenthal

The Bookseller's Sonnets intertwines three love stories with a tale of religious identity and mystery spanning five hundred years and three countries.

Paperback: 978-1-84694-342-3 ebook: 978-184694-626-4

Birds of the Nile

An Egyptian Adventure

N.E. David

Ex-diplomat Michael Blake wanted a quiet birding trip up the Nile – he wasn't expecting a revolution.

Paperback: 978-1-78279-158-4 ebook: 978-1-78279-157-7

Blood Profit$

The Lithium Conspiracy

J. Victor Tomaszek, James N. Patrick, Sr.

The blood of the many for the profits of the few… *Blood Profit$* will take you into the cigar-smoke-filled room where American policy and laws are really made.

Paperback: 978-1-78279-483-7 ebook: 978-1-78279-277-2

The Burden

A Family Saga

N.E. David

Frank will do anything to keep his mother and father apart. But he's carrying baggage – and it might just weigh him down ...

Paperback: 978-1-78279-936-8 ebook: 978-1-78279-937-5

The Cause

Roderick Vincent

The second American Revolution will be a fire lit from an internal spark.

Paperback: 978-1-78279-763-0 ebook: 978-1-78279-762-3

Don't Drink and Fly

The Story of Bernice O'Hanlon: Part One

Cathie Devitt

Bernice is a witch living in Glasgow. She loses her way in her life and wanders off the beaten track looking for the garden of enlightenment.

Paperback: 978-1-78279-016-7 ebook: 978-1-78279-015-0

Gag

Melissa Unger

One rainy afternoon in a Brooklyn diner, Peter Howland punctures an egg with his fork. Repulsed, Peter pushes the plate away and never eats again.

Paperback: 978-1-78279-564-3 ebook: 978-1-78279-563-6

The Master Yeshua

The Undiscovered Gospel of Joseph

Joyce Luck

Jesus is not who you think he is. The year is 75 CE. Joseph ben Jude is frail and ailing, but he has a prophecy to fulfil ...

Paperback: 978-1-78279-974-0 ebook: 978-1-78279-975-7

On the Far Side, There's a Boy

Paula Coston

Martine Haslett, a thirty-something 1980s woman, plays hard on the fringes of the London drag club scene until one night which prompts her to sign up to a charity. She writes to a young Sri Lankan boy, with consequences far and long.

Paperback: 978-1-78279-574-2 ebook: 978-1-78279-573-5

Tuareg

Alberto Vazquez-Figueroa

With over 5 million copies sold worldwide, *Tuareg* is a classic adventure story from best-selling author Alberto Vazquez-Figueroa, about honour, revenge and a clash of cultures.

Paperback: 978-1-84694-192-4

Readers of ebooks can buy or view any of these bestsellers by clicking on the live link in the title. Most titles are published in paperback and as an ebook. Paperbacks are available in traditional bookshops. Both print and ebook formats are available online.

Find more titles and sign up to our readers' newsletter at http://www.johnhuntpublishing.com/fiction

Follow us on Facebook at https://www.facebook.com/JHPfiction
and Twitter at https://twitter.com/JHPFiction